A DAWN OF EIGHT NOVEL

EMPATH

EMME DeWITT

For every bleeding heart and empathetic indigo child, may you find your inner strength and inner peace sooner rather than later

ISBN- 978-0-578-57649-7
ISBN- 0-578-57649-X

Iron Sparrow Media
www.ironsparrowmedia.com

ONE

The lights clicked on above me, the loud buzz of fluorescent bulbs invading the soft half sleep I had adopted since the wee hours. My arm was draped over my eyes, so I had no problem ignoring the light. But the buzzing really killed it for me.

"What, six AM already?" I said aloud to the empty room. Other than the daily routines, I had no concept of time. The illusion of a window in the spotless white institution room mocked me from the far wall. If I opened the curtains, I would find concrete cinder blocks in place of a pastoral scene. Really, they were just rude to put the frame in there. It was a constant reminder of my imprisonment—medical observation, my foot.

Good morning, sunshine, a voice inside my head chuckled. I could only sigh, forcing myself to accept the defeat of another unwelcomed wake up call. I flung my arm wildly into the air, swatting at the disembodied voice with general disdain.

Thankfully, it wasn't the voices that awarded me such grand forced living accommodations, but rather a mega evil super secret society for evolved humans. Well, they seemed nefarious enough to me. My gut instincts carried a lot more weight than the average bear's. Or super human's.

Whatever. I was right and on my way to proving it.

Well, as soon as I got out of here, anyway.

Good morning to you, too, Stalker, I replied in my head. My eyes squinted at the blinking security camera in the corner of the room. I took the opportunity of rubbing the sleep out of my eyes to hide the soundless muttering of my curses from the camera's view. *I see your late night banter doesn't deter you from pestering me first thing.*

Early bird gets the worm. And do I detect a tone? Someone's not a morning person.

I snorted, immediately sitting up and beginning my morning stretching routine. I felt better moving while having a secret mental conversation when the other party wasn't in the room. Something about the lack of body language input made me fidgety, and I would really rather not suffer an upping in my crazy pill dosage. It didn't dampen my abilities like they thought, but it sure made my stomach churn. I was not up for digestive distress in addition to the chatty nincompoop down the hall. One or the other was punishment enough.

You know, I'm not really in the mood, Quentin. Just to put that out there.

You'll think differently at breakfast. I have news.

I could feel the Cheshire grin through our connection, and I snorted so hard this time I fell into a coughing fit. I scrambled to my bedside table, but found the glass next to my bed empty. Lurching over the bed, I stumbled toward the door, smacking my open palm against the door rapidly as the coughs caused me to double over.

I heard the beep of a security badge from the other side of the door, followed by a loud click of the lock releasing. The door slid open, falling silently into its slot in the wall. I turned my face up, as I was about mid-thigh level to whichever security guard was on duty. A hand holding a small disposable cup appeared in front of me.

"Here," Blue Eyes said, his arm shooting out from his side, nearly sloshing all the water out.

The guard kept one hand on his holstered gun as he braced for my next move, but I was too focused on the water to be offended. Several previous escape attempts did not hold me in high esteem among the security staff, least of all with Blue Eyes. He was still sporting the goose egg on his shin from our last encounter.

I choked down the thimble of water I was accommodated and attempted to calm my coughing from hacking into short fits. I did not bother to ask for more. I knew the rules. As a most beloved and highly valuable asset, my every move was measured and accounted for, even down to the last drop of water in or out of my body. I liked to keep hydrated just like the next person, but this level of obsession was a little much.

Blue Eyes cleared his throat, nudging my knees back behind the barrier of the door with the toe of his boot. I let him, even though I was beginning to think he needed a matching set of bruises for his shins. With zero empathy leaking off him, Blue Eyes swiped his badge against the box outside my room, and the door swished shut abruptly in my face.

"Thank you," I mumbled, flicking my wrist out in a mock salute before I scuttled back toward my bed. Instead of crawling back onto it, I laid sprawled on the floor as I counted the speckled tiles for the millionth time. I didn't even care if the white coats were taking detailed notes about my "extremely odd behavior."

I was bored.

I was apathetic.

I was stuck.

Breakfast would be good, but then I would have to entertain myself until the next meal break. Let the white coats wax poetic about why I was mindlessly rolling on the floor, but I was so tired of playing games. The last time I had been institutionalized, I thought by adhering to each request and exceeding the expectations placed on me that I would be rewarded. Better behavior meant less days in the brig and an expedited reentry back to my life. It hadn't been true then, and it certainly wasn't true now. Not after everything that happened since Tomas passed. Definitely not after what happened with Noah.

Noah.

I sighed at the ceiling. Better out than in, I thought dumbly to myself. If only dumb platitudes like that could improve my situation. I was stuck here sighing while Noah was stuck...who even knew where. Probably without the luxury of sighing, I was certain. A lump began to form in my throat as all horrific possibilities floated effortlessly up idea after terrible horrible idea. With my teeth clenched together, I forced out more air, making a slightly more aggressive sound. We did not have time for pity parties.

Today, for better or for worse, I was going to act how I wanted. I would not expend my energy bending myself into the mold I was expected to fit into. I would worry about the consequences later. If Quentin was worth anything, it would be one of my last days here anyway. Playing the good patient role no longer reaped the most benefits.

It wasn't too long until an orderly came to retrieve me for breakfast. Of all the formalities, I found this one the weirdest. I was already flanked by two guards as I was escorted down the hall. The orderly was excessive, and it made us both grumpy. The degree of annoyance rolling off the orderly made me sigh in exasperation. It wasn't like I demanded a personal escort. Less than quarter into my day and the emotional overload was already grating on my nerves.

As soon as I was delivered to my table, the orderly vanished along with the guards, who resumed their sacred duty of holding up the walls. Quentin was deposited across from me shortly thereafter, and I scowled at him in greeting.

"You know when you pester me, it's like someone constantly ringing the doorbell, right? Even if I ignore it, it's annoying as hell," I muttered under my breath. "Just because you figured out how to project does not mean you need to show off all the time."

Quentin returned an indulgent smile.

"If only you knew how to shield better. Honestly, it's a surprise I can even get through with all the other input coming your way," he said, picking innocently at his nailbeds. "Although, if you don't respond, I don't get to go poking around like some people."

"Thankfully," I threw back mercilessly. "You know, your loyalties concern me. I'm not sure whether I should trust Adair's good old buddy-buddy."

"Don't have much choice, do you?" Quentin said, his glasses reflecting the glare of the fluorescent lights, shielding his eyes from view. The angle of his neck was too awkward to be accidental, and I growled internally at his shady body language. "Plus, some of us don't really think so much in terms of friendship. It's a major weakness both you and Mags share, interestingly enough."

"Don't you compare me to her."

I crossed my arms, trying to make it seem like that was just more comfortable to me and not because his words landed on a sore spot.

Why was it taking so long for the food to be sent out? At least if I had food, I could be eating instead of arguing. I had to remind myself this room had cameras as well. The fact that Quentin was an asshole didn't seem to matter in my overall cooperation scores. Really, it was a miracle I didn't physically attack him instead of Blue Eyes. At least with Blue Eyes, it had been tactical. Somehow, I thought, they could at least respect that.

"And the similarities get better and better," Quentin said, his smirk twisting his mouth cruelly to one side. His expression dropped a cold stone into my gut, and I hastily slammed up a mental barrier to not influence the atmosphere in the room.

I wasn't in the mood to instigate a riot today.

"You know, you have a lot of competition for greatest villain in our generation," I said smoothly, trying to sneak in my barb behind a silky tone. Quentin's neck twitched enough to lose his strategic position and reveal his eyes from behind the glare of his lenses. They seemed leery yet desperate for some sort of validation. "It's a shame you don't have a more influential power.

You're forced to ally with us weepy saps who care about loyalty and unicorns and rainbows."

My eyes flashed a warning, and Quentin stiffened a little in his seat, his hands stilling their nervous picking. After a moment, he cleared his throat, shifting his weight to regain some of the dominance he had just lost.

"I can be quite useful. You forget---I have news." Quentin paused to allow the food trays to be set in front of us. Once the attendant was out of earshot, he continued.

"I've been doing some digging, and the older generation seems to pool their resources through a charitable organization out of Boston they've so cutely named The Association. You already knew this, but I'm just confirming it for you." Quentin stabbed his hash browns savagely.

I rolled my eyes as I shoveled eggs into my mouth, not waiting for the cool room to turn their texture to rubber.

"The deed for this building is in their name, as well as the medical center you and I often visited while at school. Now, the interesting bit is there's only one other medically zoned building in their real estate deeds, and it's way the heck out in Montana."

"Montana?" I muttered, shaking my head. "Whose genius idea was that?"

"Actually, it is really genius since it's so out of the way and it would be ridiculously easy to monitor traffic to and from that area. Also, can you imagine winters up there? No, thank you," Quentin retorted, swigging his orange juice with disdain. "Dean Moriarty is no joke."

"Don't ruin breakfast." I frowned. "Anything else?"

"I mean, can you read all the way to Montana?" Quentin said, his face doubtful.

"You worry about you, and I'll worry about me, okay?" I threw back quickly.

A small part in the back of my mind was afraid to try, but I had such a deep sense of calm that I thought I very well could read to Montana. I might put myself in a coma for a week, but I still thought I could do it. It was best to keep my range to myself though, especially until after Quentin had been properly vetted. It had been four months, and I still wasn't sure if I could trust him.

If I stayed in here any longer, I might be forced to trust him out of necessity.

"All right, fine," Quentin said. "I'll try for more, but it takes time. I can only zone out for so long before they come and check for a pulse. I try and pretend I can't help it, but they might be figuring out I'm doing it on purpose."

"Oh, they probably already know." I sighed. "Something tells me they wrote the rulebook and they're timing us to figure out how long we'll need to figure it out. You would think they'd want to help the next generation by mentoring us instead of testing us for sport."

Quentin barked out a derisive laugh.

"I forget you had a somewhat decent childhood in blissful ignorance." Quentin crushed his orange juice cup in his fist. "Love. Support. Wait, don't tell me. Were there puppies?"

"Can you not destroy something while simultaneously talking about puppies?" I said. "Even for you that's messed up. Listen, just let me know if this gladiator game method has ever worked out in the past. You know, on your spare journeys."

"Sure, that'll go to the top of my list." Quentin rolled his eyes before shoving back his chair as he stood up. "See you at lunch."

"Maybe," I said.

He paused, his hand lingering on the back of the bright orange plastic chair.

"I hear Montana is nice this time of year." For psychopaths, I added to myself. Who was I kidding? It was still frozen tundra in February.

"Whatever," Quentin said. "Suit yourself."

"I always do," I said to his back, poking at the remnants of my breakfast until it was my turn to be escorted back to my room. I loosened my grip on my mental walls, letting the feelings and energies of the people around me filter in slowly, like a theatre slowly filling up before a show. I let the volume rise in my mind, pulling the barrier tightly back into place when a hand tapped my shoulder. I blinked slowly, trying not to flinch at the touch.

It was just Blue Eyes. I got up and followed him before he could register anything out of the ordinary, if he even cared at all.

TWO

"What's she doing?" Blue Eyes said, peering at the monitor bay in the observation room. It showed the young girl sprawled on the floor with her legs propped vertically against the wall.

White Coat briefly glanced up from her note taking at the monitor in question and shrugged. The subject did not appear to be in any medical or emotional distress, so she simply typed out a note about the behavior in the appropriate comment field.

"She does that, typically after she counts the tiles. She has a fairly regular boredom routine, which is admirable considering how little stimulation she gets. The boy just sleeps all the time," White Coat stated in a flat tone, nodding her head at the opposite monitor with a teenage male lying prone on his bed. His vitals blipped steadily in the margin of the screen, indicating the steady state of a REM sleep cycle.

Blue Eyes squinted his eyes, leery of such a simple explanation. These were teenagers, after all. He rubbed his shin absentmindedly, checking the size of the goose egg the girl had given him two days before.

White Coat flicked her wrist, bringing the face of her austere Timex into sight. "Time for medication dispersal," she said, making another quick note before she left for rounds. The staccato pace of her notes indicated shorthand as she firmly pressed the enter button to save her work. Blue Eyes straightened belatedly, trailing White Coat out of the observation room and into the hall.

. . .

I FOLLOWED their forms as the pair made their way down the hall from the observation room to my nicely padded cell. The clarity of my range had not diminished with the multiple medications they pumped into me, although sometimes my focus couldn't last very long before the feed shorted out abruptly. Due to my familiarity with Blue Eyes, my mind's eye captured him effortlessly. His thoughts and moods were steady and assured, which allowed his form to fill in solidly in my head.

White Coat was a little more difficult to "see" reliably. She reminded me of Noah in a way; her rational thought seemed to stem the flow of her emotions, limiting my reading to trends of previous behavior with the caveat that her robotic mad scientist brain had the emotional depth of a teaspoon. Her physical outline was a stringboard pattern, empty of context beyond the connections of Point A's and Point B's. Once in a while, like when she caught Blue Eyes glancing at her backside, anger would flare out like a supernova. But once she had regrouped, the emptiness returned with only the barest of hints of human emotion in between flares.

I wished I could ask her if she had any shield training or if she really didn't have feelings at all. It was rude in a variety of ways, but my curiosity was getting the better of me. I had a feeling my question would just be another note in the comments section of my chart. She didn't seem the type to take anything personally.

White Coat and Blue Eyes took the direct route to my room first, presumably because Quentin was "sleeping" and incapable of swallowing meds. I wasn't sure exactly what cocktail he got, but it didn't seem to be affecting his powers at all either. Which was annoying. Almost as annoying as his self-righteous attitude about it.

I heard the beep of the security badge from the other side of the door, but I didn't open my eyes. My hair was splayed out in a halo around my head, and I was taking bets on whether it would be stepped on or not. White Coat was too meticulous, but Blue Eyes was holding a grudge. Such a thrilling game.

White Coat cleared her throat above me, announcing her presence. I had felt her come in, but I indulged her by opening my eyes.

"About that time?" I asked, feigning pleasantries as if she wouldn't shove the pills down my throat if I decided I wasn't feeling it today.

"Yes," White Coat said. "It is time for your medication."

She held out two small paper cups, keeping them just out of my reach unless I was in a seated position. Honestly, like I was dumb enough to try to swallow pills lying down. I swung my legs down from up against the wall and spun to face my captors, my back now appropriately vertical. Dutifully, I knocked back the pills with another generous thimble of water. I stuck out my tongue and flipped it up and around so they could be sure I hadn't hidden the pills to spit out later.

"Thank you," White Coat said, retrieving the paper cups from me.

"No, thank you," I said dramatically, flourishing my arms out in an exaggerated seated bow.

Blue Eyes postured at me, stepping forward slightly as if I were going to do something more sinister. I only rolled my eyes.

White Coat and Blue Eyes let themselves out, and I crawled up into my bed. One good thing about being so petite was I could sleep diagonally on the standard issue sized twin bed. My limbs jackknifed in all directions quite comfortably as I readied myself for the first of many daily naps.

The only real side effect of the latest dumb cocktail was intense drowsiness. They didn't give me much to do anyway, so I wasn't even mad about the frequent occurrence of naps. It helped me keep time. Luckily, it was a blissful black sleep untinged by nightmares. Sometimes I wondered if Adair really was that bored at night or if my own mind was doing too good of a job at showing me the worst possibilities it could cook up. I didn't really want to give Adair any credit, but the peacefulness of my daytime naps always kept me guessing.

In no time, I was asleep.

"Evie!" Noah shouted. She was running toward me, but I couldn't tell where she was coming from. Grey smoke surrounded her, and her feet seemed to be catching on the ground below her, making it difficult for her to run. My body was immovable, and I felt the heaviness of dread as I watched her reach toward me on her own.

My lips moved to call out to her, but I choked, my throat refusing to move. Panicking, I tried to claw at my throat, but I couldn't find my hands. They weren't listening to my brain's directions. I was completely bound.

Noah! I screamed in my mind.

Evie, you have to get out of here. Now! Noah's voice pierced through my head with such force, I could hear ringing in my ears.

Where? Where is here? What do you mean?

I didn't know how I'd gotten there or how to get out. I didn't know if here was even a real place.

You have to leave. Noah shouted in my head. *Go, before they catch you, too.*

They already have me. I'm in New York. It's too late.

Noah howled in frustration, her body still barreling toward me with all her might.

You have to stay hidden, she said to me desperately. *They can't know what you do, okay? You have to hide it. Hide all of it.*

I'm trying, I replied, *but I don't know what they know. The escape plan is not going well.*

Dream Noah looked over her shoulder, her face returning into view with a mixture of renewed determination and acceptance. Her mouth pressed together firmly before she let out another angry yell, this time the noise tinged with banshee vibrato. Even in this dreamscape, the hairs on the back of my neck rose up.

You have to get out. You have to get to the others before they do.

Noah called out to me, this time her lips still even in her dream form. *All of them, Evie. We have to get to them before they can.*

I know! I know. I'm working on it. My eyes darted desperately around Noah, trying to find something I could focus on for a clue. A clue to where she was. Or even where she wasn't, if this was a conversation in her Dreamscape rather than in reality. The smoke told me nothing.

I'm trying to keep them out, but I'm not good at shielding. Noah said, her urgency dying away as I felt her pull back from the connection. *They might see this. Be ready.*

Noah's emotions were barreling at me full force, but seeing her face filled me with both relief and sadness. I couldn't even help her, so how was I going to help all these mysterious kids? How could I even go about finding them? Sure, a few were at Windermere, but those known players were almost a lost cause at this point.

We needed everyone else.

An immense sadness washed over me, and all I wanted to do was reach out and touch Noah. She was my rock.

I needed to get to her first. Then we could find the others together. I was doubtful I could do it on my own.

I'm coming for you first, I thought toward Noah with resolve.

Noah's face blanched, and she shook her head ferociously, nearly tripping as her legs continued to pump in a warrior's battle charge.

No! You have to get out first. Get some people you trust. I'll figure my own way out and meet you. I already have a plan. Noah's head jerked back behind her again, and I could see her pace quickening even more.

But you have to be on the outside before that happens, okay? They might use you against me if it goes sideways. Fear lanced through my gut.

Got it?

I wanted to argue, but part of me knew what she was saying was true.

Promise me! Noah screamed, the panic in her voice piercing through the nebulous smoke cloud surrounding her.

Suddenly, she flickered. I tried to scream, forgetting my voice was useless here.

Evie! Noah's banshee scream pushed through one last time, but her form kept shorting out. Every time she was gone for more than a blink, the smoky nothingness crept in to where she had been a heartbeat before.

I gathered all the fear roiling around in the bottom of my gut, using is as fuel for what I was sure was the last transmission I could get to Noah, Dream or not.

I'll be out within the week, I promised. *Don't keep me waiting, or I will come find you and you will be very, very upset with me.*

Deal, Noah's voice whispered in my brain, her image almost completely obscured by the rolling grey mist.

I miss you.

Stay safe.

I JOLTED UPRIGHT IN BED, the sheets completely entangling my small frame several times over. I fought to kick them off. My frustration released into the room, and I tore savagely at the linen shackles, feeling the air around me crackle. The intensity of the fear that had filled the room scared me a little, but dissipated immediately once I pulled it back inside. If anyone else had been in the room with me, we would have had a problem on our hands.

I took a series of deep breaths, counting loudly in my head until my heart rate was back to normal. Tentatively, I eased out a probe in my mind's eye, checking if anyone in the vicinity had been affected by the emotional burst.

Nothing pinged back as abnormal. Quentin was still asleep, and White Coat was refreshing her coffee in the break room. I couldn't find Blue Eyes, but I didn't search very far.

No one seemed any the wiser to my half-dream, so I did my

best to untangle my sheets, make my bed, and pretend like I hadn't just gotten a doomsday message from my banshee best friend two time zones away via astral projection. Any mention of that, and I most certainly would be getting a new series of medications.

THREE

"You have a visitor," the surly orderly barked in my ear. My fork dropped onto my lunch tray after my hand spazzed out in surprise.

Dining alone when Quentin was zoned out had its perks. I took advantage of any opportunity I could to limit my interaction with him. He was such a drain on what limited energy I had, and his simpering commentary haunted me whether I was in his physical presence or not. More often than I'd like to admit, I wished Mags would have been banished over Quentin as my designated hostage buddy. At least she had some semblance of personality beneath her many, many layers of maniacal ambition.

"Goodie," I muttered into my reconstituted mystery meat. I recovered my fork and stabbed it savagely into the mountain of powdered potato mass I hadn't yet tackled, where it stuck upright like a defiant battalion flag.

I was not prepared for who sat across from me.

"Yeah, can't blame you for not wanting to eat that. Are those... potatoes?" a young male voice asked.

My eyes flicked up from the tray a millisecond after my brain recognized his tambor. My shock sent a wave of joy out from me like a bullet. The orderly stumbled in surprise on their way to the door. Blue Eyes straightened from his negligent sentry duty against the far wall of the cafeteria.

"Brendan!"

The urge to launch myself over the table to hug him was so strong I had to dig my nails into my fisted palms. I saw Blue Eyes take a step toward me in my peripheral vision at my hint of movement. As extra precaution, I wove my feet back, around, and behind the legs of my plastic institutionalized kiddie chair. I would do anything necessary to savor this visit as long as it would be allowed. Oscar-worthy performance of model patient coming right up.

Brendan returned a huge grin. "Good to see you too, chica," Brendan said, his happiness filling the immediate space around him with a light glow. I hadn't seen that color in so long; my fingers itched to reach out and touch it.

I could feel a tinge of concern begin to cloud the clear warm tones, though, and the instant dimming of Brendan's aura dampened my excitement. Reality swung back on me hard. That's right. He was visiting his childhood friend in a mental institution. Why wouldn't that worry him?

"What are you doing here?" I said in a low tone. I surveyed our chaperones through quick glances, trying to gauge their level of attentiveness. The orderly had returned to some mild cleaning busywork, and Blue Eyes was slowly sinking back against the wall, assuming my threat level had returned to minimal.

"Visiting you, silly," Brendan replied. He sat comfortably in his chair, entirely at ease in this stifling setting. His shirt was clean and pressed, although it was a casual style. Just like always, his hygiene was impeccable, and the clean scent of his favorite aftershave calmed me as it slowly replaced the antiseptic stench in my nose. "I heard you had a little setback this week, so I thought a visit from a friend would encourage you to be on your best behavior."

His words slapped me in the face.

"If you're talking about me attacking a guard, it was a misunderstanding," I hedged, not wanting to sour such a nice visit with a lecture about proper behavior. It took all the rest of my available willpower to keep the pout out of my voice. "And they've changed my medications to help with some of the...side effects that led to the misunderstanding."

I tucked a strand of hair behind my ear, letting my fingers trail down the silky length to calm me. Even though it was Brendan, I was still embarrassed to have to talk about medications and side effects—mainly the hallucinations that haunted me waking and dreaming. Alarm bells of anxiety were beginning to grow louder in the back of my mind. I was struggling to focus on the present, the positive.

Brendan nodded in understanding, a mild smile still spread across his face. "I know, and you're doing so well," he said, reaching his hand across the table, palm up.

I reached for it hesitantly, not sure if I was allowed simple courtesy like a reassuring touch. My eyes darted around while my fingers inched slowly to meet his. He held my hand, giving it a comforting squeeze. Blue Eyes remained stoic against the wall.

"Just keep up the good work, okay? Once you're doing a little better with the medication, they promised I could take you on a day trip."

A weight dropped in my stomach.

"Day trip?" I asked.

How much longer was I going to have to wait to get bailed out? I asked myself. Something told me the promised day trip would never happen, constantly dangling just out of my reach. I couldn't get too excited about it. Just in case.

"Cool, right?" Brendan said, providing me another modicum of strength as his hand squeezed mine. "Any ideas on what you might want to do? We'll have to get it approved, but I'm sure we could do almost anything. Maybe a bookstore? Or a picnic?"

"Yeah," I said. The corners of my mouth pulled up shakily in a weak attempt at a smile. I nodded my head as I tried to clear the lump in my throat. My hand grew clammy in Brendan's firm grip. Walls of panic closed in on me as I spiraled down into a hole of anxiety. Fear colored my every thought, and all I could do was think about how I needed out. Like, now.

"Sounds great." The voice was mine. I was pretty sure. The noise in my head was too loud to be certain.

Brendan's smile faltered when he caught on to the dimming behind my eyes. The corners of the room were slipping away from my vision until I could barely see the impaled pile of potatoes only inches away from my face. The emotions of others I had kept at a distance rushed in as my protective barriers finally broke under the weight my panic. The orderly's bitterness over the dried used gum on the underside of the tables. Blue Eye's idle musings about which pizza he would order for dinner. White Coat's anger about...something...

I felt a pressure against my cheeks, and I could feel my brows furrow in annoyance. Why did my face feel so weird?

"What happened?" a voice said.

Female?

Angry.

"We were just talking, and she shut down. I thought you said the new medication was working!" a different voice said.

Boy.

Frustrated.

Brendan?

Why would Brendan be in the mental hospital?

The back of my neck felt cold. My face was being moved back and forth, but I didn't, and couldn't, resist. Everything was falling away from my understanding. I couldn't even be sure what was happening to my physical body. Trying to control my thoughts was harder than gripping a wet bar of soap. The harder I clung to a thought, the further it shot out of my reach.

"Where were you?" angry female voice again.

"At the door. I was watching the whole time. She was fine, and then she wasn't," defensive male voice said.

Mildly annoyed and apathetic.

Had to be Blue Eyes. I was feeling more sure about that the longer I thought about it.

My face felt better, less squished, but I still felt like I was being jostled.

Too much input, physical and otherwise.

I was ready to surrender completely to the panic and just fade out, but the discomfort of being poked and prodded left me annoyed enough not to slip over the edge and into darkness. Flashes of emotion bobbed around, further distracting me from my peaceful nothingness.

Why wouldn't they just leave me alone?

"Evangeline."

White Coat's voice sliced through my despair, her tone inciting a tsunami of rage in me. She did not get to talk to me in that tone of voice. She sounded like I was some puppy who was caught chewing on her favorite shoe. She was about to get a talking to from me, and it was not going to be pretty.

Slowly, I pushed my barriers back into place. When I was this far under tow, I had to have strong visualizations in order for the amorphous energy in my mind to cooperate. On a typical day, they just stayed put without much thought. Once the barriers were disrupted, broken, or completely annihilated, it took my best imagination to create the necessary barriers. Today I chose a rusted iron portcullis with extra spiky edges to push White Coat and all her caustic thoughts back in their place.

I felt warmth under my chin. My eyes blinked furiously to clear my vision. I needed to take in sensory information not linked to the glowing orbs of emotion burned into the back of my skull.

I was not a fan of strangers touching my face.

Suddenly, my eyes sprang back into focus, and all I could see was Brendan. He was cupping my chin, his face close enough that I could count the various dark flecks that made up his deep brown eyes. His eyelids crinkled as his reassuring smile spread across his face. Nothing but warmth was coming off him, and I lowered the hackles that had been bunching up in my shoulders.

"There's my girl," Brendan said, dropping his hand from my chin once I held his gaze.

I must have looked reproachful because an apologetic wave of guilt flickered through the relief in his aura. He knew how sacred I kept my personal space, so he inched back from my immediate breathing space and kept himself within sight. His hesitation to allow the various grumpy medical team members past my preferred acquaintance boundary did make me warm slightly back towards appreciation instead of annoyance. I was thankful, at least, for his small kindness.

"I'm fine," I said quickly, deftly blocking an attempt at a blood pressure cuff coming toward me. I was still seated in my chair, although it had been pulled slightly out from the table to allow for better access to my non-responsive frame.

Brendan was kneeling in front of me, taking up the most room. His hands rested lightly on the sides of my calves, a steady reminder that he was still here and that I was still here, too. I looked around to see a crowd had gathered behind him, noting White Coat tapping violently on her tablet a series of short notes about yet another incident with Patient B.

"That has yet to be determined," White Coat ground out through clenched teeth. Her eyes darted up occasionally from her notes to assess my condition from second to second. "We'll have to run some tests, of course. I'm concerned that you keep losing consciousness during regular activities. We may have to adjust your dosage."

"Just give her a second," Brendan said, his eyes never moving from mine.

I blushed under his intense gaze. I was mortified he had been front row center for yet another episode of Evangeline: A Space Case Odyssey.

"I'm sure the tests can wait."

"Unfortunately, that is not up to you to decide, Mr. Silva. I deeply apologize for the inconvenience, but I think it's time for you to go. Evangeline needs her rest," White Coat said, flicking her wrist at Blue Eyes to retrieve Brendan and escort him out.

Blue Eyes and I bristled at the same time, and a wave of insubordination rolled off him in a huff. Too bad I had to beat him to the punch.

"I thought you said you had to run tests? Clearly I'm not going to get any rest, and he's more of a help than you are in terms of my stress levels." White Coat stiffened.

"Also," I continued, "you can stop pretending you care about me for any other reason than your research paper. You should really save yourself the effort. You're not very good at faking emotions." I laid out the last comment with a little added pinch of agitation. Maybe in another context I would have gotten a response from the crowd, but the power dynamic was not skewed in my favor.

The room remained silent. All the medical assistants were collectively holding their breath, waiting for a response from the boss lady. Brendan emitted a wave of disapproval with a matching stern downturn of his eyebrows, but he gave my legs a reassuring squeeze, trying to direct my attention back to him.

"Oh, wow, did I miss a proposal?" Quentin said, sauntering into the lounge in his robe and pajamas. His entrance broke the mounting tension in one swift pop. Quentin openly surveyed the scene. His body twisted slightly as he took in Brendan on one knee, White Coat pale with rage, and the frozen school of medical assistant guppies. "Congratulations to the happy couple!"

"You have literally the worst timing. You know that?" I snarled, directing a bullet of rage toward Quentin, and Quentin alone. His appearance derailed what little control I had gained post-disassociation hubbub.

He doubled over with my blow, but covered it well with a rolling fake laugh. His face peered up, a knowing grin pulling one corner of his mouth up into a lopsided smirk. His oily forehead shone a little brighter under the harsh lights.

"I take it she said no," Quentin directed at Brendan. "Tough break, Romeo."

Brendan stiffened, his face stoic as he surveyed the posturing between Patient A and myself.

"Take a seat, Quentin. We'll get you some lunch," White Coat said, her eyes closed to slits in an attempt to read the social interaction between her two surly patients. She tapped distractedly on the case of her tablet, unsure of what note to describe the encounter best. "Everyone else is dismissed."

The medical staff gave one another knowing looks but made a swift exit before they could be called back. The gossip mill would be in fine spirits tonight, I realized, and I would be at the very center of it. Quentin sunk into a nearby chair, his legs crossed and bouncing while he was waited upon. I rolled my eyes hard and snorted, completely beside myself with his audacity.

I took a deep breath to steady myself. I pushed another ounce of strength into my barriers as a soothing reminder that they were in fact there. They couldn't help what came across my face, though, so I concentrated on removing all tension from my forehead and cheeks. In and out. In and out. I was in control.

Brendan gave my legs one final squeeze before getting up. I turned my attention back onto him as his aura pulsed through a quick succession of shock, embarrassment, and forced relaxation., much like I had just done internally. He was on edge now because of Quentin, and I glared at the psycho extra hard on Brendan's behalf.

"Give me a minute?" Brendan asked White Coat, who nodded assent.

Blue Eyes lingered for a few beats, but followed White Coat toward the door and resumed his stance against the wall, this time a little more defiant than surly. With the immediate space around us vacated, I felt like Brendan and I had a modicum of privacy, at least for a few brief moments. White Coat, taken by a burst of inspiration, began typing out the encounter on her tablet in the doorway, certain to maintain a good vantage point.

Brendan scooted his chair to face mine, resuming his owner-ship of the foot of space directly in front of me. He kept his hands folded between his legs, but I saw them flex toward mine but deciding at the last moment to leave our respective hands to ourselves.

I sighed.

"I'm sorry," I said, the air rushing out of me dissipating the remaining fight left in me. "Kind of ruined your visit, huh?" My unoccupied fingers hooked another loose strand of hair around my ear again, and the soothing trail down to my many split ends gave me something else to focus on other than Brendan's intense stare. Shame rose up to warm my cheeks.

"No need to apologize," Brendan said, his thumb tracing around his cuticles in his own absentminded tick. It reminded me of all the times I had seen him do that before.

I bit the inside of my cheek at the wash of memories that invaded my mind, causing my throat to close up again. I felt like I was failing him. I was still just a burden that needed looking after. At least Brendan bothered to come visit. No one else did anymore.

"I really am trying to do better," I said, half to convince him and half to convince myself. I was controlling it better, wasn't I? Even with the drugs inhibiting my barriers? I just wasn't going to promise what exactly it was I was doing better. The truth felt too taboo.

"I know. I can tell," Brendan said immediately, assuming I meant cooperation and submission. "And I remind your parents every day that you're working hard. Maybe I can bring them next time." Desperation muddied the flare of hope in Brendan's aura. Seeing that so clearly with my abilities only made me feel worse.

"We both know they won't come," I replied, fidgeting with the ends of my hair. "It's okay. I understand." I had to remind myself to breathe.

"No," Brendan said with a firm shake of his head. "They will come. I'll convince them."

"Brendan," I said, a heavy sigh escaping my mouth unexpectedly. "I don't expect them to come for me, ever."

"They need you," Brendan pressed. "Especially with Tomas…"

"Especially because of Tomas," I cut in. "I might as well be dead, too. At least to them, I guess I already kind of am."

"They only lost one child," Brendan argued. "The other one is sitting right in front of me."

"Just take care of them, okay?" I replied, not wanting to argue any further.

My mouth spasmed in a brief smile, but the facade was too much for me to maintain for long. Quentin was making too little noise in his effort to eavesdrop, and I didn't need his rendition of the exchange to be thrown back in my face later. "That was our deal."

"I know," he said. "I am looking after them. Just until you get back. That was the deal." Brendan's face searched mine for confirmation, but I had a hard time meeting his gaze.

Brendan pulled my fidgeting hands away from my nervous hair inspection and cupped them in the tight space left between us. I froze. If I yanked free of him too quickly, I would hurt his feelings.

"Your brother would kill me right now if he could see what's happening to you," Brendan said, a short bark escaping from him. His bitterness leaked into his aura, changing the color and the clarity once again. "It's my fault you're not better taken care of. Tomas would be doing such a better job."

It was my turn to grab his hands to comfort him. I pulled my hands away from his, bringing them back to cover the outside of his. I raised our hands slightly to draw his line of sight up to meet mine.

"You are not responsible for me," I said sternly, keeping his eyes locked with mine. His eyelids drew up a little, and I could tell his resistance was already making my speech futile. "Tomas wasn't responsible for me either. If that's why you're suffering, then just leave me here and don't come back. I can't take your life away from you, too. You have so many better things to be doing with your time than visiting your dead best friend's little sister in an insane asylum."

I was determined to have him hear me this time. If only I could underline my words with a little command. But I had made a promise. No funny business with Brendan. My words alone would have to be enough to convince him.

"Treatment center," he qualified.

"Loony bin," I shot back, making my eyes bulge out in a goofy face.

"Treatment center," he argued, a smile slowly spreading across his face. A pulse of joy cleared away the murky hesitation from moments before.

"Mental institution," I relented. "This is a place of learning, after all."

A huge pause filled the air between us. The moment felt like a long inhalation, when everything was suspended and the expectation of the next moment left a lag in time. All the judgment, fear, and shame were forgiven for those fleeting seconds, and we could just pretend that life was normal. It was perfect.

"Behave yourself, okay?" Brendan instructed, the lightness gone from him. Time lurched back into normal speed. His smile faltered as he began the difficult process of saying goodbye.

"When have I ever behaved?" I said with a small laugh. I squeezed his hands together before I released them.

"I'll see you soon," Brendan said, standing up and putting his chair back in its original place on the other side of the table.

Before I could get up, he leaned in and placed a kiss on my forehead. Suddenly I was drowning in his aftershave, the smell of home and safety wrapping around me once again. By the time I pulled myself out of my reverie, Brendan was already out of sight.

I sat there for a minute, biting the edge of my thumbnail in an attempt to reign in the tears that threatened to overflow. Now was not the time. I didn't know if I had the energy left to pull myself out of another spiral so soon after the last one.

A derisive snort jarred me from my concentration, and I remembered I wasn't alone.

"Honestly, you should have said yes," Quentin said, harping back on the proposal gag from his overly dramatic entrance. "If I wasn't so hungry, I think I might have vomited from the sight of the two of you. Sweet Jesus, let a man eat in peace."

"Stuff it, Quentin," I said, my voice bored and distracted as I followed Brendan in my mind's eye through the building, down in the elevator, across the parking lot, and finally to his car. Once inside, his emotions crackled like fireworks, spinning and flickering through everything he had kept from me during the past half hour. I felt like a voyeur, but I couldn't look away.

His emotions cycled in a faltering loop as his mind tried to decode what I had said and how I had acted. There was a lot of worry, but there was also hope and affection. After a while I had to pull myself back. It was getting too tempting to pry beyond recognizing basic emotions, and that fell under our do not disturb pact. Of course the one person I had been dying to know the inner mind of since I was ten was off limits. But a promise was a promise.

At some point, I was escorted out of the cafeteria and back to my room. I didn't even register Quentin's sassy salutation when I left, but I'm sure I would get teased about it later. Ad nauseum. And they wondered where the animosity between us came from.

I collapsed onto my bed, biding my time until the next test by following Brendan on his winding commute home, the scenic way, the one he showed me shortly after Tomas's accident to help me relax after a particularly bad series of night terrors. I wondered if he did it on purpose.

FOUR

"Evangeline."

Evangeline.

Evangeline.

My name echoed loudly against the endless variety of institutional white tiles in my room. My fingers clenched the pillow so hard my lips kissed my knuckles, and I suppressed a strong urge to fling one of my lone remaining comforts at the speaker. I was going to pay for my outburst in the lounge, but I was already thinking offense. Whatever White Coat had coming my way, I was ready to parry and then some.

A great reservoir of rage teemed just under my conscious self. The waves rocked violently enough that I could access it easily at each cresting of every new wave. Part of me was concerned by how readily I could repurpose my growing darkness, but I knew what kept me in check was stronger. But White Coat and I had no love lost. I didn't feel as morally obligated to protect her from myself.

"Evangeline," she said again, a slight edge to her tone.

"What?" I replied crisply into the air.

I didn't have to speak loudly. There was probably one microphone for every one of my fingers and toes. That was true for the cameras based on my mental eaves dropping and limited peeks of White Coat's tablet screen. Honestly, if they missed the opportunity to bug my bed frame, someone should find another line of work. Observation was clearly not their strong suit.

"We're going to need to run some simulations," White Coat said. "Please present yourself at the door for your escort." The speaker squawked when she disengaged her microphone. On second thought, maybe the budget didn't allow for updated audio surveillance from this century.

"And if I don't?" I asked, unable to keep the waver of fear from my overspent bravado. The fingernails of the hand buried under my pillow dug into my palm. I tried to slow my heartbeat from its gallop. Simulation was the best euphemism for torture I had ever heard.

I was curled on top of my bed and had been dealing with Quentin's wheedling monologue for the past hour. Apparently, our lack of interaction at lunch had really ruffled his feathers because he would not stop talking over our unfortunately crystal clear psychic hotline. Quentin had many thoughts and opinions about young marriage, particularly within the supernatural community. My nerves were already beyond raw.

"Then your escort will be forced to retrieve you. Staff have been instructed to use whatever means necessary to make you comply. It's up to you," she said, clicking off again.

"I'll show you whatever means necessary, you psycho bitch," I mumbled.

Okay. Deep breath. Options?

I could resist, but I would have a second episode in so many hours. My guilt over ruining Brendan's earlier visit was still fresh. Doors were not going to magically open for me if I made a run for it. Running wasn't really my style. Or strength. My only strength was currently in need of desperate recharge. Rage licked up at me, but I pushed it back down reflexively.

No decent excuse for this outburst came to mind. I wanted to save my rebellions for worthy moments to maximize impact and energy expenditure. This one was not passing the bullshit test.

White Coat was saved for this round, but I couldn't keep up

this saintly act forever. Following directions that were against my best interest really irked me. I may comply today, but the balance owed to me by The Association was getting higher and higher the longer I stayed.

The beep of the security badge sounded from the other side of my door, and I sighed.

Before they could open the door fully, I had rolled myself out of bed and stood, sulking at my escort. Blue Eyes looked equally as pleased as I was that we got to spend so much time together.

"Don't you ever get time off?" I asked him. "Your compensation package sucks. You should really consider renegotiating that at your next review."

His face remained blank as he held the door open for me. I moved out into the hall, and his inner monologue filtered into my head as clearly as a podcast.

Oh, you have no idea. Pay seemed worth it at the time, but damn, this place gives me the creeps. Damn Johnson spraining his ankle. He owes me for covering his shifts. Damn know-it-all kids and the spooky science shit's got my skin crawling. Once the debt's paid off, I'm gone.

"Same," I said out loud, eliciting a full body spasm from Blue Eyes. I savored a smirk and used the opportunity to tuck a strand of hair behind my ear.

We continued down the hall that would lead to our final destination: my least favorite room in my least favorite hall on my least favorite floor of my least favorite place. On my numerous visits, I had counted the floors of people in the building around me. I could track their movements, whether horizontally along the floor or in the elevators in manic little short trips between the only occupied floors.

No one took the stairs.

Of all ten floors, only the top three seemed to be occupied. We never left the eighth floor, so I assumed the other floors mirrored this one in terms of offices and rooms. I wondered if some day all of the rooms would be occupied. If, just like Windermere, The

Association had kept them, knowing full well who would be coming and when.

I shook my head to dislodge the thought. It was not one I wanted to keep ruminating on. Blue Eyes cycled through his complaint list again, and I tuned out of his emotional feed as well. It was time to wall off as much as I could anyway. Some part of me needed to survive to piss Blue Eyes off another day.

He opened the door to the observation room, which was dark except for the eerie blue glow of the open sensory deprivation tank. I bit the inside of my cheek hard and reminded myself to breathe.

God, I really hated this wing.

"You know the drill," Blue Eyes said, not waiting for me to get in the door before he started to close it behind me. I scooted in quickly, an indignant yelp escaping from my lips as the coldness from the steel door neared the thin cotton of my pajama bottoms.

"Bon Voyage."

The door clicked shut firmly behind me.

With the florescent glow of the hall lights gone, only the dim blue of the sensory deprivation tank was left to guide me to this afternoon's particular round of doom.

I rubbed the goosebumps from my arms, feeling the soft hairs resist my transient comforting. Without any further instruction from the hidden squawkbox, I disrobed. I was allowed to keep my underthings on, which I always did.

It was weird enough in the tank; I didn't need the added anxiety of having to fight my way out naked. Who knew you could get such small comfort from panties and a tank top?

Dipping my toe in, I grimaced and recoiled. All the hairs on my body rose in protest.

It was slightly warm, the water heavy with whatever material was supposed to engulf me and turn all my senses to white noise. I hissed as I lowered each leg in against all my fight or flight instincts. Each time it was a little worse getting in, knowing exactly what would happen next but then again never quite knowing either. It was one thing to lose your sense of sight, but a whole other thing to completely lose your hold on reality. Before coming here, I hadn't been afraid of the dark or of small spaces.

Enough time in the tank could change just about anything.

My fingers gripped the side of the shell, and my heels bounced off the bottom of the chamber. Without warning, the lid groaned alive, slowly encasing me in the pod and cutting me off from the crisp air of the over air-conditioned laboratory. I had to yank my fingers away from the edge before the lid shut on them.

They didn't stop the observation if you were bleeding, I had learned. Blood and whatever this water mixture was did not mix well. It hadn't killed me, but it hadn't felt great either.

The lid clicked home, and I was in total darkness. The bluish glow that had emitted from the tank had blinked off automatically as soon as the lid closed. I was immersed in darkness, an oddly warm liquid, and the thoughts of me and my closest one hundred neighbors.

I had been lectured on the procedure of the observation tank enough times that it played like a scratchy old recording in my mind.

Lie back.

Relax.

And focus.

It was supposed to be time for me to reconnect or whatever, but honestly, I knew they were testing my range. I was never quite sure how they knew, but I had a feeling they had planted people on the outside and determined how far out I could sense based on the readings they got from my own reaction to them. Today, I was not into playing their games. If they wanted to test my range, then I would give them a test.

I let the barriers I had so sloppily crafted after Brendan's visit fall away. Immediately, I had a sense of the techs behind the two-way mirror, monitoring me. I could sense Quentin down the hall attempting to communicate with Adair again. I even found

Brendan driving on the expressway home, about thirty miles away.

Not only that, but I could sense everyone in between.

So I pressed further.

As the feelings and life forms pressed into my mind's eye, I let them fall away into blurs. It was like I was zooming in with a high-powered lens, letting the background blur to hyperfocus on my target. Easily enough, I found my tia in Detroit. Back at Windermere, when I first found her, I had absolutely freaked out. Now, I used her as an anchor to keep going.

Usually, I did my best to hide my range. The how's never seemed to matter, as The Association figured out about my range enough to know I could cross at least one time zone. I often thought I should dig around more to find out what they knew about me for certain, but right now, the only thought I had was Noah. Could I reach her? Montana seemed like it was on the other side of the world from my little tank in New England.

Abuela was in Chicago with another aunt and uncle, so I focused on her next. Could I get to her?

I pressed past Tia's consciousness in Michigan to my next anchor, and the edges of my focal point wavered in protest as I stretched and stretched. Suddenly, I felt as if I had hit a wall. I felt my body jerk in the tank, but no sound lapped back at me to know for certain.

So many people.

So many *supernaturals*.

It was naive of me, I realized, to think supernaturals wouldn't all group together. The concentration had been high at Windermere and in New York City, where I liked to wander in my other tank visits, but somehow I hadn't thought beyond that.

Maybe finding my gifted peers wouldn't be as hard as I had thought. Sure, not all supernaturally bent individuals had high enough concentrations to be considered Elevated, but I had had no concept of just how common our bloodlines had become.

Maybe the readings I was picking up were supernaturals. Maybe they weren't. Maybe they were just regular people.

The problem with my far-reaching range was always details. I knew there were people, and the clear broadcasters drew my attention easily enough, but beyond the basics, I had very little idea who I was actually sensing. I just knew there were a lot of them.

The wall of bodies grew denser the harder I pushed. The focus of my powers had degraded to the point that the edges shook harder than the frames of a video shot on an old flip phone. I was starting to feel the pull back that was bound to happen. The laws of physics seemed to work just fine for Empaths, too.

I needed to find my abuela. Today. If I couldn't find her now, how was I supposed to find Noah in Montana? Assuming she was where Quentin and I thought she was. And that was a big if.

Ifs and maybes were fun until your immediate existence was depending on them.

I felt the pinching of a migraine coming on, which gave me a thirty seconds heads up before my mental rubber band snapped me back into my own consciousness. I had no memories of Chicago. Desperation would need to lead me home.

Please let abuela be a clear broadcaster, I wished as I flung out my last burst of energy.

My mind snagged on the South Side. It took every fiber of my being to direct my energies to where I thought I had felt a tug. I couldn't be sure it was my abuela, but I was less sure about coincidences in life these days, so I ran with it.

Her consciousness was so weak, I was startled. Was that really all I could pick up from this far away?

No, that wasn't right. I felt Tio Manuel next to her, and he was flaring bright.

Worry. Sadness. Love.

Was Abuela sick? She seemed almost asleep, her emotions blanketed by what I assumed to be medication much like mine.

I panicked.

She couldn't be sick, couldn't be dying. I had seen her only last year, and she was stronger and more resilient than a cactus in Arizona. She was the strongest person I knew. How could she be dying?

My focus on her snapped as my emotions and panic took over the majority of my mind. I was kicked out, back into myself, and my body flailed wide at the sudden change. Sludge choked me as I gasped for air against the waves of disrupted fluid.

Being unable to hear myself drowning lent an added layer of trauma to future simulations. I reached my hands where I assumed the front or top of the pod was. After several disorienting swipes, I found purchase, hitting the lid with all my might.

Cacophony surrounded me. All the noises I had wanted to hear and some I didn't came rushing at me, fighting for dominance. The noise raced to catch up with my physical sensations.

I was pulled into the freezing air by a strong pair of hands, and as soon as my throat cleared from all the fluid, I screamed until my throat was raw.

I felt a pinch on my arm and fell into blackness once again

FIVE

I woke up shivering in my bed. My hair lay in damp coils on my pillow, so densely tangled that it formed a net of knots and snarls. I was in fresh pajamas, but the cold sweat of the medication made the cotton cling to me as if I had been pulled from the pod just moments before.

My teeth chattered violently, and I could taste the blood from the cuts on my tongue and cheeks from their repeated attacks. A groan escaped through the steady metronome of bone against bone. The bright fluorescent lights blared through the small room, but I was too weak to grab my pillow and toss it over my eyes and ears. The low buzz made my ears itch.

What the heck did you do, swallow the whole tank? Quentin's voice rang in my head. His nasally tone bounced against the crumbling barriers in my mind. I tried to mentally swat it away, but my physical body reacted with a limp flip of my wrist. Well, that was no good.

I groaned again into the open air, begging to be put back under rather than deal with this fresh assault. Even on my good days, Quentin and the ambient noises of The Association accommodation put me on edge. In my current state, it felt extra cruel.

I mean, honestly, what did you think was going to happen? Did you even have a plan or think through the consequences of overreaching? Quentin's voice sent a derisive snort through the connection, and I flinched. *You don't think very much, do you? Just follow your impulses and your intuition. You're going to get killed one of these days because of it. I don't have to be an Oracle to know that.*

Shut up, I sent back. *Shutupshutupshutup.*

Constantly saying I told you so is not as satisfying as I had hoped, Quentin said with a sigh. *But I have to admit, you've got flair. The whole place is talking about you. Quite the celebrity patient. Notorious even.*

Why are you still talking? I shot back, adding a lick of rage to my missive. I felt him flinch on his side as the arrow found its target. *Leave me alone.*

I squeezed my eyes shut even tighter, gathering what little focus I could muster to repair and strengthen the core barriers in my mind. I wasn't fast enough to save myself from another Quentin tirade though.

You're a little too good at emotional attacks, you know? Makes me think you've got a little more Commander in you than Empath. Wasn't your brother a Commander?

If you do not shut up right now, so help me, I will melt your brain from the inside out, I said, my tone growing colder and colder the more he pushed my buttons. The walls were almost done, and the shivering began to calm as I focused my remaining energy on myself rather than fending off loose emotional tidal waves from the surrounding town. More had leaked through with the buzzing of the lights than I had thought. At a certain point, noise was just noise.

I'm just saying, maybe it's better off you're in here. With all your power and your volatility, you should definitely not be in public. I know why I'm here, and it's about time you realize your place as well.

The only thing making me more volatile than White Coat is you. Don't flatter yourself. You're in here because you're just as unstable as I am, and you're too nosy for your own good.

Nosy? That's rich. At least I deal in facts and actual events. You're left with ambiguous impressions and visual codes you don't even under-

stand. How are you supposed to strategize without any concrete information? Quentin continued.

And that was it.

As far as I'm concerned, I have exactly what I need to get what I want, whenever I want it, from whomever I want. Just because I'm not using my gifts to your satisfaction does not mean I'm useless. I'll figure out my issues on my own, thank you very much. You can wait for your instant replay because I'm done dealing with you, I volleyed back at him.

Before he could even blink, I made the loudest mental door slam I had ever done, locking his one way channel into my head behind several mental barriers built with enough desperation and intention to be the equivalent of concrete backed by bricks anchored with granite. It wasn't white subway tile, but my DIY renovation binge watching had finally paid off.

I released a deep breath, letting the tension melt from my aching muscles as the pent-up frustration left in a long train of carbon dioxide. Finally, I was alone enough to release my emotions into the room safely. They could only dissipate without a suitable host. The ventilation system would recycle the air into next room, free and clear of any residual angst.

The rushing noise of my breath echoed back to me, and I let the sounds of my breathing calm me until the buzz of the lighting became soothing white noise and the quiet vault of my inner mind remained silent and unprovoked. After several minutes of trained relaxation, I slipped into a dream of my own volition, thankful that this rest would be black sleep and not medicine-induced dysphoria.

I SAT on the front steps of my abuela's three-flat in Chicago. The cold cement bit into the back of my legs, which were clothed in only a pair of shorts. Looking up, I saw the sun high in the sky, the warmth tingling on my skin interrupted occasionally by clouds propelled by the licking of the lakefront breeze.

Next to me was my abuela just as I had seen her the previous summer. Looking around, I realized the familiarity rang true, like a memory. I had sat like this with her once upon a time. I knew it was midwinter in New York, where I was being held in an Association-run mental institution, but this reality seemed equally true. I pressed my lips together, trying to work out what was going on.

"Mija," a soft voice called to me, pulling my wandering train of thought back to the present scene. "Are you well?"

I turned to see her sitting in the teal rocking chair my father had made her before he died, the blanket covering her lap dancing with a brightly colored pattern. Everything seemed a little too vibrant, and I balked at her question.

"Abuela, what's going on?" I asked, my voice pitching higher and colored my question with more youth and whininess than I had intended. I had expected a calm dream after my tank adventure, complete blackness even. This hallucination was painfully real, and I could feel the prickling of frustration pushing tears to the brims of my eyes.

My body was screaming at me that something was wrong. So, so wrong.

"You came to visit," Abuela said with a knowing smile. I squinted at her bright aura, trying desperately to find what seemed out of place. "It's sweet my little birdie still thinks of her grandma when she's so far away. I thought you'd never come."

"But I haven't, Abuela," I argued. "I'm stuck in New York. I can't visit you."

"You're here now, aren't you? And you saw me earlier today as well," she said, letting the rocking chair teeter her back and forth in the afternoon breeze. A knowing smile lay contently on her cheeks, and her eyes shone with pride.

I opened my mouth to argue again, but I clammed up. Abuela was not someone you argued with, even though I knew she would never dismiss me if I had a question. My stomach lurched.

But what did she mean I had seen her earlier?

"I don't understand," I said, lifting my chin in an attempt to keep the tears from falling. I was so tired. I could not handle these crazy dreams that weren't dreams or conversations that weren't really conversations. "Abuela, please tell me what's going on."

"Little bird, come here," she said, opening her arms toward me, compassion rolling off her in radiating waves as bright as the afternoon sun above me. My body moved me to her side before I could consciously tell it to go. "It's all right. Everything will be all right."

I bent over her, holding her tightly in an embrace. She was bonier than I had remembered, but she hugged me back as fiercely as I clung to her. I wished I could climb into her lap like when I was younger, but even with my limited stature, I was too big and she was too weak for such comforts.

"Abuela, are you like me?" I asked in a husky whisper. The tears that couldn't escape my eyes had traveled to my throat. I swallowed hard. "Like Papi was and like Tomas?"

A hum escaped her lips, buried firmly in my hair. Her strong hand patted my back repeatedly until the tension cleared my froggy throat. I pulled away from her, looking her in the eyes once more. A knowing glint shone back in her warm brown eyes.

"You have a very important purpose in life, mija. You must remain strong, like your abuela. Being a de los Santos comes with a lot of responsibility, but we hold it with grace and pride, eh?" Her hand cupped my face, and my lips trembled. Tears threatened to break through what little resolve I had mustered. I could only nod my understanding.

"Why didn't you tell me before?" I finally managed, immediately worried from my previous memory of her fading essence. "There's so much I want to talk to you about."

"Us old folk tend to forget the suffering of the young. I thought I could not help you in your journey since it is so different from mine," she replied, stroking my hair. "I was foolish. Can you forgive your abuela?"

"Of course," I said immediately, perplexed at her admission. "But you can help me now, can't you?"

"Ah, of that I am not certain," she said. "Of our family's many gifts, immortality is not one of them. I need to join your father and brother soon. They need me."

"I need you," I replied. "I don't know what to do. I don't even know what I don't know, Abuela. There are so many people like us, but they're not like us. They want power and money, and I don't think I can do anything about it."

The words tumbled out unedited. I hadn't realized my greatest fears in all this was how powerless I felt. How alone.

"There will always be those people, mija," Abuela said, her knowing smile growing serious for a moment. "But you must remember there are also many people like you. People who care for others, who live with kindness. You find those people, mija, and you bring them together. Love is always stronger than fear."

"How will I know? How will I find them? Abuela, it's too much," I said, hanging my head and refusing to look her in the eye. Tears had started to run down my cheeks, and I worried I would completely lose it if I showed any more. The same feeling that had told me this was no normal dream pulsed again. Time seemed to be slipping away, and I did not want to regret any wasted time.

Abuela clicked her tongue at me, rubbing my arm for comfort.

"You are de los Santos, Evangeline," Abuela said. "You have everything you need in here." Her hand rested against my heart, and I clung to it with both of my hands.

"I don't want you to go," I said, a dark pit opening in the bottom of my stomach. The brightness of the false summer day flared up, and I could barely see anything anymore. My eyes were drawn to Abuela's brown eyes, framed in pillows and creases from years of happiness and memories.

"Going? Who said I was going anywhere, little bird?" her voice said, the light blinding my vision even from her eyes. "I am simply coming home."

The afterglow of light haunted the black of my eyelids as I dropped back into unconsciousness. The remaining tears I had been holding back from her escaped down my cheeks, leaving my pillow even damper than before.

SIX

I had started counting the tiles for the tenth time since dawn before the lights finally clicked on. After a fitful half sleep for most of the night, the memory of my abuela seemed to burn away all the other nightmares. Probably for the best.

Unlike my usual routine, I stayed in bed until Blue Eyes beeped in. I felt the air stir with his agitation as soon as he reached the bed and found me wide awake and fully noncompliant.

"Time for breakfast. Let's go," he grunted, his shoulders jerking toward the door, as if I didn't know where the only way out was.

I ignored him.

"Evangeline," White Coat's voice buzzed over the intercom, the click of disengagement hitting me like a smack across the face.

Blue Eyes flexed his hands, itching to grab me from my bed and haul me out the door.

"Evangeline," White Coat repeated. Again, her tone indicated not only her impatience but also her severely limited interactions with anybody under the age of thirty. Didn't she know teenagers were supposed to be contrary? The more she said my name, the more I melded my will to my mattress.

I blinked my eyes slowly and resumed counting the tiles. It seemed to be the most important thing to do in order to retain my sanity, so I didn't question it.

"If you don't get up right now, I'll be forced to drag you out of bed," Blue Eyes said. A tinge of excitement rolled off his body, eager to set the undisciplined child straight. He looked up toward the box, as if pleading for verbal approval to haul me out against my will.

"Evangeline," White Coat said in a crisp voice, over enunciating in an attempt to hide the crackle of anger in her voice. It was useless. I could feel it radiating off her from the monitor room down the hall. "Enough."

A tear escaped down my cheek, but I didn't flinch. Nothing was going to move me today if I had anything to do with it. I sent a little more oompf to my barriers in preparation. As stubborn as I was, White Coat was that much determined, if not more. I never liked an easy win.

Blue Eyes raised his hand to his earpiece, nodding an affirmative at the directive he received. They tried so hard to keep things from me, as if I wouldn't know about it since it wasn't broadcast over the loudspeakers. Sure, sometimes it wasn't full sentences, but intentions spoke louder than words. Knowing what was unsaid was always more important when dealing with people. Especially Association people.

I felt the disturbance of the air as Blue Eyes pushed off his heel to start toward me.

And that's exactly how he stayed.

I didn't need to turn my head to see him freeze out of the corner of my eye. Another tear escaped, but I let it fall without interference. The intercom squawked a feedback noise before White Coat broke through.

"Evangeline!" A tinge of panic leaked through in White Coat's tone. At first pass, you would hear anger, but I could tell White Coat was starting to feel out of control.

It was interesting how even though The Association cronies couldn't prove it was me, they somehow figured it out. No, I can't physically block people from my presence. About all I can do is enable a mute button in my brain so I can tune them out, but I was able to influence them in another way.

If Tomas were here, he would scold me for using my powers against adults, but honestly, it's his fault I could even externalize anything. If he were still here, it would be his power.

But he's not. So it's mine.

This much I had figured out before Tomas's accident, and it was a lot compared to what Noah had parsed out or even what Mags had known all along. I guess those of us who come from supernatural dynasties got a little edge. Sort of.

While I knew the basics of the planes of power, I knew that each face of the Eight came with an external and an internal wielder. As balanced as the planes were, the powers could not be held by one person alone. It was just too much. Two could handle it, or at least had a better shot. Their chances of surviving improved tenfold if they were together and got along with one another.

No one had quite explained that to my parents, though.

Abuela had been gifted, it seemed, but my mother was not. As soon as my father passed, she had taken me back home to her parents in New York City, leaving my brother Tomas with Tio Manuel and Abuela in Chicago.

It wasn't long before my mother remarried and changed my last name, doing her best to cut me off from my father's family, who she blamed for not only my father's death but also the problems both my brother and I seemed to be having. Tomas developed his Elevation early, so my mom abandoned him with the family "like him" who "knew how to handle" him. Being younger than my brother, I showed no signs of these gifts, so I was removed in the hopes of growing up untainted.

Tomas, however, was never one to be deterred. He always found me, no matter how many times we moved. One time, he even hitchhiked from Chicago to surprise me on my birthday. Mother had been furious. The very next week I had been shipped off to Windermere for my newly blossomed "behavioral issues," and Tomas was left to search for me yet again.

It had been the last time I had seen him alive.

I had my first full-blown breakdown when Tomas died. That breakdown was the catalyst that spurred everyone in my life into motion, mainly against one another or in direct opposition to me.

Mags and I were never the same. She thought it was because I was weak, but honestly, the power that had surged into me the moment Tomas died nearly took me along with him. Trying to keep it all together…well. Honestly, it took all of my energy not to explode, never mind keep a friendship going with someone who turned out to be merely allies of convenience.

Blue Eyes started to purple beside me, his breath becoming more and more ragged. My tears had dried up, but his face was wet with a combination of sweat, tears, and snot. He was bawling like a baby, but his body was rooted to the floor, so overwhelmed all it could do was maintain.

The door burst open, an alarm going off raucously behind White Coat, who had stormed in without properly beeping through security protocols.

"Evangeline, you stop this right now," she directed, pointing her tablet at me. "Any longer and he's going to need a crash cart."

"It's nothing he can't handle," I said, my voice devoid of any inflection or emotion. It was the tiles or Blue Eyes' brain or my social etiquette. I couldn't be sure which would be the first to break. "It's what I've been dealing with for years. He should be fine."

"Stop this immediately," White Coat said, holding back a pair of medical associates, one clearly poised to sedate me and while the other resuscitated Blue Eyes.

I could feel their hesitation. What would happen if they sedated me before I dropped my connection? Would Blue Eyes be stuck in that state permanently? I hadn't thought about it either, but no one moved. It seemed like we were not going to find out today.

My interior walls were strong, not letting anything in. I was numbed to everyone around me. All my energy was solely focused on the external, which in this particular moment was all my sadness and pent-up anxiety beamed directly at Blue Eyes. I felt hollow. It was almost as if I was observing from afar; my body and mind seemed so foreign and out of control. I had no more to give, and I was having real trouble finding a reason to care.

Suddenly, there was an outburst at the door.

Quentin shoved past a member of the medical team, marching right into the center of the melee.

"What the hell is going on?" he said, his voice bouncing off the freshly counted subway tiles. He sounded big and important. His question was answered only by the sniveling groans of Blue Eyes, who remained teetering on the brink of collapse.

"Evangeline," White Coat said evenly, ignoring Quentin. "You need to stop. Now."

Both of her arms were out in front of her. Her tactic appeared to mirror that of an animal control officer attempting to detain a rabid raccoon.

"That's your tactic?" Quentin snarled. "Scolding her? You've got to be shitting me."

He shouldered past White Coat, who had remained a safe distance between Blue Eyes, the door, and my bed. Quentin didn't feel the need for such physical boundaries.

He walked straight up to my bed and promptly flipped me, along with my mattress, onto the floor.

And then everything happened at once.

I yelped in surprise, my concentration breaking the control I had over Blue Eyes before I could even hit the ground. While I was trying to claw myself out from underneath the mattress and various bed sheets that had trapped me, I could hear the medical team assessing Blue Eyes, dragging him from the room so they could treat him before I could get any more ideas.

"The next time you want to throw a tantrum, Drama Queen, try not to ruin someone's life in the process. And you," Quentin said, rounding on White Coat, "better get a handle on her before she really goes off the reservation. If you push her to do that again, I swear to God I'll ruin you in direct proportion for the massacre she'll bring down. She's not even the worst of them, and you can't even control her outbursts."

I threw the last sheet over my head, finally clearing my vision. Quentin was drawn up to his full height, a posture he rarely took advantage of considering his lanky frame. He towered over White Coat, but she seemed to be holding her own space well, save for the obvious reddening of her cheeks.

"If it's all right with everyone," Quentin continued, "I would like to eat breakfast now." He shouldered past White Coat again, this time stopping at the door.

"Are you coming, or do I have to hear your hunger pangs through the wall?" Quentin directed at me, pointedly ignoring White Coat and the lone remaining technician, who was frozen, unsure if it was the time to leap forward and sedate me or if she had missed her window. "Your Highness?"

"Don't you dare call me that," I shot back at him, kicking my way out of the rat's nest of sheets at my feet. I dashed toward the door, keeping my feet light in case I needed to switch to an all-out sprint. I eyed White Coat warily, but she remained rooted to her spot, the tension rolling off her and permeating the small room. I didn't think anyone needed to be an Empath to feel the ocean of rage she was drowning in. Once I was past her, I ducked first into the hall, leading the way to the lounge and our breakfast, which was probably cool and rubbery at this point.

I cleared my throat as we walked, trying to figure out the best way to break the ice.

"Thank you," Quentin said, a twitch of a smile flashing across his stoic face. "I believe that's the phrase you're looking for."

"Call me Your Highness again and I'll throttle you," I shot back, jabbing out an elbow to his ribs. "Tantrum. Yeah, right."

"Spade's a spade," Quentin said, opening the door for us into the lounge. "Just imagine what you could do with some training."

"We're not talking about that right now," I said in an overly cheery voice. My skin crawled just thinking about the depth of emptiness I had felt at the expense of all that emotional energy. "It's never going to happen again."

"If you say so," Quentin said, taking a seat. "But for the record, I called it."

"Called what?" I said, slumping into my own seat. "We didn't have a wager going of who was going to crack first. That seems like a lose-lose situation for the both of us."

"You'll be the one to lead us all," Quentin said with an evil grin. "And Mags is going to hate it."

SEVEN

I was scheduled to be in the immersion tank that afternoon, but hours passed, and no one came to get me. Lunch came and went without an escort, and I had the displeasure of thanking Quentin mentally for at least getting me out for breakfast. They were probably drawing straws for who had to deal with me now. Instead, I spent the afternoon making a pros and cons list on whether tank time would have been a good thing or a good-thing-my-parents-signed-a-waiver thing.

The barriers I had erected after my tantrum remained solid, blocking Quentin's annoying chatter, leaving me with a rare peaceful afternoon devoid of people and the constant ebb and flow of emotions.

Well.

Peaceful minus being stuck in a mental institution.

The beep of an unexpected security badge made me tense from head to toe.

Who would come for me now? It wasn't dinnertime. I glanced at the speaker in the corner, but it remained silent, meaning the beep wasn't White Coat adjacent. Even on good days, she only came after it was clear she had to visit in person rather than conducting her business over the speaker box. I still felt fragile from my earlier battle of wills. I didn't dare lower my barriers to get a few seconds' heads up on my newest visitor. My stomach felt sour. All data suggested this was not a good surprise guest.

My unease caused me to sit upright, my legs still caught up in my sheets. I chewed on the inside of my cheek and secretly hoped this was not one of those times where my limited self-defense training would be necessary. My legs were frozen in place, and a brief comic montage of me trying to run away but tripping and falling on my face completely entangled in sheets shot the bile from my stomach up into my throat. This was not good.

The first thing I saw about my visitor was the slate grey hair pulled back in an elaborate chignon. A set of razorblade cheekbones and steel blue eyes followed as the Dean walked in, tucking the security card neatly into the pocket of her blazer.

My face went numb, lips tingling as cold took over the rest of my frame. The hair on the back of my neck and arms stood at attention. A shiver ran down my spine, and I made quick work of untangling my legs and stood at the foot of my bed. Before Dean Moriarty could take as many steps, I had already tucked my hair behind my ear twice.

"Evangeline," she said in a warm voice. "You're looking well."

I had to bite the inside of my lip before a smart comment slipped out unattended.

It was one thing to sass White Coat, but a whole other thing to sass Dean Moriarty. I felt a slight pulse of calm radiate out from her. Its ripples filled the room from bottom corner to the ceiling tiles like water filling a new vase. I could feel the pressure of the emotion push at me from all directions.

The energy seeped into my skin, stopping just short of my heart. It took all the energy I had left to block her emotional command, and I worried my other barriers would fail if I had to keep up the emotional defense for too long.

My recent victory of reaching Chicago felt tainted and inconsequential now.

The smile plastered to Dean Moriarty's face faltered for a microsecond when I did not visibly relax. My posture remained rigid, and I clasped my hands tightly in front of me so they would be less likely to shake. Noah's voice echoed in the back of my head, chiding me for not faking better. I returned a watery smile, more in spite of my internal monologue. If only Noah knew how strong the Dean really was.

"Please, take a seat," Dean Moriarty said, offering her open hand in direct solicitation.

I slid hesitantly in front of my messy bed and perched on the edge of the mattress, ready to pop up at the slightest direction. I thought of how rich it was that she was acting like a host in my own room and I almost scoffed aloud. Checking myself, I realized the whole building was really hers. Who was whose guest?

"I have some unfortunate news for you."

Another bucket of imaginary ice water chilled my bones, but I remained silent, bracing for the news.

"It seems your grandmother had taken ill some time ago. I'm not sure if you were aware of her condition," Dean Moriarty said, pausing to read my energy. The tone of her voice told me she was not really interested in a verbal reply, thank God.

I clenched my teeth as imperceptibly as I could. The weight of tears started to press against my lower eyelids, and my tongue was stuck pushing all my fear into the backs of my bottom teeth.

Count to three.

Exhale.

Deep breath in for another three seconds. I continued the cycle, praying silently my blood pressure didn't escalate enough to pique her interest. I imagined a lake, its surface placid and smooth, reflecting light like a mirror.

Don't let her feel your panic, Quentin's voice said in my head. Damn it.

Not. Helping, I replied, trying to shove him back in his place mentally. My barriers were decaying at an alarming rate. I couldn't hold it all together much longer. Not that I was doing a great job anyway. My face was as readable as a flashing neon sign.

"Unfortunately, she passed away last night in her sleep," the Dean continued. "I'm very sorry for your loss, Evangeline."

My mental barriers dropped down, shattering like a window

slammed shut violently by an errant gust of wind. Emotions rushed in to fill the void. Quentin's voice was lost in the chaos as I took in every minute detail of everyone's not-so-rich inner life in the building, the surrounding residential areas and roadways.

I couldn't hear myself think. I couldn't feel my body any more, or any sensory information to where I was. Evangeline the person was lost.

Abuela.

She was gone. Our final conversation echoed in my mind. I grasped tightly to my half dream like a precious memory, not allowing anything else to occupy my thoughts. I could build myself back with that as my center.

I had to. Abuela had let go because I had found her.

Had she been waiting for me?

What was I supposed to do now?

I no longer knew where I was in relation to my bed, my room, or even the institution. Without any barriers, I could easily lose my way back to myself. My overwhelming grief for Abuela's passing reminded me I had a self to go back to, but the over-whelm of every single other thought and emotion and annoyance from the thousands of consciences surrounding me overwrote all my own, puny little thoughts.

In the mass of colors of auras and flickering fires of emotion, I watched as a curious black spot approached me. Seeing it niggled some part of my brain, poking at the logical side of myself. Logic helped sift through competing emotions and sorted them nicely according to person, direction, and intensity. Even within one person, it was good to separate out general emotion and person-ality from situational and fleeting feelings. The black spot frag-mented and scattered the auras it broke through, becoming larger in my field of vision.

"Evangeline," a voice said through the chaos. The voice seemed garbled, as if talking through water or over a line of static.

"If you don't contain yourself, I'm going to have to have Dr. Novak sedate you," the voice stated, no hint of malice or indignation. Merely stating the fact that sedation was next. Even with the straight tone, I bristled with anger that they dare sedate me whenever they felt like it. "I will give you to the count of ten. I recommend boxes. I personally find them easier to manage than walls."

Using the flicker of anger as my base, I shoved the different emotions into their own corners. I felt as though I was climbing a mental mountain of trash, my intentions slipping like feet unable to find purchase in the non-corporeal mass.

Ten seconds to sort through all of this? I was being set up to fail, and my anger flared again brightly. Grief was my base, but anger became my fuel.

Boxes don't make any sense, I argued. *How many boxes am I supposed keep track of? What size? Am I supposed to label them too?* What useless advice.

"Four," the voice broke in, a little less watery now.

I growled in frustration.

"Three," the voice said. Panic stuck me in my tracks, throwing my monkey brain into complete shutdown.

I can't do this.

I can't do this.

Oh my god, what if I really can't do this?

Suddenly, I had an idea. I remember shoving all my toys into my closet when I was younger and supposed to be cleaning my room. It counted so long as you couldn't see it, right?

"Two."

I imagined a line of doors, shoving all the pent-up anxiety in one, the grief of losing my abuela in another, and finally, my anger in another. I slammed all the doors shut, leaving me with a sense of calm and a mild smirk of accomplishment.

"One," the voice said.

I opened my eyes.

I had settled back into my body, and I flexed my fingers, wiggling my toes in my slippers to make sure they were functioning as well.

"Excellent," the voice said, and I looked up, realizing it had been the Dean's voice all along. A chill snaked across my skin, but I kept the surge of bile down, swallowing hard.

With all my scattered emotions stored away, I allowed a little emotional energy to seep through as a test. I counted the bodies in the building, checking in with Quentin as well. Although I could see the Dean with my own two eyes, her emotions didn't ping my radar.

In fact, she was the black hole that had scared me back to my senses.

"What are you?" I whispered, biting my cheek savagely once I realized the words had escaped my lips. I tried to school my features before they betrayed my disgust, but I knew before I had the thought that it was pointless. Even Adair---sick bastard that he was---had an aura.

"I should be asking you the same thing," the Dean replied, her features schooled even more diplomatically than usual. "I have a feeling we'll both be finding out together."

I took a deep inhale through my nose, trying my damnedest to distract my tongue from lashing out with a snarky comment. My flight sense was pinging, desperately imploring me to run as far away as I could get from this black hole of emotional energy. Not a single hair lay sleeping on my frame. My skin tingled like an exposed live wire.

I could not lose control again. Not in front of her.

Ever.

"Yeah, okay. Whatever," I said finally. "So when can I get out of here? I'd much rather be studying for the ACT than finding myself or whatever you all had in mind. I have to get scholarship if I want to go anywhere decent. I'll be sure to get back to you on the soul searching thing once I figure it out."

I kicked myself internally. No baiting the senior emotional energy wielder. As much as I could mess myself up, I knew Dean Moriarty could supernova me into a zombie in the blink of an eye. Wasn't a big fan of eating brains. Unfortunately, my smart mouth decided on a different tactic without consulting the rest of me first.

"Well, I had considered you going to Chicago for your grand-mother's funeral, but I'm concerned it will be too much for you. I won't be there to keep you in check. I think it's best you stay put for a while."

Her Warm Smile™ did not reach her eyes.

"No," I said, anger clipping my voice short. I felt the word lunge out like a whip, licking the Dean's anti-aura before rebounding. "I can handle it." The Dean raised an eyebrow just enough to betray movement, but I knew attacking her would only prove her point more valid. Too late to take it back now.

"Perhaps we can come to an understanding then," the Dean said, crossing her arms, her face slightly inclined in thought.

"And what would that be?" I ground out through my teeth, my lips pressed tightly together. Internally, I was begging my anger to cool it. I pushed harder, forcing the emotion back behind its door. Better than a box, but still in need of improvement, I noted.

"You will have leave to attend your grandmother's funeral, provided you have an escort," the Dean said, stepping forward within arm's reach.

The darkness that surrounded her pressed up against my personal space bubble, making me itch. I clenched my fingers so tightly together, I'm sure they were beyond white. I didn't break eye contact with her to check.

"Fine."

I focused on my breathing. The air felt thinner all of a sudden, and I tried to silence the alarm bells of my mind. Just a few more moments. Nothing we couldn't handle.

"You will go, pay your respects, and return immediately," she continued.

A wave of anxiety and excitement made my stomach flutter. I inhaled to cover the spike, and luckily, the Dean had stepped forward again. Her head cocked ever so slightly, reading my anxiety as a perceived threat of her physical presence.

I began counting to guide my breathing. Any other conscious plane Elevated would crack up how audibly I was screaming numbers in my head. Desperate times, desperate measures. I couldn't let slip the plans my brain was starting to churn out.

"If you should encounter any...issues," the Dean said, "you return immediately, regardless of the timing, and you will comply with all medical personnel until such a time that you can keep your tantrums under control." I bristled at the word tantrum, but I managed to exhale my anger before it could shoot out of my mouth.

I was going to get out of here. I was going to Chicago, and I wasn't going to look back.

I held the Dean's gaze. After an extended war of not blinking, I sealed my fate.

"Shouldn't be a problem."

God help my escort.

EIGHT

Brendan kept sneaking peeks out of the corner of his eye while we drove. I was still frazzled from my tiff with the Dean, so as soon as we got in the car, I laid my seat back, put my hoodie up and blocked my face from the setting sun's intense scrutiny. Even though I was supposed to be the navigator, I knew Brendan didn't need me. He knew the way by heart. I tried to sleep, but a persistent cloud of anxiety kept bumping against me like an annoying pop-up ad.

"You're going to kill us if you don't keep your eyes on the road."

Brendan jerked the wheel a bit in surprise, assuming my silence meant I was asleep.

"See? Told you."

"I'm fine," he said, flexing his grip on the wheel. "I didn't mean to wake you."

"And yet," I sighed, groping blindly around for the lever to raise my seat. Clearly feigning sleep was not the most stress free way to get through the next few hours. The seat back sprung up into place, and I resigned myself to staring out the window and making occasional small talk. With my legs crossed and bouncing occasionally against the glove compartment, at least I was showing signs of life.

"How are you feeling?" Brendan asked, attempting to make his tone light and cool.

It didn't take an Empath to figure out what he was thinking or feeling. His fidgeting alone would have driven anyone mad. I just had the added benefit of sharing the car ride with his intense worry filling every inch of the car. Riding with Blue Eyes would have been more peaceful.

"Fine," I said aloud, leaving a big enough gap in response time that I flinched in response to another spike of concern. Everyone knows fine doesn't mean fine.

"Good," Brendan said, clearing his throat. He tapped his fingers on the wheel in time to a nonexistent beat.

"Want me to DJ?" I reached for his phone without waiting for a response. He nodded after a while and watched me scroll absently through some options.

"Good idea."

I groped along the floor for the end of the auxiliary cable. Somehow the retractor had broken, so the cord had become a loose tangle caught between the cup holders and my bag. It was easy enough to find, considering how neat Brendan kept his car. Not a speck of dust could be found on his console, and I wondered if the debris I had tracked in with my boots would drive him crazy until he could vacuum it out.

Brendan's car was not a beauty, by far. An older model sedan, it still ran well enough with minimal concerning sounds, but the care with which he maintained it made it seem much newer than it really was. I had no doubt it would get us reliably to our destination, much like Brendan.

Finally, I found purchase and plugged in his phone to the console. I went back to scrolling through the available options, keeping one mental eye on Brendan's body language and overall anxiety level. It seemed to have tapered off a little, but I reminded myself to be careful not to let it ramp up again.

I gave up trying to find something I recognized. I hadn't been paying much attention to music since the beginning of the school year. I missed out on Windermere's winter break being institutionalized, so I had very little concept of what was currently happening in the outside world.

I hit shuffle all and hoped for the best.

"We'll have to stop overnight, but I was thinking a rest stop, not a motel," Brendan said, his words choppy and unnatural. Somehow, it sounded like he was apologizing and asking permission at the same time. As the almost hostage in this situation, I didn't know what I was supposed to say.

"Sure."

Honestly, it's got to be better than my eight-by-eight hamster cage, I thought to no one in particular.

"We can find a truck stop with a shower if you want," he continued. "It's no problem."

"Can't we just shower at Tio's? We'll be there in plenty of time before the wake. I'm sure they won't mind," I said, distracted by my rush to skip a particularly annoying dance song.

Brendan's gaze lingered on me, but he didn't say anything more. After a minute, he just nodded, his focus temporarily back on the road.

I let my hair fall forward, framing my face to act like a privacy curtain beyond my hood. Between his emotional waves and his fidgeting, I was constantly aware of when he was looking at me. I was expending extra energy to limit my awareness to just that, instead of the list of all his worries. Something told me I had more than my fair share of space on that list.

Brendan had always kept an eye on me growing up. He and Tomas had been inseparable for as long as I could remember, so his presence in our house was more than commonplace. Since Tomas died, I could feel the weight of responsibility in every glance, in every hand gesture. Even his smile seemed heavier as he tried to be two big brother's worth of protection.

"Your hair's gotten so long," he said, almost to himself.

I tucked one side behind my ear so I could see him properly, but he had clammed up. His cheeks puckered from a failed attempt to school his face. Brendan wasn't much for blushing, but I imagined his cheeks were bright red under the surface. His hand flexed on the wheel again, and I looked back down at his phone, pretending to search for a good song.

"Really?" I said innocently, not wanting to make the interaction seem more awkward than it already was. "It's hard to remember, it's been so long since I'd noticed. It probably looks wrecked since I haven't gotten it cut in a while."

I grabbed a chunk, inspecting for split and dead ends. My hair had always been long, even when I was young. It was never shorter than my shoulder blades, but since I had been at Windermere and now the institution, it had gone unattended for a while. I checked a length of hair, measuring it down to my waist.

"Huh," I said.

"It looks great," Brendan said, the words falling out of his mouth in a rushed exhale. "I mean, it doesn't look bad."

"I'm sure I could walk in to a salon and get a trim if we have some extra time," I said, twirling the ends in my fingers. "Or I can pin it back for the wake so it looks nice."

"I shouldn't have said anything," Brendan said. "Now you're going to think it looks bad."

"I'm sure there will be many opinions when we get to Tio's," I said, making a point to engage eye contact, giving him a knowing look. "The truth will come out eventually."

I flexed my most encouraging smile.

Brendan laughed nervously and grabbed the back of his neck with his free hand.

I skipped another bouncy song, settling on an acoustic guitar ballad with a raspy vocalist. Brendan's hand fell to his lap, where he wiped imaginary sweat from his palm. I promised myself I wouldn't go digging around in his head, so I wasn't sure exactly what was causing his nerves to fray so easily. If anyone should be an emotional ball of nerves in this car, it should be me.

I stared out the window, my own wave of concern threatening to leak out into the stuffy tension.

I can do this. I can do this. I can do this, Brendan's inner monologue said clearly, cresting a fresh wave of anxiety into the car. My eyes flickered to his lips, unsure if he had spoken aloud. That's how direct the feeling had been.

On impulse, I grabbed his hand.

It stilled on his lap, and I sent out a small calming wave before he could swerve unintentionally again.

"Thank you," I said, looking across the car at him. His body was rigid, all focus and intensity directed at the road in front of him, minus the alarm bells going off in his head. "I honestly don't know what I'd do without you."

It was true. Without Brendan, my escort could have been Blue Eyes or White Coat herself. Without his visits, I really would have gone off the deep end, with or without Quentin's encouragement.

I squeezed his hand, emphasizing my gratitude. He squeezed back.

"I'm here for you," he said, his eyes still trained on the car in front of us. "No matter what. Right, Evie?"

"Claro que si," I said, lifting my hand slightly in an attempt to let go. It had been a while since anyone called me Evie. Only Noah and Tomas.

Brendan still held my hand firmly in his, and I didn't want to rip it away and cause another emotional spike. The contact seemed to have calmed him some, and the anxiety in the car was slowly being replaced by contentment.

Although I was relieved we finally worked through the high stress anxiety cloud, I felt guilty for wanting to remove my hand when it seemed to help him so much. The playlist continued with a variety of mellow songs, and this time, I really was getting lulled to sleep by the flat open road and the warm fuzzies coming from Brendan.

I dozed off to the rhythm of Brendan's thumb stroking my knuckles and the steady thunk thunk of the equally spaced asphalt strips. For just a little while, I would focus on the present. This present did not include Dean Moriarty, The Association, or those damn ceiling tiles. I would hold on to this illusion for as long and as hard as I could. It didn't take an Oracle to know it wouldn't last long.

NINE

The vending machine made a concerning noise as I jabbed savagely at the coffee button, muttering to myself through half-slit eyes about the audacity of withholding caffeine from the needy.

We had slept overnight at a rest stop, and I was in charge of caffeination and breakfast. My fists were jammed full with quarters, and all the vending machines were being temperamental. I wasn't particularly excited about the stale honeybun I was about to consume for breakfast. This coffee was my last hope in making breakfast bearable.

I glanced outside, worried Brendan would come inside again looking for me. I had a certain sense of pride in being able to handle things myself, and Brendan always seemed to jump in at the slightest difficulty, fixing all variety of minor problems. I just wanted to get back on the road and hopefully on to much tastier food. My stomach growled in agreement.

Brendan was leaning against the driver's side door, talking on his cellphone. Probably checking in with Tio. Or White Coat. More likely White Coat. I sighed, returning my attention to the coffee machine with a quick kick. The quarter that had been stuck rolled home, and a cup finally dropped, filling with hot instant coffee. The smell was amazing, and I clung to its comfort tightly as I repeated the routine for cup number two.

I tottered out to the car with my elbows tucked tightly to my sides. I had pinned the several varieties of prepackaged pastries against my body with sheer will, and tried desperately not to lose any while also avoiding spilling coffee all over my gloveless hands. The bracing winter wind whipped my hair against my numb cheeks, and I squinted, trying to keep my pace without accidentally wandering into a half melted snow and ice bank.

"We're heading out now," Brendan said into his phone, staring at his feet scuffing the ground. "With morning traffic, it'll be another few hours. I'll call again once we've made it."

I presented myself and my bounty in front of him, and he hung up immediately. His hands reached out instinctively to steady me as I slipped on a small patch of ice.

"Got you," he said, a reassuring smile illuminating his features against the dull grey morning sky.

"Thanks," I said, handing over a coffee and offering my armload of pastries for his inspection. He picked his coffee from my extended hand, and scooping up the slipping packets of snacks effortlessly.

"Let me get these," he said, leaving me to cradle my coffee in both hands.

A big yawn escaped him, contorting his face for several seconds. He shook it off, but I looked him over again. His eyes were puffy, and dark circles were forming after only one night of poor sleep. His energy seemed off as well as he tried to rally after moments of exhaustion.

"Did you sleep okay?" I asked, already knowing the answer.

"I'm good. Once we get back on the road, it'll be better." Brendan nodded, another yawn stalling him once again.

"Why don't I drive the rest of the way?" I offered. "I slept just fine, and the navigation system will guide me through all the highways and construction."

"I'm fine," Brendan said, standing up straight. "I promise."

I gave him a scathing look.

"Driving tired is stupid. Get in the car," I said, directing a nice mental push his way. He was already on the other side of the car before he could argue. "Keys."

He threw them over, and I yelped as I moved to catch them, holding the coffee out delicately so it wouldn't spill or burn my hand. I managed to catch them before they fell into an icy puddle, and my hand remained coffee free. I took a big draw from the tiny cup in celebration.

"Are you all right?" Brendan asked, his body sagging with guilt and exhaustion.

"Perfecto," I called out, hopping into the driver's seat and securing my precious caffeine in its cupholder. Brendan got in and settled himself long before I was done adjusting the seat and the mirrors. I scooted the seat all the way forward, even adjusting the back to get me closer to the wheel.

A dry chuckle escaped from Brendan's half-asleep form.

"I see you got your mother's height," he muttered. His seat was already extended and reclined to cradle his long frame comfortably.

"Thank you for that novel discovery," I said. "Now, eat your breakfast and go to sleep. I'll wake you once we get to Tio's."

"I'll just sleep for a little bit. Then we can switch back," Brendan said, the words becoming one long muddy phrase as he lost the battle to remain conscious. My soothing energy was guilty of his immediate descent into sleep, but honestly, he didn't need much of a push. A light snore escaped from his nose, which was pressed against the plastic wall piece protecting his seat belt retractor.

I grabbed the vending machine packets and stashed them in the center console, not wanting them to slip where I couldn't reach them while driving. I checked the navigation system to make sure it was loud enough and set it to Tio's address once again. We were off before rush hour began, but I had a feeling would hit traffic regardless as we got closer to Chicago.

I left the music off, enjoying the peaceful hum of ambient road noise and Brendan's sleeping murmurs. It was almost as quiet as my room back at the institution, but there was something more lively about it. It might have been because I was going seventy miles an hour on a highway in the complete opposite direction of my captors. Probably.

All too soon, my coffee cup was empty and I wished I could stop for another cup. I promised myself I would only stop if I had to pee, mostly because any stop would wake Brendan, who would immediately demand to drive again. He was so peaceful when he slept, and I knew he needed to rest more than I needed coffee.

Congestion started to build when the LED signs warned of impending construction. We hadn't lost a lane yet, but knowing the orange barrels were coming must have caused the other drivers to slow down in anticipation. I toyed with the idea of impressing upon them to get out of my way, but I was nervous they might wreck themselves if I had too little control over them. The horrific images of what could go wrong filled my head, and I shook them loose, resolving to deal with the traffic like everybody else.

The navigation system piped up, telling me in a few miles I was going to have to exit to a different highway. The system was filled with outdated information, though, and I almost missed the exit. They had created a new lane much earlier than suggested, and I almost hadn't made it over in time. Once I was in the correct lane, my eyes darted to Brendan, hoping the careening of the car as it scooted over three lanes in quick succession hadn't woken him. He was still dozing, completely unaware.

I sighed, checking my mirrors again that no great massacre had occurred with my aggressive movements. Not many folks were heading in this direction during the morning rush, so it seemed like I was on my own.

I looked ahead on the exit ramp and noticed the van in front of me slowly drifting toward the edge of the curve, getting alarmingly close to the embankment between the highway and our merging lane. A partition resumed closer to the highway, so if the driver didn't correct enough, the van would hit the concrete blocks even if it missed the embankment.

The driver didn't seem to be correcting the van, and I opened my tightly shuttered mind, sensing three people inside the doomed vehicle. They didn't feel right, though. I couldn't put my finger on it, but they weren't in a normal state, panicked or otherwise.

I didn't have time to investigate further.

The van continued to drift, the momentum of the vehicle on the curved plane sending it speeding even faster toward the very solid partition. My eyes bounced back and forth, analyzing the speed and trajectory. My stomach dropped, along with my jaw.

Without a doubt, I knew they were going to die.

Panic erupted from me in a loud subsonic boom. My exclamation point warning was directed at the people in the van, but no miracle happened. They did not correct course or bail out of the out of control vehicle.

I looked at Brendan, still peacefully asleep, and I swallowed hard. I sent a small apology his way, but I had to act fast.

Speeding up, I raced to be alongside the van. It was tough with the curve, but I managed to meet the front of my car with the back of theirs. They were drifting, but not fast enough. So I gave them a nudge. With Brendan's car.

My body jolted with the contact of the cars, and I turned the wheel with all my might. The van wiggled, as if something else was trying to correct the change in direction my car was providing. I clenched my jaw and accelerated, sending my will along with the physics of my car to guide the van into the shallow snowed-in valley of grass prior to the concrete partition.

The van slid into the snow, and I watched it stall out, a whoosh of noise and vibration echoing back. I slammed on the brakes in a series of frantic kicks and put on my hazard lights. I slid to a full stop just over the rumble strips, parking in front of the partition I had been trying to save the van from.

I opened the car door, leaving it ajar as I sprinted toward the van. I slid down the embankment, my legs getting soaked immediately with the snowmelt and grunge of turned-up grass and dirt from the path of the van. The resistance of the snow and my short stature made the trip stretch out in what seemed like half time, my breath ragged in my ears as I tried to get enough oxygen to power me to the crash victims. The hood of the van was smoking.

The slippery mud and snow sent me crashing into the back-side of the van, and I clawed my way around to the driver's side. I had felt three people inside, and I was determined to get them out before the van had any other funny ideas. I peered in to assess the passengers, but the windows were heavily tinted. I tried the handle of the sliding door, but it wouldn't give.

I flung open the driver's side door without much resistance, and I stared at the impossible.

The seat was empty.

I climbed up onto the driver's seat to peer inside and found nothing but rags and a few personal items strewn about the cabin. My ragged breathing sent out billowing clouds of mist in the chilly morning air. Every time it cleared, the empty seats stared back at me.

"Who the hell are you?" a voice said behind me.

I turned to find the owner of the voice. Stepping down from the van, I faced outward, noticing the trail of smoke from the engine quickly getting darker and thicker. My eyes blinked away tears as the smoke choked my throat and field of vision.

A form came forward in the thickening cloud, and my anxiety spiked again when I realized yet again this person was not quite right. I slammed my mental barriers up fully, double barricading my mind from this stranger, whose rage caused their aura to flicker like a flame. An aura tinged with pure white, which could only mean one thing.

The empty van was the least of my problems.

TEN

"Do you know what you've done?" the voice said again. My body buckled from the level of anger emanating from the approaching form. I was halfway into a protective ball before my logical brain told me that was not a good idea.

My face tingled, and I reeled as if I had been slapped. I blinked furiously, trying to clear my sight. I reached out mentally again, trying to poke around for anything that could help me. Beyond knowing the stranger was supernatural, I was getting a surprisingly low level of information off their emotional state. I had encountered people before that I couldn't quite read or could read only the foremost feeling they had. But I hadn't met a supernatural, other than the Dean, who could block the flow of information so well.

My stomach was almost in my throat, the tension and the fear building in a tidal wave of bile. Puking from my anxiety was not really a great strategy at this point either, so I swallowed it down.

"Hard to say," I choked out. I hoped I could gain a better understanding of what exactly was going on here from the mysterious person's words since I was striking out with the emotions. "Why don't you tell me? We can see who's right."

"You ruined a perfectly good fake death for a battered wife and her two children, you idiot," the voice said, its nebulous form remaining just out of reach as the smoke cloud thickened. "Way to go."

"Sorry," I said, coughing. "To be honest, it didn't seem fake to me. I was just trying to help."

A snort echoed from the cloud. I could no longer see in front of me at all. Belatedly, I realized I should really get away from whatever was about to blow up.

"Just get out of the way. Luckily, Plan B is about to clean up your mess. Unless you plan on dying today, I'd recommend you begin running. Like, now," the voice said, pressing forward toward me.

I gasped in surprise and was promptly rewarded by another round of coughing. A hand grabbed my upper arm and yanked me off my feet. I was dragged back through the snow, following the path the van had taken once it exited the highway. Just as we cleared the noxious cloud, a large crack rang through the air. I tried to look back, but my head was jerked violently forward, choosing the path of least resistance from the person dragging me away at a fast clip.

The voice spoke again, this time, clearly directed at someone else. "Requesting transport. Yeah, I'm aware. Thank you," the voice said, a snort escaping easily even with the slight jogging pace. "Tits up, as you like to say. Can you just come get me now? I have a passenger."

We stopped suddenly, and I finally looked up at my captor.

"Well I can't just leave her here," the young woman said, her face contorted with frustration. She blew away a stray chunk of white blonde hair, but it fell right back in place, continuing to obscure her face. "She's got some explaining to do anyway. You've got ten seconds before I call him directly. Old fashioned is much messier."

I tried to wriggle out of the woman's vice-like grip on my arm. I could no longer feel my fingertips.

"Be still," she said, glaring down at me, the speaker of the phone directed away from her words. "Or I will incapacitate you, and I will be very happy about it."

Another crack was released through the air, and the woman sighed as I jumped in response.

"Any day, now, Niko," she barked into the phone, hanging up.

Suddenly, a man appeared in front of me, and I screamed. His large frame blocked my view of the exit ramp and my car. I considered sending out an SOS to Brendan, but I worried he'd try to act like a hero. Everything was all happening too quickly anyway.

The large man raised his eyebrow at me, giving no other indication that he was surprised that I was surprised he appeared out of thin air.

"Finally," the woman growled. A faint spike of amusement rolled off the man, but he was similarly unreadable and returned to a faint hum of calm almost immediately.

Before the woman could rip into him any further, the van behind us exploded. I could feel the heat running to meet us, and my eyes widened in shock. We were not far enough away. I was going to be burned alive. The sudden realization pushed my input overload to the max, making me go numb with terror.

I felt another hand on my shoulder, and then everything went black.

I BLINKED HARD, trying to clear my eyes.

This couldn't be right. It made no sense.

I was in an alleyway. My eyes grazed over the graffitied brick facade of the surrounding buildings, noted the trash strewn in, on, and everywhere except for the dumpsters that lined the small alley. I could clearly read the warning sticker on the side of the dumpster on how to best avoid pests, realizing the words repeated in French immediately below. Most of the trash on the ground seemed frosted over, clumping together in various random piles. Where was I?

"Just because you can transport at a moment's notice does not mean you have to wait for the absolute last possible moment to do so!" the woman shrieked, jarring me away from my intense scrutiny of the dumpster.

The pair stood near a rusted metal door, clearly picking up where they had left off in an argument that felt like one of many reincarnations of the same conversation. The man's blank features clued me in that this was not an uncommon occurrence.

"Well, maybe if you would stick to the plan, I wouldn't have to drop everything I was doing to come save your ass at the very last moment," the man said, his voice thick and stilted, his accent causing him to enunciate much more clearly than a native speaker. It made him sound more formal, and I cocked my head at the pair's dynamics. I felt like I was interrupting a private moment, so I stood quietly, taking in the scene. I would have averted my eyes, but I was too invested in seeing how this played out.

Suddenly the man nodded in my direction. "Better grab the little mouse before she runs," he said, opening the door and leaving me to the seething woman. A bolt of anger shot off from the woman and followed the man, Niko the woman had said, inside as he rudely disengaged from their conversation. Turning her attention to me, she growled, grabbing me again by my upper arm and frog marching me through the same back entrance.

"If I promise I won't run, would you let go of my arm? I can't feel my fingers again," I said, the words escaping in a rush before I lost my resolve. The pain in my shoulder was nothing compared to the look I got, but the woman let me go, shoving me in front of her.

"Left," she directed, up a narrow staircase that glowed red. We were out onto the next floor before I could decide if the red was from the paint or the lighting. The close proximity of the narrow hallways made me sweat, and the aftershocks of anger permeated the small space enough for me to have trouble breathing.

"Left," she said again. Her breath was hot on my neck, and I really did feel like a mouse, trapped in a maze I could never escape.

If I wasn't so afraid of her reaction, I would have attempted to send out a calm wave to lessen the assault on my senses. I took a chance and glanced back, trying to formulate a plan. One second of eye contact from the woman made me discard my brilliant idea almost before I could complete it.

"In," was all she said, reaching around me to open a door, shoving me through the opening.

The ominous bang of the door shutting behind me made my whole body cringe. It took me a moment to realize she had not followed me inside, and a wave of relief flooded my frame.

I felt a different presence nearby, and I tensed again. I slowly lowered my barriers, just enough to recon the room. It was dim, not quite dark, but I could see the outline of chairs in the distance and a bar along the far wall. The ceiling seemed abnormally high, and the chill of such an empty space sent a shiver down my spine. Only one other person was in the large space with me, but my barriers slammed back up as soon as I felt him.

He was a void.

But he was normal.

ELEVEN

My heart raced ahead in a stuttering sprint, the pounding so loud in my ears I could hardly think. Every half formed thought was interrupted by another. My brain could not put the pieces together.

What on earth was going on?

If he had been a supernatural, I would have assumed he was along the same lines as the Dean. Either he was considered a Commander, just like Tomas had been, or he was able to shield so well that he had to be somewhere on the sentient plane like I was. Like Adair.

Another shiver ran down my spine.

Maybe now wasn't the time to remember Adair.

But all that didn't really seem to matter. This guy was human. Normal as normal could be, as far as I could tell. If he wasn't Elevated, that lack of emotional pulse pointed to the only logical conclusion.

The man was a sociopath.

I shoved my clenched fists into my jeans, trying to contain the variety of panic waves circling my mind. My whole body was shaking. I longed to put up the hood of my jacket, but indoors that made no sense, even in such a cavernous room. Whoever I was about to meet would not be deterred by a hood on a petite young woman who barely hit the five foot marker. My eyes tracked along the furniture, but in the limited lighting, I couldn't find a strategic hiding spot.

Idiot.

I shook my head, trying to shake loose some sensible thoughts. *Deep breaths,* I told myself. *Just breathe.*

If I kept panicking like this, I was going to have an episode. I didn't know how far one of my emotional atomic bombs could reach, and it was not the best time for a field test. There was no one here to help me and only a long line of people I could hurt, even if the rude woman was at the front.

That thought sobered me a little, and the bile in my throat settled back down into my stomach. I stretched my neck slowly, rolling it around from shoulder to shoulder, continuing to breathe deeply.

Be Noah. Think like Noah. Be strong. Confident, I coached myself. *Alpha behavior. I could handle a sociopath, right? Right.*

"You all right?" a smooth voice asked from across the dark ballroom.

Fear sliced through my gut, and I wondered briefly if I had peed myself a little.

Nope.

Guess I couldn't handle a sociopath by myself.

A shadowy form got up from a curved, plush booth and walked toward me.

The blood rushed to my ears again, and I took in deep breaths through my nose, letting them out in bursts through my sandy-tongued mouth. I was not doing well in the anxiety department, and I was kicking myself, thinking how useless it would be if I passed out right now. Tears pricked at the corners of my eyes.

I had clenched my eyes shut as soon as he had spoken, not wanting the spinning room to get in the way of my centering practice. I probably sounded like a distressed moose in labor with my patterned breathing.

"Please sit," the voice said again, hands bracing my shoulders as I was guided to a nearby chair. My legs gave out right as I was poised over the seat, and I could feel several trails of tears that had leaked down my cheeks.

When had I started crying?

The close proximity to the gaping black hole made me even woozier. The short spike of panic I felt disappeared immediately. The warm hands on my shoulders held me securely, so my feet rested solidly on the ground while my mind remained among the fluffy dark clouds.

Thoughts and emotions were falling through my fingertips like running water. All the tension I had been holding in my shoulders and neck was leaking through my ears in a slow drain. Although my panic was lessening, my more subtle feelings like curiosity of the building and the people who had transported me were melting away as well.

"Stop!" I said firmly, my hands launching out of my pockets and connecting with the man's shoulders. It wasn't a hard shove, but it took both of us by surprise. He took a small step back.

My eyes flew open and immediately locked onto a pair of ice blue irises, rimmed with dark lashes and the slightest hint of gold at the centers.

"I need you," I said slowly, trying to keep my emotions from clouding my serious tone, "to back up. Slowly."

The man, who I realized was only a little older than Brendan, tilted his head slightly.

"If you don't move right now," I continued in a too calm voice, "I will most likely flare like a supernova and promptly pass out. I don't know what will happen to you or anyone close by, but it won't be pretty. It will be chaos. Please." My voice dropped low as tears caught in my throat. Of course I would be a sobbing wreck the moment I dared to be assertive.

The man lifted his hands high in surrender, as if trying to convince a rabid animal he was no threat. He wasn't wrong. Thankfully, he did take a few steps back, and I could feel the darkness back off with him.

I shuddered.

"What is even happening right now?" I whispered aloud to myself, hanging my head in exhaustion. I covered my eyes with my hand and tried to push the barriers in my mind as high and hard as I could. I imagined a maximum security prison, with concrete behind barbed wire, behind another high and thick wall that would actually keep out the Huns. I had no other plan.

The man crouched silently just far enough away that I could still see the lightness in his eyes, even in the dim room. It was the first thing I noticed once I pulled my hand from my face.

"I should be asking you the same thing," the man said tentatively. The creases near his eyes and the tilt of his head led me to believe he wasn't angry, more curious. I had seen warmth in his eyes, though. Could a sociopath fake human empathy that well? I worried that I couldn't be sure. It had been too long since I had to rely on such little information to know how a person truly felt. The realization left me feeling naked and inept.

"Do you know what I am?" I asked, clenching my teeth while bracing myself for a response. He wasn't nearly freaked out enough to be ignorant of the supernatural, especially with his two minions who had essentially kidnapped me. I hadn't met so many new adult supernaturals in a twenty four hour span before. There was no way this man was unaware.

"I think you're an Empath," the young man said, "but I wasn't too sure until just now."

A bitter laugh escaped my lips, and I shook my head. I wiped my eyes savagely again with my sweatshirt sleeves. He cool eyes continued to assess my every move.

"I think there are more polite ways to check," I replied. "Ways that don't require an almost meltdown."

"How old are you?" he replied instead. His question had almost interrupted my snide remark, and my eyes narrowed. There was definitely impatience and curiosity in his expression. He wasn't hiding it very well at all.

"I see my age is more important than my name," I flung back at him, sending a wave of disdain with me.

"Well, your name would be good, too, but I just haven't met an Empath with such little control of her powers before. I've only met the two, though, so I guess my sample is a little skewed," the man said with a shrug.

"That's nice," I said. "But I really would like a name from you before I continue. I don't know if I can trust you, talking about these things."

"Fine, we'll exchange family names on the count of three. I think that will clear up a lot of confusion," he said. A halfhearted smile flickered across his face, but he still managed to look sad. I didn't realize a grown man built like an MMA fighter could look so sheepish with such a simple request.

"I have three, which one do you want?" I quipped, reeling from my lapse in emotional defense. Now was not the time to wax poetic about the sociopath.

"All of them," he said simply. "Three."

"Two."

"One."

"Herrera de los Santos Patrick," I said softly, hoping to hear his over my own voice.

"Navratil," he replied, his head jerking back slightly in response to my own name.

My blood chilled at the sound of his last name.

"Navratil, like the mob bosses Navratil?" I said, my voice going shrill at the end. His pursed lips told me all I needed to know.

"Yes, well, it's not often you meet a de los Santos anymore, although your most recent last name intrigues me more. Is that your stepdad?" he said, his bluntness making me scoff in indignation.

"Why do you ask questions when you already have the answers?" I shot back at him.

"Why do you not like answering simple questions?" he replied. A smile spread across his features. "This is definitely going to get interesting."

He leapt up from his squatting stance, his distance still close enough I could feel the dynamic change as he towered over me. I scowled up at him, immediately regretting giving him my name.

Something told me I was vastly underprepared for the world I had just entered, as if the exploding van or teleportation hadn't been a big enough sign.

Noah, help me.

TWELVE

"Do you like burgers?" the Navratil sociopath said, sauntering away toward the bar.

I remained in my seat against the wall of stacked chairs, arms crossed in silent resolution. He was not going to get away with this so easily.

"What kind of question is that?" I said, raising my voice enough to be heard across the room. The space was large, although sparsely furnished. I refused to shout, but I was even more resistant to following him.

"A simple one," he said, bending over behind the bar, disappearing from my line of sight. I straightened on my chair, ready for anything. He popped back up, his hand stuffed with takeout flyers and menus. "I assume Empaths eat."

"Nah, we just feed off human souls," I quipped. "Less calories."

"One of those," the man said, his head nodding knowingly.

I snorted. "Hardly," I murmured, out of earshot.

"There's a place around here that fries cheese inside the burgers. Can't remember what they're called, but they're pretty good. Want one?" he asked, spreading the flyers out in front of him and snatching up the one he wanted after a quick glance. "Or are you veggie vegan whatever?"

"Dead things don't have feelings," I said, bristling at his tone. "If that's what you're getting at."

"What?"

"You implied because of my abilities that I most certainly would be 'veggie vegan whatever.'"

"When?"

"Just now," I said, raising my voice. "What does being an Empath have to do with my eating habits?"

The man had taken out his cellphone, and I caught his frown in the glow of the screen. I snorted, amazed at how audacious he was. From what I knew of the Navratils, the behavior was not out of character. Arrogance was clearly a beloved family trait.

"So is that a yes?" he asked, typing on his phone and avoiding eye contact.

"What?"

"Yes, I should order you a burger. Got it," he said, ducking back down below the bar. "You thirsty?"

"Did I say I wanted a burger?" I said, annoyed he had completely ignored my question.

"You said you didn't not want one, which means you want one," he said with a shrug. "What are you having? The fountain gun's working again, so I have the full gamut of soda flavors." He leaned forward on the bar, his attention returned to me in full force. His clasped his hands loosely in front of him, his phone nowhere in sight.

I waited silently in my chair, seething about his dismissive attitude. I hated being told what I wanted. If he was going to be like that, I wasn't even going to engage.

"Ah, right, you mentioned calories. Water?" he offered, grabbing a glass from the hanging rack. I scowled at him. My throat was scratchy, and I was actually hoping for a glass of water. Now that he was offering it though, I considered suffering to spite him.

"I'm not like that," I blurted out, not lasting more than ten seconds of silence. Good job, self. "I just happen to like water."

The man raised an eyebrow, but continued pouring the glass.

"So what should I call you?" I said, hoping being on the offensive would be more productive than our food conversation.

"Master Navratil? Boss Man? I don't know the terminology for gang hierarchy."

"Neither do I," the man responded, coming from behind the bar to deliver my water to me. He reached his hand out before I could ward him off. The floor tilted under my feet, and I immediately shut my eyes. "You can just call me Aleks."

I felt the cool glass in my hand, and I gripped it reflexively. Suddenly, my head cleared and I opened my eyes. Aleks had retreated back behind the bar.

"You're really going to need to work on that, you know," he said. "I can't stay thirty feet away from you at all times. It'd look weird."

"What are you talking about?" I said, pinching the bridge of my nose. Sometimes jabbing the pressure points along my inner eye socket helped with tension, but that trick only worked for non-human entity headaches.

"Well, special guests typically sit next to me in the VIP booth. Also, I can't protect you very well when you're out of arm's reach. It'd just be much easier for everyone if you could stick by my side," Aleks said, straightening the mess he had made with the takeout menus. He stacked them neatly, then tossed them back under the bar.

"Why would you need to protect me? I'm sorry, I must have missed something," I said, shaking my head, hoping it would clear the remaining cobwebs. "Your people kidnapped me."

"I guess you could look at it that way," he said, resuming his relaxed pose on the bar. "Or I helped you escape a hostage situation. Forcible containment, or whatever you want to call it."

"With Brendan?" I asked. "I was going to my grandmother's funeral."

"Were you or were you not held in an Association medical facility against your will not twenty-four hours ago? I'm sorry, I must have the details wrong," Aleks said, the glimmer of the can lights making his eyes glow in the shadows. I wonder if he knew how disarming those eyes could be.

"Yes, well," I replied, re-crossing my legs. "I was handling it."

"Ah," he said, his eyes bouncing up and down in the shadows.

"I had a vague plan," I argued. "I just wanted to see my family first."

"Was knocking out your boyfriend part of it? Because I'm pretty sure he wouldn't have let you go unless he was also six feet under," Aleks said. "He'll probably never let you out of his sight again."

"He's not my boyfriend," I said, frowning into the darkness at his tone.

"According to you," he replied, letting his words hang in the air before continuing. "I would just be careful with him. Guys do a lot of stupid stuff because of girls."

"Thanks for the advice?" I said, my voice hitching up in a questioning tone. "Like I said. He's not my boyfriend. We grew up together."

"We'll see," Aleks said. "But I was serious earlier when I said you're going to have to figure out how to deal with me in closer proximity. We're a small operation, and I can't afford to have anyone else babysitting you. Can't let them be distracted."

"Then let me go," I said, my heart jumping into my throat. This wasn't the exit strategy I had thought of, but beggars can't be choosers. "I'll get out of your hair, and then you won't have to worry."

"You could go," Aleks mused. "You won't get very far though. You're a little young to realize this, but it really is about who you know in the world. If you want to get what you want, you have to know who's going to give it to you."

"I'm old enough to know whatever it is you're offering won't come for free," I said. "I'll figure it out. Thanks."

"In your eight-by-eight observation room, sure," Aleks said, not unkindly. "I'm just offering an alternative. One where you're more free to grow and be challenged instead of running a maze for the white coats."

"So I'd be one of your lackeys? Like that angry woman and

what's his name?" I asked, pushing back against the condescension I was feeling. Aleks' new tone smelled a bit too much of gaslighting. His tone implied I'd be an idiot to turn him down, and I hated being called an idiot. Or naïve. Especially naïve.

"Eli and Niko? I'd hardly call them lackeys. Business associates," Aleks said, his face bobbing back and forth in internal debate. "It's not like they're forced to do anything they don't want to do."

"Blowing up vans and kidnapping people. You're saying they wanted to do those things?" I asked. "Those are very, very illegal."

"You're missing a very, very large chunk of context," Aleks said. "It's not really my place to divulge their reasons though. I promise they are very noble aims. More than I can say of the Association."

"Yeah, well, at least the Association has a clear moral code," I snorted. "Living in grey areas can be chaotic."

"The whole world is in grey. Treating it any differently would be naïve at best," Aleks said, straightening from behind the bar. Blood rushed to my cheeks, and I bit the inside of my cheek hard. I would not let him see the comment land on a sore spot. "At least those who work with me have a say in what they do. It's more like a loose co-operation. Calling it a gang doesn't really do justice to the others."

"Being led by a non-gifted person must really be thrilling for them," I said, my eyes honed on Aleks' body language in the hopes of getting a clue off the barb I had sent his way. It was immature, but I couldn't help it.

"It works quite well, actually," he said, not rising to my bait. "It's kind of nice knowing the guy calling the shots has no ability or desire to overpower you or take away your agency. Like I said before, though, it's a very loose power structure."

"Don't you have brothers?" I asked, trying to think back to what Abuela had said about the Navratils. I had been young, though, so she hadn't shared much. I wasn't ready for those sorts of truths, especially after what had happened to Tomas. "How did the only ungifted Navratil end up heading the organization?"

"Sheer survival instincts. Luck. Being the only surviving member does wonders for the division of assets," Aleks said, his words falling flat and emotionless. I flinched.

I had forgotten. Somewhere in the midst of my grieving, I had heard the news. Only now did the dots start to connect.

Aleks sighed. "I do still have a cousin floating around out there, but that's what infighting among supernaturals tends to do. If I remember correctly, a de los Santos died a few years back right? Your cousin?" he asked.

"Brother," I said, my mind absently trying to build the Navratil family tree in my memory, the sting of my brother's death barely prickling my conscience.

"I'm sorry," Aleks replied, sincerity in his words. "Although that does explain your boyfriend."

"Not my boyfriend," I said reflexively. I drew the family tree in front of me in the air, trying to remember which cousin Aleks had mentioned. My hand stilled in the air. This would be so much easier if I had paper.

Tomas first. Then Aleks's brothers. And Colm. The hairs on the back of my neck and arms stood at attention.

Hadn't that been around the same time of the power surge at Windermere?

"Hey," I said, my hand still frozen in the air. Aleks walked out from behind the bar, stopping five feet away automatically.

"What is it?" he asked.

"When did your brothers die?" I asked. "And did they die all at once?"

"One passed three years ago, the other two about eighteen months ago," Aleks said, his arms crossed over his chest, the dim light throwing his strong angular features into sharper contrast. "Why?"

My timeline was spot on. I was afraid to assert my next guess.

"Did their abilities happen to be on the vitality, sentient, and temporal planes? In that order," I said, my hands drifting slowly to my lap.

Aleks shifted his weight from one foot to the other.

"But you didn't inherit their powers, right?" I asked, searching for his eyes in the darkness.

"No," he replied. "What are you thinking?"

"A quote unquote mysterious outbreak of powers happened at a secluded prep school run by the Association at the exact time of several unsolved supernatural deaths," I said to Aleks, our eyes locked in understanding. "Those energies don't just disappear, you know."

"Oh, I know," Aleks said. "I know exactly what you're talking about."

The door burst open. Both Aleks' and my necks snapped to the new threat, and I was already on my feet. Niko appeared in the doorway, his nostrils flaring as he tried to steady his breathing.

"Boss," he said. "We've got problems."

THIRTEEN

"Problems? Like, what kind of problems?" I said, my voice cracking in immediate panic. Could they have found me so quickly? "I thought you said no one called you Boss."

Aleks raised his hand toward my face, his focus hawklike on Niko.

"Immediate physical threat?" Aleks asked, taking a step toward me reflexively, obscuring my eye line to the door.

"Eli says your uncle is on his way. She's estimating five minutes or less," Niko said, his head inclined emphatically. Apparently, that answered Aleks's question, but didn't give me any indication what level of screwed I was about to be.

I frowned. How did Aleks' uncle play in to everything? He had mentioned a cousin earlier, but not an uncle. Aleks' face grew stormy, and the dark energy surrounding him slowly seeped out. He stood in a cloud of murky black aura, almost like a storm system with his body as the eye. My arms prickled with electricity.

"Aleks," I said through clenched teeth. The wave of darkness began encroaching on the rest of the room, shrinking the safe zone we had built between one another. He turned his head slightly toward me, as if he was listening, but not enough to be fully distracted.

"Who's with him? Do we know?" Aleks directed the questions toward Niko, who replied with a simple shrug.

"She called me at the widow's house. I had to hop three time zones. Didn't offer details," Niko said, his chest still rising and falling steadily to catch his breath.

"Aleks," I said, my voice sharp with command as his dark energy got within six inches of my scuffed sneakers.

He whipped his head around, the anger in his eyes now fully focused on me.

"What?" he said. I took a step back from the venom in his voice. I moved away from the stacks of chairs toward the wide-open dance floor.

"You're..." I faltered, trying to find the right word. "Leaking." My hand waved unhelpfully at him, and I shuffled back slowly step by step.

A look of pure confusion crossed his face, but the anger returned after the briefest of flickers.

"Boss?" Niko chimed in unhelpfully. "What's the plan?"

Aleks' gaze remained locked on mine.

"This would be much easier if you were a little better trained," Aleks said, frustration pinching his features.

"That's nice to think about. Is there some sort of secret academy I don't know about? I'd be more than happy to go," I shot back, eyeing the progress of his energy seeping out toward me. "Maybe a nice afterschool program?"

"How should I know?" Aleks said. "Not exactly qualified for all the Elevated trade secrets."

"Your family is just as much supernatural as mine. Even more so," I argued. "Do they have a handbook? Maybe a wiki page of some sort?" As much as it seemed like a sassy comment, I really would be quite desperate for a textbook on Empaths right now. Studying I could do. Winging it? Not working out well for me right now.

"Of course not," Aleks said, his arms crossed. "Is this Boy Scouts?"

"Yeah, well, you're not doing great in the control department either," I continued. "For not being supernatural, you sure have a lot of power."

"You're the first one to mention it," Aleks said.

Out of the corner of my eye, I saw Niko flex his hands impatiently.

"Listen, if you can't control your energy, I need to go. Far away," I warned him. "I'll go wherever you want. I won't cause trouble. I promise." My back hit a structural column, and I braced myself for the onslaught of dark energy that had nearly filled the room, my hair falling like a curtain over my turned face.

I should have aimed toward the nearest emergency exit, I thought in hindsight, the carved plaster biting into my shoulder blades. I was always the worst about new places. I bit my lips together to keep from whimpering as the dark mass licked at my rubber insoles.

Aleks let out a guttural noise, his energy flaring briefly. I started to feel dizzy. I couldn't feel my toes anymore.

"Niko, take her to the widow while I deal with my uncle," Aleks said. "Go now and stay there. I'll call once it's all clear."

"Boss?" Niko said, his eyes wide, not wanting to contradict an order he thought he misheard.

"Now, Niko," Aleks said. He ran his fingers slowly through his hair, already on to the next immediate problem. His eyes were clouded over with thought.

I blinked, and Niko was next to me. I jolted, unnerved at how quickly he got to me.

"It's better if you close your eyes," Niko said softly into my ear, his hand already on my shoulder. "Count of three. Like a bandaid."

Niko glanced back toward Aleks, giving him an affirmative nod in some unspoken agreement. As I waited for Niko's countdown, I thought idly about where I had been only yesterday. Could I really be missing the poking, the prodding, and Quentin's unending monologues? I tugged the cuff of my jacket down to hide my hands, looking down at my dirty shoes one more time before I surrendered to the leap, refusing to think about the institution any more. An eerie calmness had settled over me, and I understood Aleks' dark energy had sapped me of my panic, stilling my animal brain.

Serenely, I thought it wouldn't be the worst thing to puke on my shoes. Something told me I would be needing proper boots if I were to stick around in Aleks' world, and my beat up sneakers were the very least of my problems.

FOURTEEN

My knees slammed to the ground hard. I was able to catch the rest of my upper body with my wrists, but the shock jarred my whole body, the gravel cutting into my hands and shredding them.

"Sorry," Niko said. "I'm not used to such a tiny passenger."

I groaned, doing my best to push myself to an upright position. The world turned underneath me, and I yelped. Niko had grabbed me and set me right, as easily as a doll. A doll with blood staining her hands and knees. I wiped my scratched palms on my jeans to get rid of the debris. The cuts were superficial and stopped bleeding at the lightest pressure, and I let out a huge sigh.

"Come inside," Niko directed me, leading the way down the gravel path to the old bungalow. I followed, attempting to look natural while still scanning my surroundings.

The small house sat on a hill surrounded by jutting rocks and rolling expanses of green. The grass seemed more moss like than the blades I was more familiar with, and I wondered where I was. I could hear the winds howling down and around the many hills and valleys, and the salt gathering on my face told me the ocean was nearby.

Niko's frame filled the entire doorway, and he had to duck to enter. The small house was clearly old yet well kept. It blended in with the nature around it, becoming one instead of commandeering the landscape.

I brushed my fingertips on the mantle of the doorway,

assessing people more my size had built it. Immediately I felt comforted, the soft wood cushioning my fingertips like velvet. My palms still stung, but the familiarity of the house soothed the aches I felt. My anxiety drifted softly down like silt in a stream. It felt different from Aleks' own dark energy, but a small itch in the back of my mind did wonder if it wasn't also supernatural.

Niko's face loomed in front of me, startling me out of my reverie.

"Come inside," he repeated, turning back around in the narrow hall.

I followed the path of slate before me and was reminded of the layout of the Landing. Something about the rickety stairs, this time downward, and the kitchen residing at the back made me wonder if the same builder hadn't been involved. My fingers trailed down the crumbling plaster walls as I was guided to the back of the house. The timing seemed right.

A wall of warm, spicy aroma greeted me as soon as I crossed the threshold into the kitchen. A kettle was near whistling, and I could smell a variety of herbs, some of which were hanging above the windowsill in neat bouquets. *Abuela would be able to identify them all,* I thought. A lump formed in the back of my throat as I reminded myself that I would not be able to ask her.

"I'm going to grab more wood," Niko said, indicating the empty pallet near the wood smoke oven. "Stay here."

I nodded and watched him step out the back door and down into the nearest copse of trees. A shed was nestled in the shadows, and I could make out a pile of logs under a tarp. The view was distorted, though, the glass old and bubbled. I retreated to a small wooden table against the wall to wait patiently, as promised.

The chairs were sturdy but imperfect. I wondered if they had been handmade, and if so, how long ago. Time and many human hands had smoothed them down, and they shone in the fading evening light. I looked around for a clock but couldn't find one. The kettle whistled, and I leapt from my seat to take it off before my ears bled.

A teapot sat waiting with leaves in a mesh basket. I poured the hot water carefully over the dried flakes, careful not to propel them outside the basket and ruin the tea. A more potent version of the smell I had first been greeted with filled my nose, and I smiled. It had been a long time since I'd had tea like this.

I set the empty kettle back on the stove, careful not to leave the burner on. The lid of the pot was not on the counter, so I bustled about, pulling out drawers and opening cabinets in an effort to find it.

Suddenly, I heard a rattling in one of the far drawers. I hesitated. Did they have dangerous rodents wherever this was? What could possibly be making such a ruckus in the drawer?

I braced myself, taking a deep breath in and opening the drawer upon exhale. The lid sat rattling furiously, stilling only when my fingertips brushed it.

Then it hummed.

My fingers froze just above it, as it had stilled. After a long moment, it began fidgeting again.

I clamped my palm around it, picking it up, and it hummed again before I dropped it securely into its intended spot.

"It likes you," an old voice croaked out behind me, causing me to spin around, my hand knocking over the teapot. I cried out, trying to right the teapot, but it was unnecessary. It was frozen in midair between the counter and the floor. My hands framed the teapot in midair as I froze, too, realizing it had saved itself.

"Go on, then," the voice said. "I'd like a cuppa if you don't mind. Mugs are next to the spice rack."

I turned my head, keeping one eye on the frozen teapot and the other on the old woman, who sat contentedly at the small table. She had on what seemed like several layers of shawls, and her feet dangled from the chair like a child's, her feet in leather mules stuffed with hand knit stockings.

She gave me an encouraging nod, and I grabbed the handle of the teapot delicately, lifting it from its invisible cushion and setting it back on the counter. I plucked two stoneware mugs from the hooks she had indicated, and the weight of them took me by surprise. I almost dropped them as well.

I recovered, ferrying the items to the table and setting them on top of the worn floral pattern lacework doily. I poured the tea out into the two mugs, my hands shaking enough to cause the top of the teapot to rattle in response. I stilled it with a few fingers, and I felt a surge of warmth in response.

Once the pot was empty, I walked it back to the counter, scooting it far enough from the edge there would be no way for it to fall again. I grabbed the small tea service tray, noticing the sugar lumps and cream already set out, along with a variety of small cookies. I slowed my normal walking pace, trying to ensure the cream didn't slosh out of the miniature pitcher on the tray before I set it delicately on the table.

I sat across from the woman, and she greeted me with a warm smile.

"I love a good cuppa," she said, her body dancing with delight as she grabbed a cookie from the platter. "Soothes for whatever ails you." Her legs continued to swing merrily beneath the table. My feet did touch the floor, amazingly enough, and I sat silently, trying to guess exactly how petite this woman was and how she appeared from nowhere just in time for tea.

Niko appeared suddenly, letting the door bang open as he carried a large armful of wood from the shed. My hand flew out in surprise and almost knocked over my tea cup.

"Sorry," he said, moving to deposit the load. A crisp breeze followed him in, and I abandoned my tea to close the door quickly. The old woman continued munching on her cookie as if nothing had happened. "See you two have met."

I looked at Niko with a confused expression, begging him to tell me who she was before I had to ask. He surveyed the two of us, his face ambivalent.

"Grab a cuppa," the old woman said, waving at the teapot from her seat. I blushed.

"I'll make another pot," I stammered, indicating the chair I had just vacated. "Here, have mine."

Niko shrugged, taking the offered seat as I headed back to the counter. He grabbed two cookies and several lumps of sugar, offering one to the old woman.

"No thank you, dear," she said, her smile never faltering. "Not much for the sweet stuff."

Niko raised his eyebrow as she took another cookie, giving in with a shrug. I turned my focus to filling the kettle and getting a fresh basket of tea leaves.

"Birdie!" a voice called from across the house, startling me from my task. I didn't remember being so jumpy.

I let down my barriers, scanning the house for inhabitants. I scolded myself for not doing this immediately upon my ungraceful landing, but my scattered mind was out of practice in new spaces. Other than the kitchen, two small blips came up, both of them ringed in white. Not a single soul in the house was merely human. I bit my cheek, trying to school my features into oblivious calm.

The two little blips rocketed toward the kitchen, and I laughed out loud when I saw they were children, a possibility I had overlooked in my nerve-shocked brain. A young girl with fraying braids and what looked to be her younger brother, with dirt obscuring the freckles on his face. Their eyes flickered toward me briefly, but their attention was immediately diverted to the tray of cookies.

"Yes, dear," the old woman, Birdie, said, directing her gummy smile toward the little ones.

"Sebastian pulled my hair," the young girl said, her face immediately contorting in a pout. She even had tears forming in her eyes, her lip quivering.

"Did not!" Sebastian, the freckled boy, shouted. He crossed his arms in protest. "Vivvy pushed me down first."

"First?" Niko said, taking another bite of cookie. "So you did pull her hair."

"She was sitting on me!" Sebastian crowed. "I couldn't breathe!" Sebastian mimed his near death experience, his eyes bulging from his head as he made a choke collar with his tiny hands.

The little girl's waterworks began in full effect, her sniffling cutting through her brother's shouts.

"Both of you apologize," Birdie said, blowing on her steaming mug to cool the tea. "And then you can have a cookie."

"Sorry!" both shouted at each other, sobering up immediately at the prospect of a cookie. They held out their tiny hands in offering. Birdie placed a cookie in each, and the two scurried away, taking their bickering back into the other part of the house.

I stood still against the counter, too overwhelmed to move. The kettle whistled behind me, and I slowly moved to complete my original task.

"Never mind them, dear," Birdie called out to me. "It'll take the sea and the stars to separate those two."

"I remember," I said softly, clearing my throat, "what that's like." Tomas and I used to shout and play rough like that. I took in a deep breath, releasing all the tension and anxiety that had suddenly welled up in that breath. I had to be careful not to get overwhelmed again. Until the ultimate Elevated manual appeared out of thin air, I would have to do more to catch up in controlling my abilities. Aleks' warning had already buried itself deep in my mind.

I grabbed a mug and joined Birdie and Niko at the table. The familiarity of the scene was palpable. I couldn't help but wonder what alternate universe I had gotten myself into where strangers felt like family and family felt like strangers.

And I could tell it was about to get weirder.

FIFTEEN

"So," Birdie said, leaning toward me and shading her mouth from Niko's line of sight. "What're you in for?"

Niko cleared his throat, excusing himself from the table. He wasn't much for conversation, but his body language made it clear he knew he wasn't wanted. I opened my mouth to ask him to sit down, but he waved his phone at me, indicating he would be checking in out of earshot. I snapped my mouth shut and let him go without argument.

"You seem a little young to be getting involved in this mess," Birdie said, staring off into the distance while she spun her own version of my melodrama. "Then again, it does seem to start then anyhow. Whether you're ready or not."

"Sorry?" I said.

"I was your age when I met Henry. Lovely fellow. Strong. Cute butt," Birdie said, throwing me a knowing wink. I blushed automatically, snagging a piece of hair to twist in my idle fingers. "Oh, but he was trouble."

"What sort of trouble?" I asked, intensely curious. I had always been a sucker for Abuela's stories, and Birdie's tone felt familiar and equally suspenseful. I wondered if it took decades to master the skill, hoping I would someday have the same.

"Love at first sight trouble," Birdie said with a sigh. "And of course, his family didn't approve. Even the Elevated folk tend to fall into hierarchy."

"Elevated folk?"

"Yes, dear. You, me, the young ones in there," Birdie replied with a dismissive wave. "Even that mountain of a man out on the verandah. Suppose it's not quite a verandah. Never was one for fancy terms, I admit."

The old woman's eyes clouded over as she muttered to herself about which word was most proper. I was at a loss if I should let her keep going with the argument or if I would have to pull her out of her reverie to continue the love story.

My legs had scooted me to the edge of my chair, and I hung there, suspended, waiting for Birdie to continue. No one else seemed interested in cluing me in to what was going on. I had no mentor or handbook to guide me, and matriarchs like Birdie were fading fast. A knife cut into my stomach at the thought of all the things I had missed out on with Abuela. I spun my hair faster around my fingertips in agitation.

"When you say Elevated," I blurted out, finally deciding to interrupt Birdie's monologue, "do you mean gifted? Supernatural?" The word had been thrown about occasionally in my family, but never with enough clarity for me to know what it really meant. I used it sometimes myself, but it was haphazard guesses.

"Mmmmm," Birdie hummed in agreement. "They used to say elevated, since the assumption was our minds were higher attuned to the different planes. Seems a bit snobby to me, but I suppose it's done its time. Not sure what the kids call it these days." Birdie gave me a broad grin, her eyes laughing at the futility of it all.

"Do you mind if I ask you what your gift is?" I said, the inside of my cheek now raw from all the questions I had built up. Several of them still included Henry-with-the-cute-butt, although admittedly they were lower down on the long, long list.

"Ah, I'm surprised you can't tell," Birdie replied, tapping her nose. "You'll do better in time."

"Sorry?" I said again, missing her meaning yet again. I felt like she was speaking a foreign language. Or more aptly, she was speaking to me in calculus, and I had only just mastered algebra. The chasm of missing context loomed before us.

Birdie waved away my apology, grabbing an ink pen and a folded-up newspaper. She flipped to a page covered in an advertisement, drawing four lines in a star-like pattern over a pale smiling face. It looked like the beginning of a sigil in a fantasy movie about witches.

"Each line is a plane, yes?" she began, tapping each line in emphasis. "It holds a pair of truths on each access. The big ones, you'll find, are life and death," Birdie paused, labeling the central horizontal line in her jagged cursive, "and similarly future and past. The vitality and temporal planes always have the strongest of us."

I nodded, my eyes itching from not blinking. All my attention was focused on the diagram, searing it into my memory for future reference. I had pieced some of this together already, but I hadn't thought of it like this before.

"I've heard a little bit about these," I said tentatively, not wanting to disrupt her train of thought. "Abuela, my grandmother, had taught them to my brother, and he told me some."

"Smart woman," Birdie said, nodding her head in approval. "You were probably too young at the time, but you seem ready now. Do you know the other two planes?" She tapped the diagonal lines, and I hesitated.

"I think," I said, "one has to do with consciousness."

"Spot on," Birdie said, labeling the remaining points. "There's subconscious and conscious, or some say dreaming and awake. The sentient plane can get tricky, although I have a feeling you understand that a little more than me, right dear?"

I looked up, finding Birdie's gleaming eyes boring into my soul.

I cleared my throat.

"Something like that," I said. "What's the last one called?"

"Ah, the relativity plane," Birdie said with a chuckle. "Static and dynamic, or stability and motion. This is where the fun bit is, and where you'll find my poor soul. I guess one could get in a lot of trouble on this plane, but honestly, it's difficult to do nearly as much damage as the others. I am most thankful for that, honestly, as it has graced me with a long, full life."

"Does it have a name?" I asked, indicating the whole drawing. "All the parts have names."

"Well, that's an interesting point," Birdie said, leaning back in her chair. She paused to think.

"Or are the names not really the point?" I asked.

"The gifts are passed down to each new generation, but they don't come in the same form every time or even in the same concentration. The energy likes to flow best in lines that some have traced back to supposed deities. I'm not sure if that's not just part of the lore as well though, to be frank," Birdie said, humming as she dug through her mental encyclopedia, tapping her temple lightly. "They do tend to cluster that way in families. Who I've known anyway."

"Is there some sort of record? A history of some sort?" I asked hopefully.

"Lordy, no," Birdie said. "All word of mouth, sorry to say. Only recently have we really run into each other intentionally. Having a written record may be more dangerous than helpful."

One step forward. Two steps back. My excitement fell, pulling my stomach down to the floor.

"So no one really knows," I said, my shoulders hunching over my lap. I focused on untangling the mess I had made of my hair in my excitement.

"Oh, there's a legend. Talks about the Dawn of Eight," Birdie said, tapping the ends of each line, counting the eight points. "Can't remember the specifics, but it talks about the generation that has all eight sides in perfect balance. They will usher in a new era for the lost lines of deities. Of course, balance could mean so many things." Birdie's eyes glowed again with mischief. She chuckled quietly to herself.

"Eight?" I asked, frowning and spinning the diagram around to read right side up. "I thought there were more."

"Normally the energy cannot be contained in just the one person. The purists claim the bloodline is too diluted, but honestly it's simply too much for one person to handle alone. Always was," Birdie said, dabbing the crumbs on the cookie tray and sucking the sugar crystals stuck to her fingertips. "If you're thinking internal and external manifestations, which I've experienced in my lifetime, I guess you're really looking at sixteen, eh?"

I gulped hard.

Sixteen. Quentin's obnoxious laugh rang in my ears.

I had to bring sixteen people together to have any shot in bringing down The Association. The sheer scale of the task loomed before me, punctuated with another round of cackles from the internalized voice I had of Quentin.

"But they could be anywhere," I lamented out loud in argument. "Where would I even start?"

Birdie chuckled again. Her weathered fingers tapped absently at the diagram.

"If it's your generation that's the destined generation, you'll find a way. Even if you don't, fate has a way of bringing folk together, whether they intend to or not," Birdie said, hopping off her chair.

She shuffled the tray back to the counter, and I could see the dramatic bend in her back and shoulders. She stooped heavily, her aged body losing a long battle with gravity. Even I was taller, and the realization made me feel strong and protective of her.

I got up to clear the teapot and do the dishes on her behalf, finding Birdie's height frozen at my already petite shoulders.

"I've got this," I said, grabbing the tray from her.

"I know, dear," Birdie said, patting my hand. "I know."

SIXTEEN

"Time to go," Niko said, the back door gusting open violently with his entrance. He caught the door before the glass panes broke against the wall, but the teapot wasn't as lucky. I had been drying it with a hand towel embroidered with daisies, and the shock of the door had been too much for the slippery surface. The tactile stitches clung guiltily to my empty fingertips.

"I'm so sorry!" I said, crouching down immediately to gather the shards into the damp towel. I hissed at a close call with a particularly pointy piece.

"It's just a teapot, dear," Birdie said, shuffling away to grab a dustpan. She returned, holding it out toward Niko. "Be careful to get all the little pieces. Don't want any cut feet."

Niko secured the door and took the pan and broom lightly, making quick work around me.

"We need to go. Now," he said, setting the broom aside.

"Let me just clean up after…"

"Already done," Niko said, his wrist flicking toward the broom in the corner. I looked around me, scanning the floor for any stray pieces. Except for the two right in front of me, I couldn't find any indication the teapot had broken the minute before.

"His efficiency worries me sometimes," Birdie directed toward me, her words a little muddied, but the volume too loud to be a proper aside.

I held back a snort, not wanting to hurt Niko's feelings. Birdie and I had the same sentiment.

Niko cleared his throat. I ducked my neck in response, scurrying to toss the larger pieces in the trash before I left.

Birdie shuffled forward, grabbing my hands in hers.

"I need you to promise me one thing," Birdie said, the sparkle in her cloudy eyes turning sharp, all smiles gone from her usually bright face. Niko exhaled impatiently through his nose.

"Of course," I said immediately, hoping belatedly it was something I could actually follow through on. Although our time together was brief, I felt a special bond with Birdie. I hoped that one day I could be as old and happy as she had been, but her earlier comment about the less powerful making it longer left a bitter taste in my mouth.

"Take care of yourself," she said, her hands squeezing mine tightly. "You Empaths have the worst trouble with it, but you won't last long if you don't. You know by now to trust your gut, but it won't do you or anyone else much good if you're not around to follow it." Birdie locked gazes with me, her eyes sincerely concerned.

"I'll try," I replied honestly, my throat closing as tears welled up. For once, I towered over an adult, but I felt so small and so young. I didn't know if I could keep my promise, but her words echoed in me like the warnings Abuela used to caution me with as a child.

It was that simple, and it was that hard.

"Oh, and do find your other half. Sooner rather than later," Birdie said, making me blush. "Most people caution against falling in love young, but for us, it's our only saving grace. Bit of fun, too."

I nodded, my cheeks still flaming from her advice. Niko cleared his throat again, and a wave of impatience shot out into the room. My eyes widened.

"No need to be rude," I scolded Niko, still caught in Birdie's hands.

He tried his best to remain impassive, but his curiosity began to needle its way into my brain, poking out cautiously like a cat batting a new toy.

"He's just following orders," Birdie said, patting my hands again and releasing them with a final squeeze. "I hear his boss can be quite the dictator."

"All the more reason to keep him humble," I murmured so Birdie could hear. A bright laugh escaped her, and the music of it echoed through the house.

I hugged her suddenly, and she hooted in surprise. I made sure not to squeeze her bent frame too hard, but she returned a firm press, and I was able to surrender fully to the hug. I basked in the love for a few long moments, wanting to recharge for my next meeting with Aleks, which, due to my delay, would begin with an argument. It was all worth it. Something about grand-mothers gave them the ultimate hugging skill, and I was sorely in need of a great grandma hug.

Before Niko could interrupt and spoil the moment, I pulled away. I stepped toward Niko like an obedient child, waiting for him to zip us back to wherever we had been.

"It was a pleasure meeting you, Birdie," I said, my happiness leaking through every pore in my body. "I hope to see you again soon."

"Take care, dear," Birdie replied, a tinge of sadness radiating from her.

Before I could make anything of it, Niko's hand was on my shoulder, and we were gone.

SEVENTEEN

"Where have you been?" Aleks' voice thundered toward me before I could even open my eyes. Even if I hadn't been an Empath, the vibrations in his tone would have slapped me hard enough to get the picture.

"Whoa," I said, pinching the bridge of my nose to steady the room. Niko had literally just flickered us back into existence, and I hadn't closed my eyes before the jump as I should have. My stomach was rioting against my ribcage, threatening to make an appearance. "Can you give me a second?"

Even with my eyes closed, I could feel Aleks' anger redirected toward Niko, who gave the most audible shrug I had ever not heard. More amusing for me, Aleks wasn't even angry. Not really. Niko must have been able to sense that, too, since he didn't seem cowed by the volume or animosity.

For once, I could read Aleks through his inky barrier. It wasn't anger I was sensing; it was fear.

"So," I said, dropping my hand from my face and hoping for the best, "how's your uncle?"

"Don't," Aleks said, his hand blocking any future words.

I bit the inside of my cheek to reign in a cheeky smile. I looked toward Niko, who shrugged again. His underlying zen calm was back, so I decided if Niko wasn't worried, I shouldn't be either. Birdie had been right to call him a mountain. He made me a little nervous with his imposing frame, but since I could temporarily put him in the ally category, I was able to be less diligent.

"If you don't need me, can I go take a nap?" I asked, feeling the itching sensation of a migraine coming on. Today's overload was finally catching up with me, and I realized belatedly that any medication I had been under was working itself out of my system. I didn't want to deal with withdrawal right now, but that's how it was looking.

At least I had remained awake so far all day today. That was new.

"A nap?" Aleks shouted, causing me to take a small step back.

"Or sleep in general," I said, frowning at his volume. "I honestly don't know what time it is."

"Just," Aleks said, his hands framing his eyes as his head rested against them. He sat slouched in an overstuffed circular booth, the weight of his conscience seemingly held up only by his elbows resting on the table. He sighed heavily.

I heard a buzz of commotion and turned to figure out what was happening. The lights flickered and came to life, and staff moved into their assigned places. The buzz amplified as a bouncer slipped through the door.

Was I at a club?

I whipped around again to face Niko, both of my eyebrows raised in question.

"Remember when I was in a hurry?" Niko said, his deep voice almost nostalgic. His head inclined toward the door.

"What am I going to do with you?" Aleks said, definitely intending to be rhetorical.

"I'm underage. I should probably go," I replied simply. "I hear they're pretty serious about catching minors these days."

Aleks sighed again.

"Niko, get one of the girls to help her out and then bring her right back," Aleks said, raking his hands down his face in one last moment of vulnerability. Slowly, as he spoke, the hard crusted facade was built back in place. "Don't let her out of your sight."

Niko nodded, gripping me lightly by my upper arm and propelling me toward a side door.

"Help out how?" I asked to the stony-faced teleporter.

"Look less," Niko replied, appraising me from head to toe, "underage."

"I am not consenting to a hooker makeover right now," I argued, bucking slightly against Niko's grip, which only tightened more painfully. "I refuse."

"You have to blend in. It's safer," Niko said with a shrug, completely ambivalent to my plight.

"Or I could just go to sleep," I said, trying to catch Niko's gaze. "I'm very cooperative when I'm asleep. I don't even try and go anywhere! It's a win-win!"

"Here," Niko said, shoving me through a doorway that read DRESSING ROOM in silver painted script. "Don't be difficult." Niko slammed the door shut in my face, standing sentry outside. I turned around, my back plastered again the wall as I took in my surroundings.

A bustle of women were moving at warp speed. Most were half clad or in the process of dressing. Those not fighting with clothing or shoes were focused intently on mirrors, applying all varieties of make-up. I squinted at the outfits, trying to decide on which level this strip club was, but I couldn't tell. My limited media experience left me somewhere between burlesque and Playboy bunnies. Most of it looked too difficult to rip off, but there was a lot of corsets and fishnet stockings.

"Ah," a soft voice said in my ear. I startled, not realizing a girl had come up to me so quietly. "You must be Evangeline."

I squinted at her, curious as to how she knew my name. Clearly, Aleks had known more about my family than he had let on. I had never given him my first name.

"Hi," I said curtly.

"I'm Gaby. Here, let's get you changed. Cute jacket!" the girl said, taking my hand and leading me into the heart of the storm. I looked down in confusion, trying to remember what I was wearing. It was a simple black winter jacket I had thrown over my crusty hoodie, which did not help me decide if she was being sincere or merely polite.

Hands helped me undress, and I froze. Internally, I was ninja kicking them all away, but my limbs froze at the awkward sensation. I was in my bra and underwear---and awkwardly only one sock---in no time. I hugged myself automatically, bowing my head to shade my flaming cheeks.

"Let's see what we're working with," Gaby said, her appraisal soft and diligent without a hint of malice. She turned me to the side, checking my profile, humming in approval. "Ariel, grab me your spare bodycon. She's almost your same measurements, I think."

A dress appeared in the circle of women, and Gaby offered it to me.

"Straight over the top," she directed me with an encouraging smile.

I reached out a tentative hand and took the dress, skeptical such little fabric would cover my whole butt. It reminded me of the embroidered tea towel I had held less than an hour before. Bile rose again to my throat, but I did my best to wiggle into the dress.

Hands immediately came to the rescue, tucking and pulling until the dress was indeed past my butt and encompassing all of my womanly features, plentiful or not. Gaby took a step back, clapping with delight.

"Perfect!" she crowed. "Let me grab a few things while we get you done up, hmmm?"

Gaby led me toward the vanity, shoving me into a seat and the waiting hands of another girl with large eyes and a cascade of artfully curled tresses.

"This is Ariel. Gosh you guys have a lot of similar features," Gaby said, comparing the two of us with a few quick glances. "Bottom heavy, big eyes, and long hair. We should rename you Night and Day!" A chorus of laughter filled the room, and my cheeks flamed again.

"I would kill for your eyes though," Ariel said, her voice a little gravely. "They are the most beautiful shade of brown."

"We can trade," I said, clearing my throat awkwardly. "I can't even tell if your eyes or blue or green. It's so pretty." Ariel waved my comment away in the air.

"Grass is always greener, right?" she said with a raspy giggle. "Now. Do you trust me?"

I gave a short nod, my lips pursed in anticipation. Ariel smiled and turned the chair around, away from the mirror.

"We'll do a reveal like all those reality shows," Ariel said. "Now close your eyes, and don't flinch."

I tried my best to follow her directions, but it was clear who was the pro and who was not. After a few botched attempts to put on false eyelashes, Ariel gave in and decided some well-sculpted mascara tricks would have to do. My clammy hands remained tangled in my lap, as I was not allowed to touch my hair. I felt like an alien with my hair bound up in large plastic curlers, but I did my best to keep calm.

The energy in the room was contagious, and everyone seemed to be in a great mood. Instead of allowing my anxiety to take over, I relaxed, the positive energy waves washing over me. My barriers were slightly lowered, my curiosity getting the better of me, but surprisingly, nothing bad happened. My doomsday thinking was thwarted for once, and I sighed internally with relief.

"Finishing touches," Ariel said next to my ear, waking me from my semi-trance state. My hair was being unbound, and hands were fluffing and twisting my locks into an acceptably manufactured mess. She turned me back toward the mirror and squeezed my shoulders.

I opened my eyes fully and yelped, clapping my hands to my mouth.

I looked like a social media influencer.

The girls screamed with joy and excitement at my reaction, deeming the pity project a success.

"You look foxy," Gaby said in approval, high-fiving Ariel with a broad grin. She held out some thick stockings and a pair of boots that reminded me of Noah. A small sad smile flickered across my newly painted lips at the thought.

"But not too sexy," Ariel said, grabbing a comb with a birdcage netting attached to it. She secured it in my hair, directing the netting to obscure part of my face. "Some nice armor for you."

The subtle effect bolstered my confidence, hiding just enough of my face for me to feel like I could go unnoticed. Against all these beautiful ladies, I had no doubt I wouldn't catch too many eyes.

"Stockings go up to your mid thighs, and they're warm. You're going to be sitting and not running around like the rest of us, so it does get chilly. Here," Gaby said, shoving them into my lap while she bounded away. She returned in a moment, holding a cropped jacket. "This also has a high collar, but it's very chic. I promise."

I yanked on the stockings, slipping into the booties as I stood. I hung my arms like a scarecrow, and Gaby threw on the jacket, turning me around and doing a final assessment. She nodded in approval, and Ariel stepped in to give me a quick hug.

"All set," Gaby said. "Go get 'em, killer." She winked at me, scuttling me toward the door and out into the corridor. The din of the women getting ready died away immediately once the door was shut, and I stood facing Niko yet again.

He glanced at me and my new outfit. I must have passed a test because he nodded, holding his hand out for me to go first. I scowled at him.

"Oh, now you're nice about it," I said, storming ahead. Luckily, the booties were wedges, so I didn't ruin the show of power by wobbling or falling over. I felt a little stronger with the few extra inches, but I was skeptical if I could run long distances in these. I felt a pang for my practical street clothes lying in a heap in the dressing room.

"Don't want to ruin everyone's hard work," Niko said, his

tone amused. I tossed my hair back over my shoulder so I could glare at him. "No pouting. You look your age when you do that."

"I am my age though," I said with a scowl, making the pout deeper.

"Not tonight you aren't," Niko said, pausing at the side entrance to the club. "And don't say anything. Just listen." Niko raised his eyebrows, giving me an intentional look.

I swallowed hard, shaking out the last nerves in my fingers as I did a mental check of my barriers. Not knowing what I was walking into, I prayed silently that Niko was offering sage advice.

I nodded to Niko, and he opened the door, ushering me into the unknown.

EIGHTEEN

I felt lightheaded as I walked across the dance floor. The lights pulsed along with the music, and I was so overwhelmed with the vibrations of the bass that I tripped a few times over nothing but my own nerves. Niko was only a step or two behind me, and his steady hand on my back was a small comfort as I teetered my way toward Aleks' VIP corner booth. I used the bouts of darkness in between the strobe lighting to steady my breathing, flexing my hands nervously before he came into view.

Aleks' head was inclined toward another man in a dark suit. Although the stranger seemed older than Aleks at first glance, Aleks' presence was clearly the one radiating dominance. The other man's posture was more extreme, contorting to accommodate Aleks' slightly inclined head. The other face was obscured, but Aleks was frowning in concentration at his guest's words. The inky black aura around him tickled at their ankles, but remained sequestered inside the booth's perimeter.

I froze, causing Niko to bump into me slightly. I had forgotten about the black aura. How was I supposed to sit next to him for a minute, let alone the whole night? My legs went cold, and I couldn't feel my toes for a moment.

The pressure of Niko's hand between my shoulder blades propelled me forward, and my stiff legs managed to move in spite of the alarm bells ringing in the back of my head. In two breaths, we were at the bottom of the steps leading up to the VIP booth. A behemoth of a man stepped in front of me, taking up the majority of the width of the stairs. I squeaked in surprise.

Niko stepped forward, exchanging words with the man. With the din of the music and the raised cloud of voices of the patrons, I wasn't sure how they could hear one another. After a moment, I realized they were laughing like old friends.

Niko clapped the man on the shoulder, and the other one cracked a toothy smile, letting me pass. Niko stayed at the bottom of the stairs with his friend, and I was left to climb the stairs alone. I took a deep breath in through my nose, belatedly hoping the bodycon dress didn't make me look like a stuffed toad with the expansion of my stomach. It was dark, I reminded myself. No one could see anything.

I squared my shoulders and ascended, trying to exude a cool confidence to match my new duds. I tried to freeze my face like those fierce runway models, but I had no idea how successful I was. Not knowing who the other man was, I kept with Niko's advice and said nothing.

Aleks' eyes caught mine on the last step, and I slowed down, hoping for a cue as to what I was supposed to do next so I could move with grace and confidence. Or at least try to.

Does one curtsy for His Royal Highness? I thought to myself. Aleks' lips twitched, trying to hide a smile. His attention was no longer on the man speaking to him.

Aleks' guest, sensing a shift, looked up in my direction. I could feel his gaze assessing me critically, his thoughts broadcasting sporadically. Upset that I had interrupted. Not as upset as his eyes lingered on my accentuated frame. The moment he leaned back from Aleks, his broadcasting was clear as a bell.

My head tilted in curiosity, and I hoped the movement wasn't too obvious. As much as Aleks' dark cloud scared me, it seemed to have its uses. I tabled my hunches and put them in the back of my mind. Now was not the time to be daydreaming. I had to remain vigilant.

Both men had stopped talking, and I waited to see what would happen next.

Aleks, realizing his faux pas, stood, one arm indicating the seat in the booth next to him while the other held his jacket shut. The other man stood, mirroring Aleks' manners, bowing his head slightly in greeting. The top of his dark head shone with product, and a lock of hair fell free of its shellacked prison, causing the man to nervously swipe it back into place. I nodded back, smiling without my teeth, as I sat as daintily as I could manage in the restricting dress. The dynamic in the booth was interesting, and only about to get worse.

"Would you like a drink?" Aleks asked me, and I nodded. His hand rose, and a woman appeared from the shadows, her attire more austere than the ladies in the dressing room. She placed a tumbler in front of me, something clear and fizzy with red marbling. I inclined my head to her in thanks, and she was gone again immediately.

Aleks bent his head toward mine, and I only had to turn slightly to hear him.

"It's a Shirley Temple," he said. I could feel his smile against my hair. "Non-alcoholic. And poison-free. I promise."

I dipped my head again to acknowledge I had understood him. He chuckled at his own poor joke falling flat.

He lingered, and I felt a slight zing of nervousness as the silence dragged on.

"We have to stay here for a bit. Let me finish up with Akira and then we'll be able to talk freely," Aleks said. "You look great, by the way."

I nodded, glad my hair and the dim lighting hid my blush. This whole not talking thing was much harder than Niko made it seem. I clenched my hands together in my lap, determined not to ruin my hair even though the urge to twirl a strand was over-whelming.

Instead, I focused on Aleks.

I had never been this close to him before, and I was thankful his shielding was working better than it had earlier. He wore a tailored black suit, almost a severe cut, which complemented his strong jawline and cheekbones. I could hardly imagine this had been the man to greet me less than an hour ago.

Confidence rolled off him in waves, and he had a subtle way of carrying his authority, which really did remind me of a prince. His aftershave was subtle, almost woodsy, like a piece of amber I had found in the forest once. The smell seemed softer than Brendan's, since his was almost overwhelming in its sharpness, but there was no mistaking its masculinity. I bit the inside of my cheek.

Brendan. I hadn't thought about him much since our separation.

A wave of guilt crashed over me, and I had to work hard to compose my face once again. I tried to shove the emotion in a box and hide it in my mind. I clasped my hands even tighter, willing my self-control to swing back into place.

Later, I promised myself. We could think about everything later.

Brendan. Abuela. Tomas.

Please, just not now.

Aleks placed his hand gently on top of mine. I stiffened, but didn't move it away. He was still in deep conversation with his guest, the man Akira, but he managed to send a wave of comfort my way. All thoughts of Brendan slipped away as Aleks slid his hand between mine, breaking the tension I had centered there, taking my hand in his. All my thoughts scattered as he laced his fingers through mine, bringing our hands to rest on his leg in a cradled, relaxed position.

He squeezed my hand softly in solidarity.

I opened my mouth, unsure if I could say anything. I closed it slowly, biting my bottom lip. What was happening right now? Aleks was still mid-conversation, letting no indication of his actions leak through to his other interaction. I was left to wonder alone.

Finally, Akira inclined his head toward Aleks, shaking hands in parting. The action seemed stiff, and I wondered belatedly who the man was. As Akira walked down the steps, he turned back toward me, bowing in parting to me as well. I did my best to reciprocate, but I had no idea how to act. Niko and the other bouncer stepped aside for him, and he was lost to the crowd before I could think on it much more.

Yet again, my tumultuous inner world had taken over, and I had not been paying enough attention. I let the frustration wash over me, letting my scowl bore holes in the inch of skin showing between my dress and the stocking socks on my upper thigh.

Another squeeze to my hostage hand brought me back to the present. I looked up, and Aleks' full attention was on me, assessing every line on my face.

"What?" I said, feeling the hairs on the back of my neck stand up in defiance. He shook his head, a light chuckle escaping through his half smile.

"You're amazing," Aleks said. I looked at him skeptically, and he laughed again.

"Is that why you won't let go of my hand?" I asked, attempting to subtly remove my warm fingertips from his. He held on, ignoring my hint.

"What do you think about all the time?" he asked suddenly. His eyes were searching my face again, and I bit the inside of my cheek. I was doomed if he was able to read my expressions.

"What are you talking about?" I asked, hoping my deflection would work.

It didn't.

"You're so animated when you're in a conversation, but when you aren't, it's like you're in sleep mode. I was a little worried I was too overwhelming again," Aleks said, my eyes catching on the creeping black aura obscuring our feet. It remained a small nebulous cloud, and I tried to ignore it.

"Well, your shielding was much better than earlier," I said. "I was only a little lightheaded."

"What shielding?" Aleks said, his head leaning closer toward mine as the bass dropped in the background. Even in the VIP area, the vibrations were overwhelming.

"You," I said loudly, over enunciating in the hope Aleks could read my lips before I shattered his eardrum. "Your black aura was under control. Weren't you shielding the whole time?"

Aleks shook his head.

"I don't know how." He shrugged.

"Then how..." I trailed off, snapping my mouth shut. I focused on our clasped hands once more, my confusion channeling through that focal point.

"But I could hear you," Aleks said, his fingers lightly touching my chin, redirecting my gaze back up to his face.

"I didn't say anything," I argued. "Niko told me to be quiet."

"No," Aleks said, pointing to his temple. "Here. The Your Highness comment. Remember?"

I froze, my mouth dropping open as another tidal wave of confusion crashed over me.

"And the other things. Some were feelings. Some images. Something about the woods?" Aleks' eyes shone with curiosity, and his head fell to the side. "How do you do that?"

"I am so sorry," I said, my voice wavering. Once again, I tried to pull my hand away from his grasp, but he held on. I could feel tears prickle in the corners of my eyelids, and I tried desperately to contain them. "I'm usually very good at shielding. I didn't mean to...I'll try better next time. I promise." I let out a shuddering breath, my constant attempt to pull myself together unsuccessful yet again.

"Hey," Aleks said, catching my chin again, forcing my wandering eyes to swing back to focus on him. "It's okay. Shhhh. No one got hurt. Nothing happened. No one else noticed. You're safe."

I hiccupped. I groaned, mad at my pitiful state. Aleks just smiled, releasing my chin from his light grip.

"Starting tomorrow, we'll get a whole work up done," Aleks

said, his voice strong against the buzzing cacophony on the floor behind us. "I know you're really overwhelmed right now, but we just have to focus on getting through tonight. Then we'll be golden. Sound fair?"

I nodded, hiccupping again, my face immediately resetting into a pout. Aleks laughed.

"Shut up," I quipped, hiccupping more violently. Aleks tried to sober up, but his smile broke through his failed attempt to stop laughing. I shoved my shoulder against his. "Stop!"

I hiccupped in the middle of the word, and it only set Aleks off more.

My jaw dropped open in indignation, and he looked at least a little chastised. He raised our clasped hands to his mouth and kissed mine in apology.

"Let's get you some food, huh?" Aleks said, flagging down our personal waiter. The woman appeared out of the shadows again, scaring me. I jumped, and Aleks went off again with laughter. I went to shout at him and realized my hiccups were gone, which made him nearly inconsolable for several minutes.

Once he could speak again, he ordered us a late dinner, wiping the tears from his eyes with his free hand, never letting my hand go. I surrendered to his infectiously happy mood and tried to stay in the moment. The dark thoughts lingered in the back of my mind, but I did my best to keep them behind the curtain. Like Aleks said, we just had to survive tonight. I could go one night without worrying, right?

NINETEEN

"Get up, Sleeping Beauty," a voice said immediately before my head was assaulted with an overstuffed goose down pillow. I squawked, burying myself deeper into my various blankets and comforters, trying to avoid not only getting hit again, but the frigid temperature of the room.

"There's this invention called an alarm clock," I called through my layers of covers. "It's very handy."

"Well," the voice said, yanking all my comforters and me along with them onto the floor, "it's not nearly as satisfying."

I looked up at Eli from my nest of comforters on the floor, my face mostly obscured by my ratty, product soaked hair. I had forgotten how dirty I could feel after waking up with make-up and hair product residue. My crustiness level was reaching maximum overdrive at this point, and all I wanted was a hot shower. A deep steam would be needed to slough off the many layers of gunk, grime, and various pigments.

"Good morning to you, too," I grumbled, trying to fight my legs free of the mess to stand properly.

Someone had dumped me fully clothed into the bed the night before. The leggings had slid down to bunch at my calves, and I was thankful it was Eli waking me up, since I was definitely flashing underwear and ass cheek, the tight dress from the night before having ridden up above my hips.

I peered through my bleary morning eyes, not daring to rub

my face for fear of extreme panda eye mode being activated. Eli was smirking enough; I didn't need to add to her enjoyment.

The room was built like a hotel suite, and I could see a bathtub across the room through the doorway of what I assumed to be a very posh bathroom. I was having trouble finding purchase to stand on the silken sheets and duvet. Eli did not move to help.

Her arms were crossed in front of her, and she stood like a statue as I barreled past her, my toes sinking into the lush red carpet.

"Did you come with anything useful," I muttered, "or are you just here to gloat?" My filter was never intact this early in the morning, and a flash of annoyance sobered me a little as I remembered the Eli of yesterday.

No, we didn't want to push her to full anger, I decided. Not until after breakfast.

"Change of clothes and toiletries are in the bathroom," she sneered at me, marching toward the door. "Be outside in fifteen or else."

I snorted as she slammed the door behind her.

Just in case she returned to get her revenge, I locked the bathroom door behind me. I decided at the last moment to draw a hot bath instead of a shower. Eli's time limit grated on my last nerve. A full soak would be needed for me to feel clean and decrustified.

With a smirk, I flicked the stopper down at the base of the tub and cranked the hot water handle to firehose-level pressure. Even so, it would need more than a moment to fill fully.

Slowly, I peeled off the tight borrowed clothing, now wrinkled from a night of fitful sleep. I tried to lay them nicely on a vacant chair, but they would honestly need a good cleaning before they were returned to their owners. Getting the dress off was an adventure, and suddenly I missed the gaggle of women around me to help.

Free from my constrictive clothes, I tore through the cabinets in the double vanity, finding a basket of bath salts in the bottom that made me hoot with pleasure. I tossed a bath bomb into the rising water and hissed as I lowered myself slowly into the scalding water. I placed a damp washcloth over my face to soak off the remaining make-up and laid back to enjoy my alone time.

I had not had an unsupervised bathroom visit in months. Quentin and I had joked about the naughty leanings of the guards who had to watch us do our business, but the awkwardness remained even though we tried to laugh it off. Just the lock on the bathroom door gave me immense pleasure.

As promised, I got another round of ground-shattering pounds on the door once my fifteen minutes had expired. The water in my bath hadn't even cooled, so I felt no obligation to hurry.

After a few minutes of silence, a more practiced knock of authority rang through the door.

I greeted it with silence, basking in the healing powers of a good soak.

"Go in and get her," Eli said loudly on the other side of the door. Her voice, though muffled, was clear enough for me to understand without straining my ears.

"I am not going in there," Niko said. "Just wait for her to come out."

"I'm not going to…"

"She's in there, yes?" Niko said firmly.

"Yes," Eli said in a clipped voice.

"And she's still alive?" Niko said.

"For now," Eli growled. "You know I can only approximate so much."

"Then she's no flight risk. Only one way out. If she's still not out in another ten minutes, I'll consider it," Niko said, his voice fading as he moved away from the door.

"I'm not getting in trouble because the diva decided to lock herself in there," Eli said, standing resolutely at the door.

"Well," Niko said, "that diva is a personal guest of the Navratils. I think they'd be more upset if she wandered away." Eli harrumphed, causing me to smile into my washcloth. "Also, she's food motivated. Tell her she's going to miss breakfast, and I guarantee you she'll be ready in no time."

I heard Niko chuckle, leaving Eli to her silent brooding.

He would be food motivated, too, if he saw the kind of crap they feed you in an institution, I thought at him, hoping he got the message. After last night, I wasn't sure how clear I was projecting.

Last night.

Aleks' words resurfaced in my idle mind, making me think a little harder about what had happened. Something about his aura must be working in conjunction with my powers. That was the only way I could explain Akira's static as well as Aleks' ease of "eavesdropping" on thoughts I hadn't been broadcasting.

Unless I had been broadcasting and hadn't realized it. I bit the inside of my cheek. I really hoped that wasn't the case.

Sighing, I removed the washcloth from my face, giggling at the various colors of my temporary facade smiling back at me. I tossed it aside, grabbing a clean one before I went to town scrubbing off the rest.

I rubbed off the first several layers of skin all over my body and diligently washed and conditioned the entire length of my hair. The shower following the bath was not anything special, but I managed to let the anxiety that had been creeping into the sides of my subconscious follow the sudsy water down the drain.

By the time I had finished washing my face and detangling my hair, Eli was back, pounding at the door.

"I'm serious," Eli called. "If you're not out here in one minute, Niko's coming in."

In response, I turned on the hair dryer, drowning out the pounding on the door. I got my hair to damp versus soaking wet by the time Niko popped into the bathroom.

He sighed, his hand covering his eyes. He looked like a bored grownup forced to play hide and seek against his will.

"You decent?" Niko asked, clearly annoyed he was sent on a fool's errand.

"Give me a second," I said with a sigh, snatching a pair of

jeans from the clean pile. So much for chaperone-free personal time. I had to dry the wet spot on my back that was left over by my hair. Luckily, I'd at least had my bra and underwear on when Niko popped in, but I threw on the henley left for me, pulling my damp hair through with another large sigh. "Decent."

Niko's hand dropped from his eyes, and he surveyed the room. Nothing out of the ordinary. He made a grumbling noise, clearly peeved at Eli for wasting his time.

"Even the institution gave me more than ten minutes to get ready in the morning," I said pointedly at Niko, who raised his hands in mock surrender. He glanced down, noticing my still damp hair.

"Do you want to finish drying your hair? You'll catch a cold," he stated, his tone factual, not concerned.

"Nah," I said with a grin. "Food might be all gone if we wait that long."

Niko snorted, lifting his hands minutely in agreement.

"But seriously, you are always welcome to bribe me with food," I said, tossing all my towels into a pile by the tub.

"Noted," Niko said, a ghost of a smile playing across his face. I pointed toward the chair with my evening clothes on it.

"Should I?" I gestured futilely at the black pile.

"Leave them," he directed, reaching for the door handle. "Let's go."

"Would you be opposed..." I began, a mischievous smile spreading across my face, "to teleporting to wherever I need to be?" I could hear Eli pacing outside the door, lamenting at her latest task. Niko squinted at me.

We locked eyes in a battle of wills, but Niko, ever punctual, gave in easily enough.

"You owe me unquestioning obedience for this," Niko warned, stepping forward to grab my shoulder.

"Totally worth it," I quipped, remembering to close my eyes before we jumped. I smiled, imagining Eli's face when she realized I had gone ahead without her.

TWENTY

"Ah, the guest of honor," a man said, nervously adjusting his glasses higher on top of his prominent nose bridge.

I froze, the devilish smile dropping from my face as soon as I realized I was in front of an audience. Niko stepped back, nodded respectfully at Aleks, and took his leave. I was left standing at the end of the ornate dining room with a large wooden table between me and the three remaining room occupants.

Aleks covered the bottom half of his face with his curled fingers, and although it seemed a lazy gesture, the lines near his eyes told me he was trying to hide a smile. My hand immediately went to my damp hair, and I tried to twist it more elegantly down one shoulder. My henley's waffle knit fabric, while comfortable, did not seem to be on the same level of dress as the others in the room.

The man with the nerd chic glasses and large nose sat to Aleks' left and wore a tweed vest, his shirtsleeves rolled up studiously at his elbows. Although he looked no older than his thirties, he dressed like someone brought up the same time as my abuela. His female companion dangled her mimosa lazily in one hand, her strong brow set in perpetual disapproval as she eyed me up and down. Her smartly cut emerald dress was powerfully elegant while still remaining feminine. I picked enviously at the hem of my shirt. I did a not-so-subtle double take, realizing her eyes were two different colors. One was a clear blue, and the other pure silver. Not unlike my main school nemesis, Mags.

I stumbled forward nervously, knowing that standing dumbstruck would not get me through this awkward interaction fast enough. Might as well jump in both feet first.

The empty place setting sat to Aleks' right, and I was relieved to have unobstructed sight lines of all the guests. This time, I did note the exits and the wall of ceiling-high windows. I had promised Niko I would behave, but he hadn't warned me the caveat attached to my food bribe. No one could fault me for being too careful anymore.

I cleared my throat nervously as I sat, a silent waiter appearing from the shadows to help me with my chair. I bobbed my head in thanks, but they were gone before I could successfully catch their gaze.

"My apologies," I said, my mind cycling through possible dialogue options and etiquette rules. "Please excuse my tardiness." I felt like an actor in a play. Is that what people said in fancy dining rooms with waiting guests? I had no idea. Sounded good to me.

"No need to apologize," the man said, his words falling over one another in their rush to get out. "Right, Jasleen?"

The woman hummed thoughtfully, taking a measured sip of her mimosa. I smiled nervously in her direction, careful not to keep her gaze any longer than socially acceptable, but not too short either. Aleks remained silent in his chair, soaking in the interaction. I could almost hear the cogs in his head turning.

"It really is such a pleasure to meet you," the man gushed, eliciting an eye roll from Jasleen. "Your family is very well respected and dare I say beloved in our community."

"They are?" I said, reaching for the cup in front of me only to realize it was empty. My slight flicker of disappointment sent Aleks' hand up, and the waiter appeared again, filling my cup with steaming fresh coffee. I scooped it up before he finished pouring, basking in the warmth and aroma like a cat in a patch of sunlight.

"Absolutely," the man continued. "Legends, practically."

I looked up from my steaming mug with a frown.

"Legends?" I parroted. My mind cranked through another new set of options. Tomas's tragic death? Maybe Abuela's? I couldn't possibly have made enough waves to be notorious already. "And I'm sorry, you seem to know me, but I don't know you. Or your companion."

I took a long sip of my coffee, catching the groan of pleasure before it escaped into the room and I ruined what little semblance of respect the man felt he owed me on behalf of my family.

"Ah, that's my oversight," Aleks said. "May I introduce Henry Wolf and Jasleen Desai. Henry, Jasleen, this is Evangeline Herrera de los Santos."

I squinted at Aleks, amused he had left off my mother's remarried name. He tilted his head slightly, locking eyes with me. I pursed my lips but kept my comments to myself. I had a feeling I already knew the reason. A small part of me wasn't even opposed to the edit.

"Yes, Evangeline de los Santos. Like I was saying, such a great history," Henry said. Jasleen reached out and gripped his wrist, silencing the beginning of what I assumed would have been a long and extensively detailed monologue.

"Before you put the girl to sleep, Henry, I think it'll be much faster to lay our cards on the table," Jasleen said, her tone rich and direct, immediately swaying Henry to her way of thinking.

"Of course," Henry said, a nervous laugh escaping him. I smiled at his energy though. Lots of bright yellow interwoven with the Elevated white. If not for the coffee, Henry's pleasant aura could have warmed my exhaustion away. "After all, you two have a lot going on. Don't want to take up too much of your time."

Henry's eyes bounced back and forth between Aleks and I. A

large unspoken shared knowledge hung in the air, and I felt a bit taken aback. The assumption was that I was in on the joke, but I was completely lost.

Covering my perplexed expression with my saucer, I took a long measured pull of coffee. Just cool enough not to scald going down, but a bit warmer than comfortable. I used the mundane action to school my face back to normal. My mind was spinning off on several tangents at once, but I didn't have the luxury of following any of those thoughts too far before I pulled myself back to the present. The nebulous Big Task ahead of me must be more monumental than I had thought. Somehow I was already mid-quest, and I didn't remember getting the call to arms officially from anyone. I was just stumbling around until enough details fell together for me to do…something. Henry seemed to know a lot of the details I may be looking for. I was already apprehensive the meeting was being cut too short.

Finally, I set my cup down, and my stomach growled audibly in response. The plate in front of me remained empty, but no one moved to put food in front of it. I crossed my legs to hide my agitation, hoping if I played my part well enough, I could finally enjoy some of the food bribe I had anticipated.

"Jasleen has seen some interesting developments as of late," Henry began tentatively, his attention half focused on his odd-eyed companion as she nodded her head in approval. The light caught her silver eye in just the right way, and I stiffened slightly. I wondered if a flare for theatrics was part of an oracle's gift, or if Jasleen and Mags just came by it naturally.

"To clarify," Aleks said, "Jasleen is an oracle." I bit my cheek to muffle the snort that dared to escape.

"I figured," I said, suction cupping my hands together in my lap as another intense urge to mess with my hair washed over me. Aleks' eyes flicked over at me briefly, but he didn't interrupt.

"Yes, well, interesting is putting it mildly," Henry said, his cheeks rosy with excitement. "In light of such exciting events currently unfolding, we decided to pay a visit to show our support and offer our services, should they be needed."

Aleks' forehead creased deeply as his eyebrows popped up towards his hairline. So much for his practiced poker face from earlier.

"We are not ones to take sides," Jasleen cautioned, shifting in her seat to directly face me. I tried to keep steady eye contact, but my mind screamed at me to look away. I focused on my breathing, remembering to blink at regular intervals.

"Sides?" I asked after several seconds of silence, clearing my throat.

"War is brewing," Jasleen said, tossing the phrase lightly into the room.

My eyes flitted to Aleks, but he had regained his aloof composure, the darkness of his aura swirling idly around the legs of his chair. If I wanted to know more, I would have to focus my efforts into breaking his barrier without catastrophe, abandoning the doomsday conversation that was on the verge of being prophetic. No, it wasn't worth it. I needed as much information as possible to orient myself in wherever and whatever I was doing now.

"Indeed," Henry said, his nervous energy turning to excitement. "Quite the kerfuffle. A showdown, if you will."

Jasleen clicked her tongue in disapproval of his word choice.

"Imminent?" Aleks asked, directing his question to Jasleen.

Her silver hoop earrings caught the light at the same time as her eye as she turned her face to the head of the table. A picture of a hydra came to mind, and I had to bite my cheek again.

"It has already begun," Jasleen said, her tone just shy of ominous. "You've seen the effects of some of the chess moves already in motion. Unknowingly, I think, you entered the match by stealing a most valuable pawn."

"Who me?" I asked, my eyes locked on the stare down between Aleks and my second least favorite seer. "Stolen seems a bit harsh. Pawn, even. I am a person, you know."

"I wouldn't call her a pawn," Henry thought aloud, his mind

caught arguing a different word. "At the very least a knight, if not a rook. In time, she could even be the queen."

The rest of the room ignored Henry's comments, but I was sidetracked trying to follow the chess metaphor. The names seemed familiar, but chess had never been my game. My impatience never let me get more than two steps ahead of my opponent, so I had quit before I even started.

"You're saying it's inevitable," Aleks half-asked. "It's already happening?"

"The momentum will build," Jasleen said, her eyes darting to me. "There's no way to stop it now."

Aleks withdrew his arms from his lap and crossed them against his chest. A series of micro expressions cycled through his face as he argued with himself in his head.

"Who exactly is in this showdown?" I asked, taking over the slack Aleks had left.

"Once, not so long ago, your family was allied to those who you are now against. If balance is not restored in this generation, all of us risk elimination. The scale is sliding dangerously in their favor, which has put everyone in great danger," she said. "For now, Henry and I must go into hiding."

"Hiding?" I echoed, my aching from continued pinging between Aleks and the two supernatural guests. "Why?"

"Remember our theory about the string of mysterious deaths?" Aleks asked, turning to face me. His expression remained stony, and I could see the teeming mass of darkness ebbing and expanding with his mood. What had been a tighter smoky haze pool earlier was now morphing into a veritable cloud of blackness as Aleks' mood shifted with the worsening news.

I threw my scattered thoughts aside and refocused, sending a burst of energy to my barriers. Immediately, I could see the darkness licking at my expanded barrier like the tide against a levy wall, a clear barrier in my mind's eye but still invisible to everyone else.

I let out a heavy sigh. I did not like where this was going.

"If the pattern continues, those with Elevated powers in the middle generation who don't ally with the Association will be hunted down and killed. Their energy will theoretically gift the next in line with their abilities. People---children---in the Association's control," Aleks explained aloud to the room, his hands hopping on the table to illustrate the trickledown effect. Henry nodded violently in agreement.

"How many generations are in the mix right now?" I asked, my voice pinching off as a lump formed in my throat. "Three?"

"The maximum the world can hold is four, which is in flux right now as the eldest die and the youngest are born," Jasleen said, pausing to let the information sink in. "If they force a hand, they could concentrate all the energy into two generations or less. That is assuming they allow the second generation to live."

"Can the energy flow the other way?" The words left my mouth before I realized I was the one speaking. My stomach clenched as if it was suddenly shot through with a frozen arrow, the answer coming to me as soon as I dare to speak aloud the question. I looked directly into Jasleen's metallic eyes, unsurprised to find no warmth. "They're killing to push the energy into the next generation, but if there's no one left young enough, would it rebound back to whoever's left?"

Silence greeted me from all sides of the table.

"That's going to be an unknown then," I mumbled under my breath, my face tingling with shock. Waves of fear swirled within me, and I was thankful I had enforced my barriers earlier with Aleks's shift in mood. It may officially be an unknown, but my instincts were screaming otherwise.

"It's never happened before," Henry said, "if that's a comfort for you."

"How would you know?" I snapped, the fear I was holding lashing out through my one unguarded space---my mouth. "There's nothing written down. No record of anything!" My voice shook with anger. Tears started to pool in the corners of my eyes, and I looked to the ceiling in an attempt to hold them back. I let out a deep breath, but I felt it catch in my throat. This was just too much.

Aleks reached out and placed his hand over mine, and I sat back, fuming. This was all just too much.

"Henry's gift," Aleks said softly to me, "is immortality."

TWENTY-ONE

"Excuse me?" I said. "Did you just say immortal?"

"It's quite a selfish gift, really," Henry said with a wistful sigh. "Not as glamorous as the films and novels seem to portray."

"And it has its side effects," Aleks said, raising a knowing eyebrow.

I glanced at Henry, his once warm pulsing energy suddenly erratic, like solar flares. A wave of pity fell over me, and I could only imagine what it could mean to outlast everyone and everything you held dear. All the bitterness that had been building inside me was immediately extinguished.

"Can I ask how old you are?" I said, sending a warning look to Aleks when he opened his mouth to intervene. "Or is that...rude."

"I don't remember," Henry said, looking to Jasleen. "Do you remember?"

"When I was younger, you told me you were born in a time before the white man," Jasleen said with a chuckle. "I suppose you didn't have calendars back then."

"Like colonists, white people?" I said, my eyes bugging out. "Or like before evolution made white people from brown people?" Henry didn't look much older than thirty, his dark hair as shiny as his dark brown eyes. I took a closer look at him, trying to ignore the semi-modern Western style clothing and just take in his features. His skin tone was similar to mine, but even I could pass as white for the uneducated observer. My brain could not reconcile this new information. There were too many assumptions to be made with so little information, and I knew I was as far off from the truth as I could be.

I couldn't decide which shocked me more: his Elevation or his lived experience. It was one thing to honor your ancestors and the pain and suffering they had gone through before you. Living through it and carrying those memories with you every day of your never-ending life? Barriers be damned, the pity I felt was so strong I felt a wave of it escape out into the room.

Aleks and Jasleen stiffened, their bodies overwhelmed with the sudden emotion. Their eyes instantly boring into me with reproach. Henry smiled weakly, his eyes shimmering with tears.

"Thank you," he whispered. "You're very kind."

Jasleen scowled at me, her mama bear instincts honing in on Henry, making sure he was all right. No physical scar remained, but I could tell that had pushed him over the limit for human interaction today. I was about there myself.

"Stay safe," I told him, locking his eyes with mine. "If I don't get at least one story from you, I will be very, very upset." Birdie's face flashed in my mind. Then Abuela's. Even though Henry's age was far beyond that of a grandparent, I put him in that beloved category. The vulnerable fourth generation category.

I smiled brightly at him, a bond immediately imprinted to him just like Noah. A shock of recognition, of kindred spirits. I knew I would never find anyone else like Henry my entire life. Somehow knowing that made our time together more precious. It already felt too scarce.

Henry chuckled at my scolding tone.

"If I can remember any," Henry said. "I promise I won't disappoint you."

Reading the emotions in the room, I knew we were at the end of our breakfast meeting. I stood and walked over to Henry's chair.

"Let me walk you out, old man," I said in a saucy tone, much to Henry's delight. I winked at Henry, and his aura blushed with happiness. He must have been on pins and needles meeting a new person and sharing his gift, even after all these years. "The adults can talk a little more about boring things like code names and bringing down the establishment."

I took the crook of his arm, and he escorted me slowly down the length of the dining room, leaving Aleks and Jasleen behind as promised. Henry, who actually knew his way around, slowly directed us toward the door. We chatted about the décor and the funny assortment of portraits along the wall, giggling and laughing like little kids.

By the time we reached the entryway in the front hall and the coats were offered, Aleks and Jasleen had joined us. I leaned in to give Henry a parting hug, thinking of him as equal parts grandfather and friend.

"You laugh just like Ana," Henry whispered in my ear, startling me. Ana was my abuela's first name. "She couldn't be prouder of you. Told me so herself." Henry squeezed me tight, and I reciprocated. Knowing he knew Abuela strengthened my belief we really were on the same side.

Stepping back, I wiped my damp cheeks behind my curtain of hair before facing Jasleen to offer a goodbye formal handshake. Just as I looked up, Jasleen caught the bottom of my chin, holding my gaze with a gloved hand. Lightning laced up my spine, and I felt all the hairs stand up on my frozen limbs.

"Don't listen to anyone or anything that doesn't resonate here," Jasleen said, pressing firmly on my stomach with her spare gloved hand. "Doubting your decisions for even a second could mean the difference between life and death. Yours, and others." Her eyes flashed in warning. "I don't particularly feel like dying this decade."

Jasleen stepped back again, moving her arm to wrap around Henry's. I remained petrified with my hand still slightly extended.

"I look forward to seeing how this all turns out," she said, a sly smile on her lips. "Don't disappoint me."

The door snapped smartly, and the remnants of cold died away, immediately replaced by the toastiness of an overactive internal heating system. I stood quietly in the hall, staring at where Henry and Jasleen had been minutes before. Aleks stood silently next to me, waiting patiently. Finally, anger shot through me, and I swiped at his upper arm in a not so playful cuff.

"Why didn't you tell me they were going to be at breakfast?" I said, my voice fluttering up and down in my higher register. "I'm practically wearing pajamas!"

"Didn't Eli tell you?" Aleks said. Upon hearing her name, Eli appeared from a side atrium, leaning against the doorframe. "Or Niko?" I turned and gave Aleks a withering look. Instead of arguing, Aleks let out a low series of chuckles.

"Why are you laughing?" I said, my tone still much higher and out of control than I liked. I knew complaining about it now wasn't going to change anything, but I couldn't seem to help it. The emotional rollercoaster of the last hour drained what little fight I had left in me.

"Do we need to have a family meeting?" Aleks said, the sly uptick in his smile creating a dimple. I sucked in a breath. How long had that been there?

"No," I blurted out, crossing my arms. "Clearly it's too late now."

"Okay then," Aleks said. "How about some breakfast?"

"Yes," I said, sagging in exaggerated relief. Aleks laughed, leading the way back to the dining room. "I thought my stomach was going to eat the table."

"I heard it," Aleks said, pulling my chair out for me personally.

"And now I'm mortified," I said, snapping the cloth napkin in agitation before setting it on my lap. A steaming slice of quiche was set in front of me, and my fork was shoveling it into my mouth before the butler's hand could move out of range.

Aleks sighed and took out his phone, attending to business while I cleared my plate with gusto.

TWENTY-TWO

"So what's the plan for today?" I asked, pressing my shoulders into the the high-backed dining room chair, my legs stretched out to give my full stomach some space. My eyelids were closed to slits, and I could feel a food coma coming on. I couldn't remember the last time I had a full belly and the luxury of time for a nap. Or at least the romance of choosing a nap over other activities.

"The consult I had requested for you seems to have fallen through," Aleks said, muttering at his phone. He had been typing furiously for the past few minutes, and the curiosity of what he was planning was eating away at me. "Apparently, your kind are either dead or in the hands of the Association."

"Excuse me?" I said, my eyelids snapping open. My few moments of peace were already ruined. "Did you say dead?"

"Or allied with the Association," Aleks repeated, his breath coming out in a hiss of agitation. "Henry had warned me, but I figured I could find someone off the list he gave me."

"And my kind are...?" I let the blank float in the air. I was trying to uncurl my fingers from the ornate arms of my chair, but my nails only dug deeper. More than one alarm bell was going off in my mind. I did not have time to explain how wrong that phrase was. Aleks looked oblivious, and I tried to soothe myself in that he was just an idiot and let it go.

"Sentient plane Elevated. Or at least that family of abilities."

"So Henry is the historian," I said, latching on to a new thought train. "We aren't completely in the dark after all." Aleks' careless phrasing and casual mention of death had set my stomach off a bit, and I rubbed it lightly, trying to work out the kinks and avoid indigestion.

"His memory isn't the greatest. Just because he was alive doesn't mean he knows the who, what, and how of every supernatural since he was born," Aleks said, dropping his phone onto the table in agitation. "Unfortunately."

Aleks' dark energy pulsed to match his mood. Which reminded me.

"I didn't get a chance to ask you, but," I cleared my throat nervously, "what exactly is your reason for getting involved? I know it's family business and all, but, you're not…"

Another fill in the blank floated in the air. My hand paused over my stomach as I waited for the answer.

"Elevated?" Aleks said, his thumb jamming into the pressure point on his orbital bone.

I was already regretting asking the question.

Aleks let out a loaded sigh.

"Obligation," he said finally after a long pause. "Even though I don't have the gift, my brothers did. My cousins did. They're pretty much all gone." He paused, and I held my breath again. Standard words of condolence caught in my throat, and I bit the insides of my lips to keep them shut. He took a measured breath. "If I didn't step up, it would be the end of our family. As messed up as this all is, I couldn't let that happen."

My eyes dropped to my lap and my newly knotted fingers. There was more I wanted to ask.

"I wonder," I said, "if all the energy draining hasn't had an effect on you. I don't read you as a supernatural, but you seem to have some sort of ability."

Aleks looked at me, his head cocked to the side. Silence weighed heavy in the air, this time as he waited for me to continue.

"Part of my ability to sense people is at the base of their soul," I began, my words syncopated as I struggled to find the right ones. "The Elevated have different colored souls than normal people. The core is unique."

"That seems logical."

"Right, well, that's where you don't follow the rules. Your soul says normal, but your aura doesn't," I argued with myself. My frustration leaked out into my tone. "Remember the other day when we first met, and I almost passed out?"

"Sure," Aleks said.

"And I told you that you needed to shield, and you had no idea what I was talking about," I pressed.

Aleks nodded.

"It was because I thought you were like me, somehow. Able to influence others with your mood. Like my brother." My eyes locked with Aleks' and I waited several heartbeats. I could see the moment the realization clicked in his mind. His whole body stiffened in response.

"You think I somehow got your brother's energy when he passed," Aleks said, carefully crossing his legs to not bump his knees under the table. I noticed his careful fidgeting-but-not-quite-fidgeting. I didn't know him well enough yet to say for sure, but I felt at least somewhat certain it was a sign that he was rattled. I was rusty on basic body language. I had been leaning on my energy reading for too long. Not that that helped at all with Aleks.

"Maybe," I said, frowning. "I can't seem to work it out though. The energy is there. It's linked to you, but it also doesn't seem to be yours either. You can't control it." The thoughts bounced back and forth in my mind. Close, but not quite. I felt like I was missing something huge. Something obvious.

"Even worse than having nothing at all," Aleks said, his finger rubbing his bottom lip. I wondered if that was a pensive tick. It didn't look as if Aleks was aware he was doing it.

"If it's not meant to be yours, then maybe it's waiting for its next host," I said, lobbing my crazy long stretch idea out into the open. "But I guess that's a lot to expect of energy. You must have just enough Elevated blood in you to withstand it, but not enough to utilize it."

I grabbed a strand of hair, piecing it out and beginning to braid the length of it.

"But with so many shifts in energy lately, we can't even be sure whose that energy really is. Or if it's only one person's."

My mind started to list out the possibilities. Slowly, I retreated into myself to work out some of the new arguments coming up. My fingers still wove through my hair, but otherwise, none of my attention was focused outwardly.

"Wait," Aleks interrupted, pulling my attention from my thoughts and back into the dining room. "Both you and your brother were on the sentient plane?" Aleks rested his hand on the table between us.

"Were," I said, a smile flickered and faded off my face.

"As an empath, you're just on the receiving end, right? You internalize everything?" Aleks said. "You just access information that others can't see."

"And then some," I muttered into the tail of my tiny braid. My back began to ache, and I found myself in an awkward slouch posture in the ornate high backed chair. Arching my back and wiggling my limbs, I shifted around until I was in a more comfortable stance.

"Earlier, though," Aleks said, "your emotion hit me hard. It was like I walked through a waterfall."

"Sorry about that," I said, my cheeks burning. "I'm still working on controlling it." My fingers twitched nervously in my hair, not wanting to give up the comfort, but having no alternatives available for my nervous energy.

"No, I mean, I felt pity for Henry and his life and the struggles he's likely faced," Aleks said. "I've never felt that strong of an emotion for anyone before. But your wave made me feel, just for a second, as intensely as you did."

"They put me on medication to dull that," I said, clearing my throat. My eyes darted around the room, trying desperately not to maintain eye contact with Aleks. I was so embarrassed about the outburst. Continuing to talk about it made the heat flare in my cheeks and down my neck. "I had no idea it was that strong. I'll try better next time to keep it in."

"Evangeline." Aleks moved his hand from the tabletop to my wrist, holding it lightly as it was entangled in my knotted hair. He moved his face to be directly in front of mine, and I was forced to lock in on his determined gaze. "I'm trying to tell you that you externalized your power. Empaths should not be able to do that."

"Abuela said that if you meet your counterpart, they can help teach you the other side a little and help balance you out," I argued, my voice squeaking again in agitation.

"A little," Aleks said. "Your powers go beyond a little."

I frowned at him, refusing to take the next step in his logic.

"Evangeline," he said softly, squeezing my wrist. "I don't think I got your brother's powers. I think you did. All of them."

"What are you even talking about?" I said, a scoff burning my throat on its way out. "That's impossible. One person cannot hold that much power. I asked Birdie. Even she said it's too much."

"Maybe not all of them, but I'm betting enough for it to really matter," Aleks said. "Your abilities are too strong and too diverse to just be an empath. I'm sure the timing is no coincidence either. Maybe I'm just supposed to hold on to a little of the energy until you're ready or until whoever is meant to share them with you in this lifetime comes around."

The timing.

I had broken down completely after Tomas had died. That was true. My sensitivity to others' emotions went haywire when I couldn't even tame my own. I had blown up in front of Mags. Our big falling out had happened then, but the next few weeks I had been heavily medicated in the hospital off campus. What little I could remember of that time was fragmented and hazy.

Had there been some aha moment where I had become both commander and empath?

"There's no way," I repeated, my eyes still locked with Aleks'. "No one person could handle all of that."

"You can," Aleks said. "You are. You just need more practice. If I remember correctly, the de los Santos line is one of the strongest out there. Henry and Jasleen think you can do it. Birdie thinks so, too."

"You're all out of your minds," I said. "There has to be another explanation. I can't possibly—"

"One afternoon with Birdie and you came back able to block me and my bad juju energy," Aleks argued over me, throwing my old phrase back at me. His eyes shimmered with intense confidence, and my mouth snapped shut, my argument drying up. "I don't want to hear that you can't. You are clearly capable of much more than you imagined."

"That's great and all, but what am I supposed to do? I'm a runaway. A big, bad evil corporation is after me, and I can't even buy cold medicine legally," I replied, trying to bring Aleks' big ideas back down to reality. His hold on my wrist started to burn, and I shook off his loosening grip.

"The world isn't going to end today," Aleks said, leaning back in his chair. "Jasleen's pretty good at these sorts of things. You just need to get on board."

"Get on board what?" I asked, my fingers pulling through and unweaving my half-completed braid. My stomach was doing backflips nonstop. Everything felt unstable and unsure.

"Well, we don't have a cool nickname," Aleks said. "But there are a few of us dedicated to bringing down the Association. David versus Goliath, if you will. We could really use your help. Apparently, empaths are in really short supply these days."

Aleks' face was filled with a mischievous smile, his dimple crowding toward the lines near his eyes. My heart stuttered, and my mouth dropped open, at a loss for words again. Any semblance of an argument I had gathered scattered haphazardly to the corners of my mind like spiders escaping the beam of a flashlight.

"Just say yes," Aleks said.

My mind was fuzzy, devoid of any thought other than dimples.

"Yes."

TWENTY-THREE

I tapped the middle of my forehead savagely, scolding myself for my flippant answer.

Boys are the devil.

Dimples are dumb.

You're dumb, for letting dimples get you into this mess.

I sat across from Eli in the middle of a sparsely furnished room. The table and set of chairs reminded me of every interrogation room I had seen on TV. This one just so happened to be on the basement level of the Navratil mansion. Of course. What powerful supernatural family didn't have their own torture room?

Eli's smirk radiated from her core, so even though my eyes were shut, my finger poking me in self-punishment, I could see her so clearly in my mind's eye I still wanted to punch her in the mouth. I knew I could land it exactly where I want to, eyes open or not.

"Whenever you're ready, sweetheart," Eli said. "Haven't got all day."

"Yes, we do, and that's even more unfortunate," I muttered, my voice low enough not to betray my words.

"Play nice," Niko's voice clicked over the intercom, the sensitivity of the microphone giving away my snark to the watchful big brother. I growled. Why did everyone have the same fritzy intercom system? The feedback noise made me itch. Another shock of adrenaline coursed through me.

"It's supposed to be subtle, Eli," I said through clenched teeth. "You egging me on is not exactly setting me up for success."

"You should be able to do this in high-stress situations," Eli countered. "Not everyone is going to go nicely when they feel their emotions being manipulated."

"I wish I were a dream walker right now, so I could take you under and leave you there," I spit back at her, her animosity coloring my own feelings instead of the other way around.

Eli laughed, her arms and legs crossed. Her right leg bounced lazily on top of the other, and all outward appearances pointed to her calm and affable attitude. At the end of her laugh, however, I caught a slight hiccup. Fear.

Had Eli dealt with a dream walker before? I couldn't think of a reason why she would have crossed paths with Adair, but it wasn't like he was the only one. Maybe being a creep ran in Adair's family.

Just like that, Eli's tiny flicker of doubt was the in I needed. There was always a chink in the armor, especially if the armor seemed impenetrable. I opened my own barriers a little, allowing my consciousness to walk in through the opening Eli had unwittingly left.

Waves of pictures flooded me, and I pawed through them quickly, finding an innocent one. Even if Eli was being a complete bitch, I didn't need to ruin her day. The exercise was meant for practice for me, and I didn't want to abuse the privilege. Just because Eli was a pill did not mean I needed to stoop to her level. I would save my destructive capabilities for the real bad people.

I was tempted, though.

I thumbed through one memory that I thought would suffice. It was a young girl playing with a puppy. Daisy. It was an adorable golden retriever puppy, and the memory was soft and warm, clearly a happy memory. I brought it up to the surface of Eli's consciousness, letting it play for a while.

Eli's outward bravado cracked a little, and I could sense her stiffening as she relived the memory briefly. Just as I was beginning to turn up the nostalgia, hoping for a smile, the doors slammed shut in my face. The memory fell away, and I was shoved unceremoniously out of her head.

I growled in frustration as the cycle continued.

"Nice try," Eli shot back at me.

A burst of air escaped me, and I pursed my lips, trying to hold in a sassy comment.

"You're acting like I tried to make you relive puberty or something," I said, my lips exploding with my pent-up frustration. So much for keeping it in. "I'm just following orders."

Eli let out a sharp laugh.

"Yeah, right," she replied. She switched her crossed legs to the opposite side, her top foot still waggling freely.

"For the record, I dug up a memory of playing with a puppy," I directed at the intercom box on the wall, my eyes sliding to the two-way glass mirror. "I don't know how many more tame memories she even has. I won't be able to continue being nice at this rate."

"Again," Niko's voice directed through the box. Eli and I squared off again.

"Any requests?" I asked, my own arms now crossed to mirror Eli's posture.

She snorted in response.

"Good luck with whatever you can find," Eli said. "You're not getting in again."

It was true. The last time had been a fluke. We had been at this exercise all afternoon, and I had only broken through to her consciousness a handful of times. Eli was difficult to read, her barriers strong and extra fortified by some misplaced hatred of me. Other than botching the accident and dallying before breakfast, there wasn't anything I had done that should warrant such strong feelings.

Maybe if I cracked it again, I could find out why. It was always good to have goals, right?

I exhaled, trying to center myself. I ignored the rude noise that came from the other side of the table, letting all Eli's drama fall away as I focused on her mental barriers.

What I had always found interesting since discovering my gift was that the barriers we put up are full body. Sure, it might make sense for it to be a concentrated bubble around our entire heads, much like a fishbowl or an astronaut's helmet, but somehow it came down to the entire energy field of the body containing our core selves and sensibilities. It's a large area to cover, even on a good day, and Eli had spent a good portion of her day feeding her energy and concentration into being as indestructible as possible. That much concentration was beginning to take a toll as our practice session extended into its third hour.

And as Eli's foot began to fall asleep.

In a pinch, I was back inside. This time, I didn't waste my time being selective of a happy memory. That's what had booted me before. I searched for the strongest feeling I could find. The memory was crisper than a high definition movie. The colors were extra bright, the lighting saturated to a blinding level.

It was Eli and Aleks. He was squatting next to her in the alley out back. He was putting a blanket around her, taking her hands in his as he tried to warm them up. I started to delve further into the emotion that was behind the memory, but, sensing Eli's restlessness, I threw it up into her consciousness quickly. Her reaction would be telling enough, I thought to myself.

Eli jumped up from her seat, the chair thrown violently behind her.

There was a stitch in the memory though, as if it were linked to another. That memory came up in the middle of this one, as if queued to play next. It was Aleks, this time with me. Last night in the club, our heads bent close to one another.

I heard Eli yell loudly, but my senses, clouded by my internal focus, seemed deadened and far away. My body felt detached from my senses, but I could still feel the breeze against my skin from Eli's guttural yells. I just couldn't hear them well.

Instead of withdrawing from Eli's memory, I turned up the

volume. The actual noise of the scene didn't turn up, but rather the emotions connected with the memory flared to life.

Jealousy.

I cranked it up, letting the feeling fill the room. I could feel the energy teetering on the brink of something, but I was so enamored with it, I followed it to the very edge. What would happen if I pushed it that much more?

Suddenly, I felt my body falling.

My consciousness snapped back into my own head like a rubber band. Suddenly, I was just me, my head bouncing on the ground as my chair bore the brunt of the fall. My neck snapped uncomfortably as the force redirected itself, but I was too concerned with Eli looming over me, her eyes wild with rage.

The cloud of jealousy was thick in the room, and I realized I had caused Eli herself to slip over the edge, or just nearly. Her body shook with rage.

"Pull it back, now," Niko said forcefully over the intercom.

I nodded quickly, ignoring the twinge in my neck as I focused on Eli's savage eyes. Even though the cloud of emotion was created from what lay within her, I would have to eat the energy to dissipate it. I swallowed hard, unhappy at the prospect of ingesting so much jealousy and rage.

It couldn't have been the puppy, huh?

Suddenly, Eli tensed, her body one second away from lunging at my throat. It was now or never.

Eli launched herself in the air, and I slammed my barriers down, allowing the room full access to myself. The negative energy rushed toward me, and I could sense the cloud being sucked into my aura, cleansing the room immediately, like some horrendous reverse gas chamber.

The wild gleam in Eli's eye vanished midair, and I pulled all the negativity from her as well before I slammed the barriers back shut. Losing her immediate desire to maim me, Eli caught herself as she landed, rolling to the side to avoid a violent collision.

Both of us were left gasping on the floor. I was the first to recover, the thick cloud of jealousy and anger rolling through me, leaving me wound tighter than a spinning top. It was a little too much, and I released a roar of my own to ease the pressure. I sprang up from my overturned chair, storming toward the door.

The handle turned, but the bolt left me shaking the door with no way of getting out. I banged my tiny fist on the door in frustration.

"Let me out!" I yelled. "Now!"

"You need to calm down a little before…" Niko's voice began, but I cut him off with another scream.

"If you don't let me out right now, Eli won't have eyeballs in two seconds. Let me go!" I yelled, trying my best to keep my jealousy and anger contained. I opened my fist, switching to an open palm smack on the door. Anything to keep the energy focused on inanimate objects versus people.

My mind began to think crazy thoughts, more paranoid than it ever had before, which was astonishing to me. If I was left alone with Eli much longer, my tenuous grip on my actions would be tested past its limits. I knew in my gut that if I didn't leave, I would cause irreparable damage.

The bolt clicked, and I was able to wrench the door open.

I sprinted out of the room and down the hall, using my sense of the bodies in the house to find the most secluded area devoid of any life. I needed to make sure I couldn't hurt anyone else until I could work through these poisonous emotions. I let myself get lost in the large mansion and ended up in a linen closet on an upper floor. The mountain of fresh sheets and towels was comforting, the scent of lavender surrounding me as I buried my face in my hands, letting the cloud of negativity slowly eek out with each falling scream and tear.

My energy spent, I curled up into a ball in the nest I had created for myself and fell asleep. Thankfully, only the blackness of unconsciousness greeted me. At least for a few hours, I felt safe and out of harm's way.

TWENTY-FOUR

"Is she in there?" I heard the muffled voice from the other side of the door.

"Yep," Eli said, her tone hard to read through the door. I focused on the scent of lavender that surrounded me instead. Much more pleasant.

"Has she come out yet?"

"Nope," Eli replied. She sighed. "If she had, I would have gotten you sooner."

"I know," the voice said.

"And yet," Eli said. A long pause stretched out between them, my brain belatedly assigning the first voice to Aleks. My half-asleep state left my barriers down, and I felt the intensity of his agitation through the door. I buried my face deeper into my makeshift pillow, willing it to go away.

"Is she okay?" Aleks asked.

"How am I supposed to know?" Eli replied. "She's in there. She's alive. That's about all I can tell you."

"You've been out here the whole time?" Aleks asked, skeptical.

"Since you told me to go find her and not leave her side? Uh, yeah," Eli said, the bite in her tone softened a little. "I've been out here. She's been in there. The whole time."

"And you're sure she's in there?" he pressed.

"Do you want to bet money? How is it that I can find someone halfway across the world and you believe me, but some little girl in your own house is just too much for me, huh? Explain that to me," Eli said, the softness gone from her tone. Whatever slight affection she had for Aleks broke as soon as he pressed too far. I could tell she was cranky though, and I wondered if she had slept at all last night. I sighed internally, not ready to start my day with that level of guilt. I was so tired of holding things for others.

"You can trick radar," Aleks said. "We don't know what all she can do."

"I'm a little more sophisticated than radar, okay? Just like I know Birdie is sitting in the kitchen in the safe house in Iceland, Jasleen and Henry are currently running through Terminal 2 at O'Hare to catch their connecting flight, and how I know your uncle is on his way, but thankfully is stuck in morning rush hour traffic. Which is why I called you," she grumbled, "as instructed."

"Thank you," Aleks said.

Eli snorted dismissively.

"Yeah, well," Eli said, her words strained as she pushed herself up from her spot against the wall. "I owe you."

"Is that what yesterday was all about?" Aleks asked.

"You'll have to be more specific," Eli said, evading the question.

"You did volunteer to be Evangeline's guinea pig," Aleks said. "You said you had it under control."

"I did until I didn't, okay?" Eli said. "I don't know what else to say."

"Fine," Aleks said. "Go check in with Niko. I need to beat my uncle to the club, but I have to take care of something first."

Eli snorted.

"Well, something is awake, so good luck," Eli said, her heavy footsteps storming down the hallway and out of earshot.

I groaned into the nearest sheet. My eavesdropping skills needed work.

I could feel Aleks' apprehension growing on the other side of the door. He was getting easier and easier to read, and that scared me. I wished for the days spent holed up in the library by myself, reading and studying. No big bad wolf. No emotional manipulation. Just me shutting out the world and living in peace.

Well, minus Mags.

I sighed in resignation, swiping blindly for the door handle in the dark. I swung the door open, catching Aleks off guard. Apparently he had not been successful in gathering the courage yet himself, but I knew he was on a deadline. I was no stranger to ripping off bandages.

"Hey," he said, his face clamming up. He was uncharacteristically nervous, which left me perplexed.

"Hey," I replied, sitting up from my rat's nest of sheets. I ran my hands through my hair, attempting to smooth down the tousled strands and bring them back into order.

"You all right?" he asked, shoving his hands into the front pockets of his pants. His black sweater pulled slightly at the hem, the nervousness ruining the sleekness of his outfit. My face scrunched in response.

"That's a deceptively simple question with some not so simple answers," I replied. "But I guess so."

"Really?" he asked, his eyes bashful in front of me for the first time.

"Yes?" I said, my tone doubtful due to his response. "Is there a particular reason why I shouldn't be?"

"Yesterday…" Aleks began, losing his words almost immediately.

I nodded sagely.

"Was a shit show," I completed for him, forcing him to crack a nervous smile.

"Yes," he replied.

"Eli seems fine," I said.

Aleks shrugged.

"Eli is Eli," he dodged. I gave him a measured look.

"Eli can be a bitch, but she still has feelings," I said, my lips and eyebrows drawn down in disapproval. "Just because she can handle a lot doesn't mean you shouldn't worry about her. It's always the tough cookies that really fall apart once they break."

"I guess I should have expected you to come to her defense," Aleks said, his hands digging deeper into his pockets. "With a food metaphor, no less."

"Just take care of her," I stated. "She sacrifices a lot for you. The least you can do is look after her properly."

Aleks rocked back on his heels.

"So that's what you saw," he said. His hand reached up, grabbing the back of his neck. "I kind of figured."

"Empath guinea pig privilege," I said, making the sign for sealed lips, miming me throwing away the key.

"I see," Aleks said. "That seems fair."

"I think it's also fair to say that Eli is relieved of any future guinea pig duties," I said, catching Aleks' eye. "I mean it. Even if she volunteers."

"Agreed," Aleks said, letting out a big sigh. "I'm going to leave the practicing up to you. Clearly facilitating was not the way to go."

"Hey, at least we tried," I said, untangling my legs from underneath me. I crawled out of the linen closet, forcing Aleks to step back out of the way. I stumbled upright, shaking pins and needles from my waking limbs.

"And now we know not to mess with you," Aleks said, his lame attempt at lightening the mood making him seem even more awkward.

I let out a laugh, overcome with his adorableness. He was trying so hard to not make things worse, even if he was doing an odd job of it. I had to give him credit.

"Yes, the tiny tyrant will make you throw a tantrum and then threaten to dig your eyes out with her baby spoon," I said, wiggling my fingers ominously in front of his face.

He laughed, the tension finally breaking between us.

"Terrifying," Aleks joked, stepping aside to leave me room to walk beside him.

"How much time do we have before you need to meet your uncle?" I asked, padding down the carpeted hallway in nothing but my socks. I was curious where my shoes went off to, but didn't waste brainpower worrying.

Aleks tensed beside me for a moment, and I caught the pause before he was able to recover.

"We," Aleks said, clearing his throat. "We need to meet my uncle."

I stopped walking. He turned back to me, a sheepish look already on his face.

"Really?" I said, my voice flat and unamused.

"Can I redeem myself for giving you enough time to shower and be presentable this time?" Aleks asked, his hands clasped out in front of him, as if praying to the angry little deity he just woke up. "I even have occasion-appropriate clothing."

I crossed my arms, refusing to move.

"We need to have a discussion about boundaries and schedules. Like telling me if I have one a good time before I magically have to be somewhere important," I scolded. "You're not doing much better than the Association."

"Ouch," Aleks said, bending over and faking a chest wound. "Noted, now can you please hurry?"

Finally, a smile reached his eyes, and I could see the lightness return. His smile was broad enough to activate his dimple, and my breath caught momentarily. Every damn time. That dimple would be the end of me.

"Words," I said, wagging my finger in his face. "We will be having words." I tried to remain serious, but Aleks' smile was infectious. I cracked after only a moment, which only led Aleks to grin even wider.

"I promise," Aleks said, ushering me down the hall, weaving our way back to my personal quarters.

Niko was waiting outside the door, glancing pointedly at his watch. Aleks and I both shrank a little with the silent rebuke, and I dashed inside, leaving Aleks in the hall with the burly school marm and what I was sure would be the most hilarious disapproving lecture ever delivered.

TWENTY-FIVE

"You call this appropriate?" I said, tugging at what could be considered the collar of my borrowed shirt. It was cut across the shoulders, and every time I moved, it slid from one side to the other. I couldn't stop fidgeting and trying to fix it. I'm sure it looked cooler on someone who didn't pick at it all the time.

"You look great," Aleks said, taking a moment to look me in the eye.

I tried to stop fidgeting, letting the line of the shirt fall where it may.

My hair was pulled back in a series of twisted buns at the back of my neck. It was an odd feeling not having my hair falling against my neck and shoulders, but I did feel a little regal. I tried to hold my neck straight and keep the buns from falling to the back of my neck. Childhood lessons in posture echoed back at me, and I smiled sadly at the mimicry of Abuela's voice.

Someone had set up a table in the middle of the club, the area surrounding it black with shadows and empty space. I felt like we were on a stage somewhere, performing an elaborate play. I clasped my hands in my lap, calling my breathing to mind as I fought to steel myself against the impending meet cute.

"I suck at acting," I said suddenly, my eyes drawing back from the black edges of the room to find Aleks' calm gaze.

"You'll be fine," he repeated for what felt like the hundredth time.

I exhaled audibly.

"Should I just not talk again? I feel better about the not talking strategy. Worked well the other night," I babbled, knotting and unknotting my fingers together.

Aleks' palm covered both my hands, and I froze.

"Just like we discussed," Aleks said. "If they ask you a direct question, you should answer them. It's okay not to initiate conversation. It's going to be a big show anyway. They're trying to figure you out just as much as you're trying to figure them out."

"Why do they care about me? I'm not anybody special," I muttered darkly.

"My uncle wants to pay his respects for your grandmother. He's also poking around to figure out why you're with me," Aleks said.

A warmth radiated from me at Aleks' words. With him. I bit the inside of my cheek hard, drawing blood. This was not the time for dimples and hand squeezes to throw me off my game.

I closed my eyes, focusing on taking long, deep breaths. I could do this. Just one more gauntlet to survive. Show the pony around a bit, and then we'd be good. No harm, no foul. I struggled to find more pep talk phrases. I was out of practice.

"Who's he bringing with him again?" I asked, trying to replay all the information Aleks had schooled me on while my hair was being pinned back. If I kept the information on loop, maybe I could retain it when I needed it. Anything to soothe me would be welcome at this point.

"He's bringing one of his interns. The intern is likely to be a supernatural, someone on the rise. Try and get a reading off him if you can. My uncle likes to think he's in the know of everything, so he gets upset when he's outmaneuvered. I've been outmaneuvering him for years, hence the...animosity," Aleks said, squeezing my hand in reassurance. "You'll do great."

The side door opened with a bang, a stream of light beaming through before being interrupted by two large shadows. Niko had been outside, guarding the door and awaiting the guests. I could make out his shadow before the door was shut. Niko resumed his guard post, this time on the inside, out of earshot. The other two shadowy figures made their way to the table, taking their time getting from the doorway into proper view.

Aleks squeezed my hand one more time. His chair slid back noisily as he stood, securing the button of the sport coat he had added to his ensemble. He walked out to meet the shadows at the edge of the ring of light. I set my chair back lightly, standing to greet the guests as well but remaining in front of my seat. My stature didn't give me much advantage though, even with the behemoth heels that had been loaned to me as a part of this partic-ular costume. Much like my first night at the club, I felt like an imposter. At least tonight I got a knee length pencil skirt for my troubles.

The two forms shook Aleks' hands forcefully, and I waited, holding my breath for the big reveal. In the back of my mind, I changed our setting from an elaborate Broadway stage play to an episode of a mob boss crime show. The only things missing were the cigars. It had to have the right amount of camp for me to not take the meeting so seriously as to vomit. Whatever spin would prevent that, I thought to myself.

The first man to step into the light was a bigger, burlier version of Aleks. His face looked as if it had been carved from a jagged crag of rock, minus the smooth sanding of an expert hand. I couldn't see his eyes clearly due to his strong brow, but the emotions rolling off him were clearer and clearer as he closed the distance between us. Eye contact would not be necessary.

While he was imposing, I felt safe enough with Aleks. Worst case scenario, Niko had been instructed to flicker me out at the slightest hint of danger.

It was the second guest that turned my blood cold. When Aleks noticed my face blanche, his demeanor instantly went on full alert as he assessed our interaction.

"Brendan," I breathed out, locking eyes with him.

He stopped in his tracks, eliciting the same raised brow from both Aleks and his uncle.

"You two know each other?" the uncle boomed, his voice echoing even in the large event space. A smirk his in the corners of his mouth, sensing somehow the tide had shifted in his favor already.

"Yes, sir," Brendan said, all the color gone from his face. I could hear the stream of thoughts barreling through his mind at 100 miles an hour. I didn't even need to purposefully access them.

What are you doing here? I thought you were dead. Oh my God. Why are you here? This is not good. What am I going to do? I thought you were dead. How did you get here? You can't be here. You can't.

I swallowed hard, trying to rein in my own whirlwind of feelings. My eyes darted to Aleks, trying to explain with my eyes the severity of this situation. His hand lifted from his side, pushing the air down slightly. The message was clear. Calm down. I inhaled deeply, a polite smile plastered to my face as Aleks' uncle reached the table, his hand out to greet me. I shook his hand firmly, trying to leave a strong impression without overdoing it.

"Marek Navratil," Aleks' uncle said, returning my handshake with a solid grip. Clearly he wasn't worried about my doll-like hand breaking in his grip. Luckily, it was a brief shake. "This is my associate, Brendan Silva."

Brendan and I exchanged glances, stepping forward awkwardly to shake hands. Brendan's gaze kept bouncing back toward Aleks, as if he were some demonic presence ready to swallow me up if I did not behave. I relaxed internally, realizing Brendan would hold his cards close to his chest in an effort to protect me. I wasn't sure he was protecting me from the right people, but I could only hope it would make the meeting end that much more swiftly.

"Pleasure," Aleks said, stepping in front of me to shake hands with Brendan. I blushed at the show of ownership, chafing at the posturing between the two guys. I wasn't completely helpless on my own. Any other time and place, everyone would be getting an earful. "This is Evangeline de los Santos. She'll be sitting in on our meeting today."

The formal impersonal language piqued my interest. Was it normal to speak to family members this way?

Brendan opened his mouth, moving to correct Aleks' supposed naming faux pas. I shook my head imperceptibly, and he caught the hint. His mouth snapped shut, his mind still trying to piece together my presence with the last time he saw me alive.

We all took our seats, settling in for a long, awkward exchange. Aleks had warned me that his uncle tended to be long winded, and I braced myself for the idle pleasantries to begin in the elaborate dance we were forced to enact. I crossed politician off my list of future career possibilities. I could already tell this was going to be painful.

"I would like to start with my sincere condolences, Ms. de los Santos," Marek began, surprising me with his formal use of my name. It took me a moment to realize he had spoken to me, since de los Santos wasn't my legal last name. I nodded in response, accepting his well wishes. "Your family has lost a great treasure this week. I'm sorry to hear Ana Maria had been sick for some time. I was unaware."

I nodded again, unsure what else I could say.

"You're her youngest granddaughter, yes?" Marek continued, his fingers poised delicately over the base of his wine glass. Measured, but deceptively innocent.

"That is correct," I managed, crossing my legs with some difficulty. I had forgotten how snug the pencil skirt was, but the movement allowed me to resettle myself, and I felt more confident instantly. "My mother was her middle daughter."

"Elena? Ah, forgive my memory," Marek said, his ego slowly filling the room with his hubris. He gave me an indulgent smile. "It's not as good as it used to be."

"I'm sure your memory is as good as it always has been," I said, trying not to let the chill shivering down my body become noticeable to the room. Marek's voice was like an eel, making my skin crawl. Aleks hadn't warned me enough about him.

At my discomfort, both Brendan and Aleks leaned toward me unconsciously. I plastered a smile on my face, trying to brave Marek's inquisition.

"Well, be sure to send my regards to her as well. It's hard losing a parent, even at your mother's age," Marek said. "So shall we celebrate your reunion? I hear the Silvas and the de los Santoses go back quite a ways."

Marek raised his hand, snapping his meaty fingers together. Two women appeared from the shadows ready with bottle service. Once they served the table, they melded back in with the shadows. Marek raised his glass, the table responding in kind.

"To family," Marek boomed, the chink of our glasses colliding raising the hairs on the back of my neck. "May blood always be thicker than water."

TWENTY-SIX

I set my glass down without taking a sip. Brendan raised his eyebrow at me, but that was unavoidable. Take a sip underage? Eyebrow. Commit social etiquette suicide by not taking a sip? Eyebrow. Just like most things with Brendan, my decisions were met with mild disapproval. He had clearly gotten over the miracle of my being alive. His subconscious stream was now focused on how everything was linked together.

Specifically, how I ended up where I had.

Which was an excellent question. Aleks was difficult to read again, and I chalked it up to my scattered state of mind. If I was calm and collected, peeking behind the dark curtain of energy was no more difficult than with anyone else. If I wasn't collected, the wall of darkness kept a solid barrier between Aleks' feelings and my fruitless pondering. I let it. There were other things I needed to focus on.

Aleks had also set his glass down, leaving Marek to drink alone. Brendan toasted the air, towards his boss, took a measured sip, and abandoned the mostly full glass on the table. Marek's posture oozed power and dominance, almost enough to fill the entire room. I took a moment to study his facial features, giving myself time to strengthen my barriers in the background. Marek was Elevated, just as Aleks had mentioned. He just forgot to mention which plane his gifts were on, which could make all the difference in a battle of wits. Yet again, I felt unprepared. I was beyond tired of surprises at this point.

As Marek guzzled his champagne, I followed the steady pulse of his gulps from his chiseled face down to the buttress of his neck, past his Hulk-esque former bodybuilder shoulders to the loud paisley tie secured with a bejeweled tie clip resembling a garland wrapped lance. A little archaic, but the image stuck in my mind. What an odd tie clip.

"Glad to see old friends together again," Marek began, his cheeks now colored a cheery red as the attendant refilled his glass for the third time.

Brendan and I shared a look, and he took the lead. My mouth was glued shut with nerves.

"Yes, it's been too long," Brendan said, clearing his throat. He finally unbuttoned his suit coat, allowing him to breathe a little easier. The move seemed to give Brendan the confidence to continue. "So much has happened since our last meeting."

Aleks squinted slightly, his arms crossed lazily over his legs. He leaned back in his chair, as if settling in for a good show.

"I thought the Silvas and de los Santoses were close," Aleks said. "In such a trying time for the family, I'm surprised you haven't been around more."

Brendan's eyes flashed at the jab.

"Evangeline was away at school," Brendan said. "High school." Brendan's head tilted forward slightly, underlining his last phrase with his body language.

The gauntlet had been thrown. I could barely suppress an eye roll before he continued.

"You know how that goes," he said to Aleks, ignoring his boss, who was sipping merrily away on his fresh glass. "All your focus goes to the next test, the next final, then the next semester. Other than holidays, it's difficult to find time for family or family friends."

"Well, some of us weren't that into school," Aleks said with a self-deprecating chuckle.

Marek joined in loudly, clapping Aleks jovially on the back.

"The Navratils have always been strong minded, Brendan. We don't do well in confined situations," Marek boasted. "My boys were all the same. Not that they weren't smart. They just weren't ones for traditional learning institutions."

"Evangeline is quite skilled in those areas," Brendan said, turning it around onto Aleks again. "Best marks in her class. Even does self-study since she's so ahead of what they can provide for her. It's a shame she's been pulled away from what she loves."

I bit the inside of my cheek hard. I was dying to say something, but they weren't really talking to me. This was clearly a pissing match between the two, and I would have to sit through it. Right now, I was wishing I had Niko's skills instead of my own. The arrogance in the room was stifling.

"If I remember, she was pulled from school quite a few months ago after a tragic accident," Aleks said, showing his cards. So he had known more about me than he let on. I hadn't said how long I had been in Association control, but he had found out somehow.

I suppressed my anger, tabbing that comment for a later conversation about privacy and espionage. We really needed to be comparing notes before the next Elevated encounter. I couldn't rely on Aleks to have all the cards. Being blindsided was about the worst thing you could do to an empath.

"Your point?" Brendan said.

"I'm just clarifying that I wasn't the one to pull her away from her studies," Aleks said with a shrug. "That was long before me. I just helped her out of a tight spot, and she has been so kind as to help me on a difficult project I'm developing. Her mind is not going to waste, I can assure you."

Brendan took a deep breath, his chest rising noticeably as he smoothed out his jacket, letting the breath out in a chuckle.

"Good to know she's keeping occupied," Brendan said, finally looking toward me again. "And that she's safe." His eyes flashed at me.

I nodded sincerely.

"Her family was a little worried when she was unable to attend her grandmother's wake," Brendan said, laying on the guilt thickly.

I pushed away the impending cloud with my mind, not ready for that kind of breakdown. I steeled myself again, resorting to my multiplication tables to drown out the needling thoughts poking through my barriers.

"I'm sure she'll be able to visit and pay her respects soon," Aleks said, his foot touching my ankle lightly. I looked up from my knotted fingers and gave him a half smile. His eyes were full of concern, but his posture remained strong. "I know how important it is to say a proper goodbye."

"Well said." Marek set down his empty glass loudly. An attendant stepped forward, but a slight gesture from Aleks had her stepping back silently, escaping the notice of the older man. "Too much tragedy gone on lately. First my sons, then your brother and grandmother. I can only imagine the difficulties you've lived through in your short life."

"I couldn't agree more," Brendan said.

Marek's ego flared with the comment. I pursed my lips, taking several deep breaths to bring my thoughts back into equilibrium. The pull of arrogance rocked my composure quite effectively. Aleks seemed to pick up the thread of conversation his uncle had tried to start before getting distracted.

"It's a shame so many of us have come to unfortunate ends so early in life," Aleks said. "The only shame is that no one seems to be stopping it from happening again."

"Accidents happen," Brendan said. "No one is immune to that. How do you suggest we protect ourselves against accidents? We're not invincible. We die just like the normal folks out there do."

"I hardly think four young men in their prime were felled so easily by natural selection, as you're implying," Aleks said, his teeth gritted in annoyance.

Felled, I thought to myself. Murdered. You mean murdered. I kept the nuance to myself.

"You're saying someone's behind my sons' deaths?" Marek asked, his fists pounding angrily onto the table, causing the glass-ware to shake and fall.

I was able to catch my full glass, hearing the emotional tremor before the proverbial quake. No one else seemed surprised by the outburst either, making me wonder if this quick-to-flare temper of Marek's was also common knowledge. Another tip I could have used ahead of time.

"Tell me!"

"I just think we need to take a closer look at our friends and those who call themselves our friends," Aleks said, staring directly at Brendan. "Particularly new friends."

"What are you even saying?" Brendan said, standing in outrage. Even in anger, Brendan was proper, taking the time to button his jacket.

"I'm only saying we need to dig a little deeper," Aleks said, a smile curling his lips as he took in Brendan's agitation. "Only those closest to you have the opportunity to stab you in the back."

"I need names!" Marek yelled, pounding the table again.

This time, I slid my chair back, using my outrageous heels to push off the leg of the table, putting me out of the line of fire when the dishware finally went flying. Both Aleks and Brendan reached out a hand to me, checking on my wellbeing first. Marek continued to roar, throwing a particularly violent tantrum.

This was too much. I was sick of this meeting and the one-upmanship. I hardly saw the point.

I slowly reached out to Marek's mind, finding it wide open and unprotected in his rage. I located the central point of his anger, buried deep within his mind. It was fueled by the grief of loss. Too much loss for one man to handle. All but one of his sons gone. A tear fell down my cheek as I felt the wall of grief crash through me as well.

I didn't dawdle.

I moved to push down the anger, centering it back into the ball of grief and fear and madness that was growing wildly in Marek's mind. I couldn't erase it completely, but I could shove everything back in its place. As I concentrated on that, I let the calmness I had been focusing on myself flow into Marek's mind. I poured all my energy into that, forcing Marek back into calm.

As I slowly extracted myself, I built a better door for Marek's mind, giving him a little more protection than he'd had before. I felt it was only fair after I so rudely barged in. I shut it softly, returning immediately to myself and a room so silent, I could hear the rustling of the barmen behind the scenes preparing for the evening.

Brendan stared at me with his jaw hanging open. Aleks' eyes were boring into me, looking for the slightest sign I was not okay. I wiped the tears from my cheeks and cleared my throat. Marek startled at the noise, his large frame frozen in his chair. The blush had gone from his cheeks, and I wondered if somehow I had sobered him up unintentionally. Only a good thing in my book.

"So," I said, looking around to the three men in a sea of broken furniture, glassware, and linens. "Was there anything else or are we adjourned for the day?"

"What are you?" Marek whispered, his eyes large and haunted.

"That's kind of a rude thing to ask," I chirped back. "I don't know what you are either, but I don't go around asking about it. Honestly, your manners could use some work."

"Evangeline," Aleks cautioned.

"You know what? No. Don't Evangeline me. You either," I said, sticking my finger out in Brendan's face. "I'm tired of everyone speaking for me. I'm not some prize you can fight over and use to your advantage. I may be seventeen, but that doesn't mean I don't know anything. And you." I swung my pointed finger toward Marek briefly before laying it back in my lap.

"Me?" he asked sheepishly, as if I were waving an assault rifle in his face.

"If you are going to visit, you should call ahead and schedule an appointment. And don't come back if all you're going to do is drink and break things. Honestly. It's a waste of everyone's time. If you want to see your nephew, be human about it." I stood.

Aleks and Marek joined Brendan, who was already on his feet, as I stood.

"I've got better things to do than to sit here and listen to you argue about nothing," I said. "It was a pleasure meeting you. Goodbye."

I walked out into the darkness of the room's periphery, leaving the men behind in shock. As soon as I got to the door, Niko stepped out of the deepest shadows, his hand over his mouth and stomach, his body shaking almost imperceptibly. I stomped my foot.

"Pull it together, Niko," I whispered angrily at him. "Help me make my exit, or move."

Niko nodded, grabbing my shoulder.

"Where to, tsaritsa?" Niko mumbled.

"Take me to Henry," I said. "I've got a few questions I need answered."

TWENTY-SEVEN

We popped into a tiny apartment next to a bustling Underground hub, where I could see the glowing sign through the smaller of the two windows. The winter evening left commuters in the dark on their way home, and most were bundled head to toe, battling the bitter elements. The windows were letting in a good stream of chill night air, the old sealant crumbling softly to the worn carpet below.

Niko and I were scrunched in the only available standing room in the place. Two twin beds and a writing desk with matching chair were crammed awkwardly against the only available wall space. We stood uncomfortably between the beds. Niko had to stoop slightly to accommodate his height.

"Nice aim," I muttered, slightly surprised I wasn't on someone's lap or foot given the square footage. Niko blew a small burst of air through his nostrils in response.

"I would say what a welcome surprise, but you know I'm not really the surprised type," Jasleen said, flipping to the next page in her magazine. Henry sat meditating on the bed, managing to find the absolute central point in the room. Niko cleared his throat, catching my attention.

"I'm going to leave you here for a bit," he said. "I need to check back in with Aleks."

"No problem," I said. "I shouldn't be too long."

"See you in twenty," Jasleen quipped, flicking another page with her long fingernails. Niko nodded, confirming the time, and flickered away. I waved my hand where he had been just seconds before. Amazingly, the air didn't seem to be disturbed like I had expected.

"He's always here, but also never here. That's why your ears don't pop when he leaves," Henry said, his eyes still closed serenely. I startled, not expecting him to speak. Looking around at the limited choice of seating, I decided to sit on the vacant bed across from him. Jasleen remained reposed on the edge of the small writing desk, ignoring the chair.

I smoothed down my skirt, picking away imaginary fuzz balls as I waited for Henry to complete his practice. My mother had gone through a meditation phase, although it didn't seem to suit her once my stepdad came around. She was too preoccupied with running a large household and micromanaging the staff to meditate. Just like prayer, I knew to remain quiet until the practitioner had wrapped up themselves.

"Do you have..." I began, looking up at Jasleen, who had appeared with a small notebook and pen. I snapped my mouth shut, accepting the offered gift with a nod of thanks.

"I picked it up at the airport once I knew you would need it. Keep it with you. I would argue with you about keeping paper records of the Elevated few, but you won't listen, so I won't waste my breath," Jasleen said, looming over me.

"Can I ask you a question?" I whispered, sneaking a peek at Henry. Jasleen rolled her wrist at me, wanting me to get on with it already. "How far are you able to see? Is one side always spinning ahead of the other?" I pointed to both her eyes, snatching my hand back into my lap when I realized how rude I was being.

Jasleen pursed her lips at me.

"Unlike most novices, I can in fact see the present out of both eyes, especially when I need to focus on the here and now. Otherwise, I let it track as far ahead as it would like. I have developed a sense for finding important occurrences, especially when it concerns either myself or Henry directly. If you asked me to look for you, I could. If I wanted to. But I don't," Jasleen quipped, turning on her bare heels and walking back to the desk.

I had begun to think of a follow-up question, but the conversation seemed closed as Jasleen gave me her back.

Henry's eyes popped open, and I leaned back in surprise. I had a sudden sense of déjà vu of me and Noah speaking internally, freaking out her aunt, Adele. Two supernaturals so in sync with their gifts, completely open with one another and using them without fear or reservation. It was uncanny from an outside perspective, but calming at the same time. It gave me hope for how the future could be. Assuming any of us wanted to be in sync with one another.

"Why hello, dear," Henry said. "What a pleasant surprise."

"Jasleen wasn't surprised," I said, feeling like a little girl arguing with a patient adult. Something about Henry made me shrink back into a helpless toddler, and I had to make sure my voice didn't follow suit.

"Jasleen and I have an understanding," Henry said. "She doesn't tell me everything so I can still be surprised. I can't imagine living life without a little mystery."

"It's not horrible," Jasleen said, idly flipping another page in her tabloid.

"I'm sure you knew I'd be back though," I said, blushing. "I've been told more than once I ask too many questions."

Jasleen snorted primly, but Henry offered a warm smile.

"Questions are good. Curiosity is an undervalued talent," Henry said. He glanced down at the notebook and pen. "I see you're prepared."

"Please don't feel pressured to answer if you don't want to. Or if you don't remember," I said in a rush, chewing on the inside of my cheek nervously. "I was hoping you could help me with some family histories. I don't know much about the main lines or who's in them. I figured if I knew the families and the known players, it could help me sort out who I may still need to find."

"That's a very studious undertaking," Henry said, rubbing his thighs as he thought. "I may remember some, but just because you have certain concentrations of supernatural energy, that doesn't necessarily mean it'll strike the same tree eternally."

"But say the energy has to have a certain threshold of supernatural blood in order to manifest in a person," I said, tapping the pen softly against my lips. "If it dries up in certain lines, like the Navratils, for instance, wouldn't it find the next best host? We could be looking at a lot of other possibilities."

"True," Henry said. "Even better though, is that the so-called Old World deities weren't even the oldest deities. Sure, a high concentration came from the Celts and the Nordic populations. They naturally emigrated, and their bloodlines with them. Jasleen and I are both outside those populations, which could open up even more you might not have thought about."

I blushed. I hadn't thought of that.

"Even you, technically, have part of your bloodline from indigenous populations. You must think globally. Although I must admit, it's easier to find the colonialist histories and bloodlines. It's easier when it's the population dictating the history," Henry said, his eyes dancing with shadows. I cleared my throat, not wanting to say what didn't need to be said. I was more than aware of the issues in historical accounts and didn't feel bringing Henry to that painful place would be worth the emotional output for either of us.

"So," I said, flipping open the notebook to the second page, leaving the first one blank out of habit. I desperately wanted to stay on track for the remaining time I had with Henry. It was already too short. I needed hours, if not days. "If we figure out the players we know, we can estimate the missing pieces and look for them first."

Henry nodded, his smile broad and toothy.

"See? Curiosity is definitely worth something."

"I do feel a little guilty though," I confessed, my pen pausing over the fresh sheet. "I feel like I'm kind of giving up on all the kids I do know. I mean, just because they go to Windermere or are related to people at the Association, it doesn't mean they're bad people. Or not worth protecting."

I bit my lip, hesitating. The war on my conscience was bigger than just me or Aleks or even Brendan. We were talking about the possibility of kids being killed for not picking the right team. Leaving anyone behind seemed too significant.

"Those who have grown up within the supernatural community will have more resources than you think," Henry said, the calm confidence ebbing from his spot on the bed. "It's not abandoning them, so much as reaching out a hand to those who have no connection to the community and who may not have any idea what's going on. Imagine being the first in your family to be endowed with powers. It's not like you can Google 'How to control my supernatural powers' and get any real help."

I started scribbling a list in my notebook. Henry peered across the gap to see what I was writing.

"What did I say?" Henry asked.

"You've got a point about Google. I can't put anything obvious out there, but some sort of SOS page could be useful," I said. "Of course, I haven't written any code in a while. That might have to go on a back burner until I have some traction on leads."

"Which is where I come in," Henry said brightly.

"Yep," I said, finishing a thought with a messy flourish, whipping the next page forcefully. "Lay it on me. Who are we working with?"

Henry gave all the names and abilities he could remember, which filled up several pages. I would have to draft out family trees later, but right now the hard data was what I needed. He was able to think back four generations, which was more than I was expecting.

Niko popped in as Henry took longer and longer to respond,

his eyes lost in memory searches for anyone he might have missed. Henry sighed, shrugging in defeat.

"That's all I have for you, my dear," he said. "I'm sorry I couldn't offer any more."

"No, please, this is great," I said, snapping the notebook shut as I felt Niko's eyes wander to my messy script.

"Remember, if your theory is correct, I would not discount some of the truly ancient deities from your parameters. Or mixed lineage," Henry said, whistling low. "That could give you a lot more to work with."

I hopped up from the bed, leaning to give Henry a hug.

"You're the best," I said. "Thank you."

I took a deep breath, a sigh escaping me in relief. I finally felt the world under my feet. There was data, there was a plan, and I was in charge of executing it. Research was definitely my element.

"Of course," Henry said, chuckling. "Don't forget to tell me how it all works out."

"I should see you soon, right?" I asked, my eyes darting to Jasleen for confirmation. She lifted a hand, warding me off.

"Off limits," she said, flicking the page in her magazine again. "No spoilers."

"Like the TV shows. People get really upset over that," Henry said, the innocence on his face bringing a smile to mine.

"Look at you being up on the lingo," I said. "You caught me off guard with Google earlier as well."

"He tries," Jasleen said, her eyes not leaving her reading material.

Niko stepped to me, his hand already on my shoulder.

"You've got another appointment," he said, nodding his goodbyes.

"Seriously? Again? What did I just say this morning about letting me know I have a schedule, I dunno, any time except immediately before I need to be somewhere doing something?" I said, my words slicing through the cheery film of the room unexpectedly. Niko offered a shrug.

"Good luck," Henry said, his demeanor unaffected by my outburst.

Jasleen waved sarcastically, and I ducked in for another quick hug from Henry.

"I'll do my best. See you around."

Niko pulled me from my brief field trip back to the Navratil mansion before I could lift my hand and wave.

TWENTY-EIGHT

Aleks was waiting for me in my room. It was weird to call it that. My room. I had only been around for three days. Three sleeps, anyway. I was having trouble reentering normal time. Aleks sat patiently on the bench at the foot of the queen-sized bed, his arms extended backward in a deceptively relaxed pose. Could he be counting tiles?

I looked up to where his eyes were directed and found the ceiling did in fact have ornate plaster tiles. Having only been unconscious in this room briefly, I wasn't surprised to find I'd overlooked such an obvious detail. The rich textiles of the room dampened my footsteps, and I had to tap Aleks gently on the shoulder to alert him I was near.

He startled, and I apologized instinctively.

"I'm so sorry," I said, withdrawing my hand with a snap back into my ribcage.

"No need to apologize. You just surprised me," Aleks said, sitting up. His eyes regained their normal sparkling alertness, scanning me curiously. His eyes crinkled at the corners. "Are you okay?"

"Yeah, why?" I asked, my hand reaching for a loose strand of hair, only to remember my hair was pinned back at the nape of my neck. I let my hand fall lonely to my side and avoided the itch to let my hair down for comfort. I wanted to enjoy the regalness of the ornate coils for a little longer. It felt like I had an added boost of confidence I wanted to use up fully.

"Did you want to change into something more comfortable?" Aleks asked, nodding at my stiff posture. His eyes pinged up and down my frame. I felt like I was being x-rayed, and all my nervous ticks and awkward body language was more see through than ever.

It was true the pencil skirt and heels didn't let me slouch, but it was kind of nice being dressed up. I smoothed down the creases in my skirt in goodbye. The magic from my hair would suffice, even if it was paired with jeans or sweatpants.

"I guess," I said, picking away a loose string at the hem. "I wasn't sure if I had other clothes. These are fine."

"Whatever you need, just ask," Aleks said. "You're an honored guest. The least I can do is feed and clothe you. The girls had fun picking out some basics for you. If they aren't your style, I can always send for more."

Aleks pointed out a large armoire in the corner of the cavernous room. I flung off my heels, tip toeing in my stocking feet to check out my new options. Although both Ariel and Gaby seemed nice, I wasn't sure their tastes would line up with mine. The outfit from the first night of dress up flashed in my mind, and I shook my head to dislodge it. I said a quick prayer for pants and hoodies.

The old lacquered wood of the armoire felt like liquid on my fingertips, and I opened the front facing doors without so much as a squeak. I had hoped for a little noise, remembering Abuela's heirloom chest that sounded like a beached whale every time I opened it. A small smile pulled at the corners of my mouth. After a small sigh, I redirected my focus to my new wardrobe.

Black. Lots and lots of black.

A loud laugh escaped me. Noah's visage popped into my mind, and I could see clearly the relief that would have shone from every pore had this been her closet. I didn't mind the color so much, but I was definitely used to a little more variety. At least

I wouldn't have to worry about matching while I was here. Trying on a new aesthetic could be fun.

"Everything all right?" Aleks asked, his voice and cologne floating somewhere behind me. An internal alarm bell went off in my head, and I kept my eyes forward. After one quick glance in the wardrobe, Aleks let out a low chuckle. "I see. Well, I'm sure we can swap out some of these for more…colors."

"No worries," I said, counting my breaths in and out as I worked to quiet the thundering heartbeat in my ears. "I'm just grateful someone took the time. Whatever is here is great."

I grabbed a hanger, pulling out a flirty skater dress into view.

"I like this," I said, my fingers pulling on the fabric. Setting the dress back on the rack, I leafed through a few more, cooing in approval. "They did a great job. You've got some talented stylists on your hands."

"Don't give them any ideas," Aleks said, retreating back to his spot on the bench. I ruffled through some of the shelves, finding a variety of pants and sweaters, along with pajamas, silken tees and a blouse or two. "I'm pretty sure they got at least one of everything."

I grabbed the equivalent of a hoodie and jeans and headed for the bath suite.

"Give me just a sec," I said.

"Take your time," Aleks said, letting his back fall to the bed, his arms crossed contently. "I'll be here."

I dashed into the bathroom, locking the door reflexively. I let out a huge breath I hadn't realized I'd been holding, shaking out the nerves in my hands.

"Keep it together," I scolded myself aloud, ripping off the jacket and skirt combo with a sigh of relief. The stockings were harder, and I had to hop around a little to pull them off successfully. I fell over with a crash, a loud yelp escaping me. I covered my face with my hand, mortified I couldn't even undress myself without causing a ruckus.

A soft knock came at the door, and Aleks' muffled voice came through the slight crack.

"Everything all right in there?" he asked.

"Yeah, fine!" I called, folding the clothes nicely, wandering around in my underwear trying to figure out where to put the clothes. Just like yesterday, there didn't seem to be a designated hamper, and I wondered if I could sneak away to do the laundry without anyone noticing. I gave up, setting the pile on the edge of the spotless tub, and went back to find my pants and sweatshirt.

I pulled them on hurriedly, relieved they fit as if they had been mine all along. Apparently seeing someone practically naked one time was enough of an indication of size. I remembered suddenly that Ariel and I were similarly built. She had probably just bought whatever she would get for herself, also having the presence of mind to get the proper rise in jeans to cover my round assets without any embarrassing crack cleavage. I sent a silent thank you to her in my mind.

The hoodie was tighter than I expected, and I realized the cut was different than I was used to. On the second try, I found the front of it, much to my chagrin. It was more of a viscose material, so it clung to me like a second skin. It wouldn't have been a problem if I had thought to grab a tee to wear underneath. Not only was the material slim, but the cut was at a bias with a very dramatic cowl neck line that dipped to reveal the top of my bra. I spent several minutes pulling it toward one collarbone or the other, desperate to find whatever option gave me the least amount of anxiety.

It was useless. No matter what I tried, I couldn't find any more coverage, and I was left to exit the bathroom with my hands on my chest awkwardly.

Aleks looked up, his eyes widening with surprise. My knees locked, and I was frozen in place. The armoire felt miles away.

"I know, it's horrible. I wasn't paying enough attention. Let me grab a blanket or t-shirt or something," I said, my cheeks on fire.

"What? No," Aleks said, shaking his head. "You look great. I just wasn't expecting—"

"My ta-tas to be out and making friends? Yeah," I said, a nervous laugh escaping me as I tugged at the only spare throw in the room, conveniently situated beneath Aleks. "Might need to talk to Ariel and Gaby about my style."

Aleks finally looked away from me, realizing I was trying to get to the blanket he was sitting on. He stood up quickly, knocking heads with me in his hurry to get out of my way. The fistful of blanket I had been yanking on swung back on me, causing me to punch myself in the face.

"Damn it!" I said, stumbling back. Aleks grabbed me by the waist, steadying me and returning me to two grounded feet. He was also less than three inches away from me, and the subtle aroma of his cologne made my head float. Between the head assault and the cologne, the dizziness was overwhelming.

"I'm so sorry," he said, the vibrations from his voice low and close enough for me to feel the words before my brain could decode them. "Are you all right?"

"Yeah," I said, my hands clutching the blanket tightly to my chest. Aleks' hands were still on my waist, and I counted my heartbeats as I waited for him to step back.

Only he didn't.

I was frozen in the most perfect version of hell I could imagine. A tall, handsome man had come to my rescue and was now holding tightly onto me. Firecrackers radiated from his hands all the way up and down my body.

Only this couldn't be happening. Not now.

I stared intently into the blanket, refusing to meet his eyes. I knew he was looking at me, but any resolve I had left would be melted instantly if I looked into his eyes. I was making this up. It was only in my head. And even if it wasn't, I didn't want to ruin what felt like my mission by crossing a line with my...patron? Benefactor? Boss? A line that couldn't be uncrossed.

Fifteen.

Sixteen.

Seventeen.

Finally, after what seemed like an eternity, Aleks stepped back, his hands sliding slowly from my waist. When he was several feet away, back on his bench, I was finally able to look away from the stitch pattern that was now permanently etched into my brain.

I cleared my throat, turning away to throw the blanket over my shoulders. Once I was more comfortable with the amount of skin showing—now next to zilch—I turned around, my face flexing in a sheepish smile.

"How is Henry?" Aleks asked. He sat back again with his arms behind him. Relaxed. Neutral. Unfazed.

I sighed in my mind, thankful this wasn't going to be more awkward than I had feared.

"Good," I quipped, taking a seat next to him on the bench, careful to leave an arm's length between us. "Lots of good information. I have some ideas of where to start, which is much more than I had before seeing him."

"Start what exactly?" Aleks asked, his face open and intent. "The friends and foes list? I wasn't sure if that's what sparked your immediate interest. Your dramatic exit earlier did leave several people speechless."

I bared my teeth guiltily.

"Sorry about that," I said sheepishly. "I didn't mean to be a diva or anything."

"No, no, please," Aleks said, his hands raised in front of him. "It worked out well for me. They left almost immediately afterwards, and I got a free afternoon. I usually have to suffer much longer with my uncle. Although I will be curious to see if he does call ahead from now on."

I raised my eyebrow. Aleks laughed.

"You left quite the impression," Aleks admitted. "And your poor friend Brendan almost wet himself."

"He did not. Brendan isn't the type to scare easily." My nose crinkled in disbelief.

"Well, he looked as if he might puke and cry at the same time, then. I guess he doesn't know you as well as he thought." Aleks shrugged. "His loss."

"We've known each other since we were kids," I said. "He's like a big brother to me."

"Really?" Aleks said, his eyes shrinking skeptically behind a squint. "Are you sure?"

"I mean, sure I had a crush on him ages ago," I said, my cheeks flushing at the confession. "But he's only ever seen me as a little sister. Especially since Tomas…well, you know."

Aleks nodded briefly in understanding but switched to a series of head shaking after a moment of thought.

"I don't know," he argued. "He seemed a little too possessive. His feelings might have changed."

It was my turn to snort.

"Okay," I said dismissively.

Aleks laughed off the denial, and I noticed the laughter made it to his eyes. We sat near enough to one another that I could tell the happiness was truly resonating from within. I shifted closer to him, happy in his happiness. It was rare to have someone's positive energy radiate so warmly from them, and even rarer when I could enjoy it.

"So what's your new project anyway? Don't you think I should know a little about it if I'm going to help you cover it up?" Aleks said playfully. "Of course, I'll pass it off as my own. Marek already thinks you're consulting anyway."

"Unfortunately for you, it's quite boring research," I said. "Lots of genealogy and mythology. Books. Lots and lots of books."

"Hey, my uncle was the one bragging about doing poorly in school. I'll have you know, I'm quite well read. I even enjoy it sometimes." Aleks bumped my shoulder with his, and I laughed.

"I'm going to have to commandeer not only your library, but also a laptop. Think you can swing it?" I said. "You do have a library, right? It's a shame to have such a big house without at least one library."

"Oh, we've got a library," Aleks said with a smile. "I'll have to relocate then."

"I was kidding," I said, backtracking immediately. "I don't need the library. I'll just bring the books up here. I couldn't kick you out of your own office."

"It's not a big deal. Just temporary until we set yours up," Aleks said. "I don't want you lugging around all those books by yourself and leaving them in weird places. Makes more sense for you to take the library for now."

"I can handle a few books," I said defensively. "And I would never abandon them just anywhere."

"Not the point. Although," he said, his eyes glimmering mischievously. "For all this effort, do I at least get rewarded with knowing what you're working on? Come on. Just a little hint."

"If I'm right," I said, dangling the carrot in front of him, "then you'll hear about it. So until then, mum's the word."

I mimed locking my lips and throwing away the key.

Then, Aleks was there.

His lips were warm against mine, my hand now braced against his shoulder where it had only moments before held an imaginary key. I froze in surprise, my lips parting a little in reaction. Suddenly, the kiss was deeper, and my head spun. I wasn't sure which way was up or which way was down. Emotion poured into me and back out. I wasn't sure which feelings were mine and which were from Aleks. Whatever combination they were, they felt good. No, they felt great.

Vertigo glued my eyes shut, the sensations too intense for my rational mind to override my own body's instincts. So it hadn't only been in my imagination. The flirting. The connection. Unless I was currently experiencing a stroke, which seemed unlikely.

A coolness overtook the surface of my lips as they were freed from Aleks'.

"I'll take that as deposit," Aleks said softly near my ear.

I felt his weight lift from the bench, the fabric bouncing back without the pressure of his form pinning it down. The door clicked shut softly, but the smell of Aleks' cologne lingered in the air.

After several minutes, I was able to open my eyes. My hand still hung in the air where the lock and key motion had ended and the kiss had started. Thoughts spun around and around, but none seemed to stick. I began by counting my breaths. Slowly, I added in a catalog of what was in my field of vision, bring my awareness back to concrete things I could make sense of. Bed. Armoire. Carpet. Bench.

Aleks' lips locked onto mine. I shook the image from my mind.

My fingers found my lips, and I slumped down into a puddle on the top of the bed. Flinging myself across the bed like a starfish, my eyes finally came to the ornate tiles in the ceiling.

"Pull yourself together," I repeated over and over again. "We can only think about kissing boys after we save the world. We've got a long way to go."

TWENTY-NINE

I woke to a boot nudging my ribcage. I groaned in protest, turning away from the intruder. My arms flailed out, and I could feel the plush carpet itching my cheek.

I sat bolt upright, looking around in a panic. Carpet. Blanket. Papers strewn all around me in a nest of scribbles and arrows. My hands propped me up from the mess, but I was at a loss as to what I was looking at. My notebook with Henry's intel was the only object I could place, but where the rest of the paper madness had come from, I wasn't sure. My handwriting stared back at me, poking my consciousness to remember.

"Did you sleep on the floor last night?"

The look of disgust overflowed from Eli's face down to her crossed arms as she loomed over me. Her presence sobered me more quickly than the many tactile sensations my mind was attempting to sift through. Funny how annoyance works.

"Clearly," I croaked, my voice thick with disuse.

"Well," Eli said, her toe nudging around some of the paper squall. "I suppose sleeping inside your room is an improvement over a linen closet."

I looked up at her blankly.

Eli heaved a great sigh, clearly unimpressed with my lack of urgency.

"You. Shower. Now," she drilled at me, hauling me up by my armpits. Luckily, my legs were pulled free of the knotted up blanket, and I found sure footing as soon as she dropped me on my feet.

I stumbled to the bathroom, then staggered back into my bedroom when I realized I had forgotten fresh clothing. Eli was already there, a clean stack in her hands, shoving the pile at me and spinning me around again.

She slammed the bathroom door shut in my face.

"Twenty minutes," Eli called through the bathroom door. "And I know how to pick locks."

"Now," I added. I scowled as I clicked the lock home, staring at it for several seconds, worried it would magically click back if I wasn't vigilant.

Grumbling, I wandered over to the shower and attempted to wake up enough to figure out the hot and cold water handle. I settled for cold at first, not willing to waste precious minutes when I had all my hair to dry.

The brutal chill made for quick work.

Even so, I was left barely enough time to dry my hair and brush my teeth. Eli was pounding on the door when I clicked off the hair dryer, so I rubbed my face a little to bring color to it, leaving my hair down and loose around my shoulders.

I flung the door open, meeting Eli's glare with my own.

"You have the patience of a two-year-old," I said to her.

Eli grinned back menacingly.

"And you look like a twelve-year-old without make-up," she shot back. "Now that we've stated the obvious, can we go?"

"Where?" I asked, grabbing a pair of skater shoes to slip into as Eli marched out the door without me. My provided uniform didn't give any indication of what would happen next. At least I knew it wasn't an audience with the President or anything.

"Breakfast," she said.

"You made me rush for breakfast?" I asked, my hair whipping behind me as I jogged to catch up with her long-legged stride.

"Most important meal of the day," Eli said, grabbing the balustrade and peeling down the staircase at breakneck speed.

"Then wake me up more than twenty minutes before you need me," I crowed to her back. "I look like death warmed over because someone wouldn't let me fully dry my hair."

"Let it air dry," she threw back, leading the way to the main dining room.

"Just get me an alarm clock already," I groaned, forced to leap down the last few steps to make up lost time. "And slow down. I'm a foot shorter than you."

"The world's not going to do you any favors, and neither will I," she quipped, flinging open the door to the dining room and waving for me to enter before her.

"That doesn't make any sense," I moaned, slowing down to catch my breath before entering the room. "You're a frickin' Amazonian war goddess, okay? Just have some compassion for us more normal-statured folk."

"Oh, I have compassion. It lives right next to my jar of dreams and unicorn tears on my nightstand," Eli said, shutting the door in my face. "Enjoy."

"Always a pleasure," I called through the door at Eli, holding back a rude hand gesture. I spun around to see the dining room empty except for a place setting for me. An envelope sat on the plate, and I snatched it, tearing it open before taking a seat. Opening the folded note, Aleks' scribble greeted me.

E,

Sorry I had to skip breakfast. Important meeting in town. Granger (butler) will show you to the library when you're done with breakfast. Have fun. We'll catch up at dinner.

Yours,

A

My cheeks flamed at the shorthand. I hadn't even thought of Aleks being at breakfast, which was probably a good thing since I wasn't sure how I was supposed to act after last night.

Pretend it didn't happen?

Warn him it couldn't happen again?

Suggestively hint I wouldn't be super mad if it did?

I smacked my hand on my forehead, dislodging that particular train of thought. Bad, bad thoughts.

Exhaling slowly, I set the note aside. A man swooped in with a covered dish and unveiled a heavenly mass of scents and textures that screamed breakfast. I cleaned the whole plate, not slowing down for the imaginary guests in front of me. No need to look cute or pretend I didn't have the appetite of a linebacker. My stomach purred in delight as it was slowly filled with delicious food.

As soon as I was done, the gentleman who served me showed me toward the door, wasting no time or words in escorting me to the library. He shut the door behind him, and I was able to exhale any pretense of decorum I had salvaged in between the end of breakfast and being shown the library. Even a week after my escape, I still felt like anyone standing around was there to watch me. Not only that, but that they were taking notes and discussing my behavior amongst themselves.

I shook off the paranoia that had begun creeping up my neck and focused on the shelf-lined walls and gorgeous stained glass windows. Being surrounded by books was in its own way a therapy. The musty smell of tree and ink wrapped around me like an old worn quilt, welcoming me home even though I had never been here before.

The desk at the end of the room was spotless and clear of any clutter. I ran my fingertips across the top, noticing the leather inlay in the center. The door opened again, and this time a female staff member came in, carrying a stack of papers. I smiled at her, the grin widening once I realized she had brought the papers I had left in my room. My notebook weighted the stack down, and the woman deposited them on the desk along with a handful of new pens.

She left me without a word, and I muttered a belated thanks as the door shut behind her.

I remained standing, my hand tracing over the ornate carved back of the wooden desk chair. An odd sense of déjà vu overcame me, and I realized the layout and furniture had echoes of the old section in the Windermere library. As I stared at the lead-lined windows, I realized the age and style was too similar to not have a connection. Knowing this house was built by the same hands that built Windermere sent a chill shooting down my spine, and I had to do a lap around the edges of the library to calm myself.

This level of coincidence made my stomach turn.

My brainstorm papers had been shuffled in my sleep, but some present part of my mind late last night had had the decency to number them. I spread them all out on the desk in front of me and stared at the names of the families Henry had listed, their names and gifts delineated by generation in a chaotic attempt at a family tree.

The intermarriages alone were a headache. I had left off trying to annotate the various unions by making symbols directing to other branches, but the cross matching was too much. I already had a headache, and I had only been back at it a few minutes.

I flipped to a fresh page in the notebook Jasleen had gotten for me. I focused on the abilities and the planes Birdie had told me about. Instead of the spokes she had used, I decided in favor of squares. After all, balance needed to come from every side equally if what the prophecy had stated would come true.

After several shaky attempts, the pile of crumpled pages growing exponentially on the floor around the desk, I had a few workable rough drafts. In the midst of my muttering, the woman from before had come in and set a thermos of coffee and a pile of sandwiches on the small coffee table between the two couches. She kept her distance from the desk, and I only looked up when I heard the click of the door shutting again.

Desperate for a different perspective, I moved to the couch with its back to the door. With a sandwich in one hand and my pen in the other, I was able to work out a few more diagrams before the light dimmed from the windows, leaving me in near darkness.

Suddenly, the lights snapped on around me, and I jumped.

"Hey," Aleks' voice said from the doorway. "It's just me."

I put my hand to my chest, realizing it was still clutching a sandwich. My eyes were blurry from so much focusing, and I blinked violently to try to bring them back into focus. Aleks sank into the couch opposite me, his hand covering his mouth. I realized his body was shaking a little.

"What's the matter with you?" I said, my voice cracking.

"Nothing," he said, clearly trying to smother his laughter. "Did you have a good day?"

I was so distracted by the convulsions in his chest, I couldn't answer his question.

"Are you laughing right now?" I said, my hand still clutched to my chest.

"Nope," Aleks said, giggling at his own horrible attempt to lie. "Not at all."

"What's so funny?" I said, looking around me at my mess of papers and open books. He sighed, trying to push out all his amusement, but failing, he reverted back to a full laugh.

"It's a tie between you cradling a half-eaten sandwich to your chest or your resemblance to Gollum seeing the light after centuries in a cave," Aleks said, trying to keep it together enough to speak. He barely managed, and I was left trying to decipher his words.

"Did you just say I look like Gollum?" I shrieked at him, hurling the remnants of my sandwich at him. "It is not nice to tell a girl she looks like Gollum! Even if she does!"

Aleks continued laughing, curling himself reflexively into a protective ball as I looked around for something else to launch at him. A throw pillow was the only unimportant thing within reach, and I chucked it at his head.

"Apologize!" I howled. "Take it back!"

"No, not the Precious!" Aleks said in the worst Gollum impression I had ever heard.

It was my turn to laugh uncontrollably.

"That's horrible," I said, sobering up. "It really is. You should definitely say you're sorry."

"I am very sorry my accurate description of your general state upset you," Aleks said, crossing his arms across his chest and wiping tears from his cheeks. "But really. Do you always get so wrapped up in your research? I was gone for only a few hours."

"Studious champion," I said, pointing both my thumbs to me. "What can I say? Go big or go home."

"How about go to dinner instead?" Aleks said, standing and offering me his hand. "Would the Precious like to freshen up or…"

I smacked him hard with the spare pillow, beating him with it all the way to the door.

THIRTY

The edge of the stainless steel counter bit into my back, right below my shoulder blades. I shifted around, trying to find a comfortable position to lean and eat my ice cream. So far, I was unsuccessful.

After Aleks had led the way to the kitchen, I finally realized how late it had gotten. A lone staff member was in the kitchen and looked panicked stricken when she realized we might need a full meal. Aleks, much to my surprise, had offered a calm smile and told her not to worry. Her skeptical eyes lingered on us as she left the industrial grade kitchen, but she ducked out as soon as she was dismissed.

"Ice cream for dinner," I said, inspecting my loaded spoon suspended in midair. "Impressive."

"I am an excellent cook," Aleks boasted.

I snorted. I didn't need any supernatural help to spot the lie.

"Fine," Aleks said, shutting the freezer door crisply. "I can burn water. But this isn't so bad."

Aleks grabbed his own bowl off the counter and walked toward the island I was propped against. The kitchen had been completely renovated to support a five-star bistro. It seemed off in an otherwise well-preserved old manor house. Where there should have been carved oak cabinets, stainless steel tabletops and shelves glared back. My shoulders ached from their uncomfortable spot.

Suddenly, I felt Aleks' hands on my waist. A small yelp escaped me, and I found myself propped on top of the prep counter like a doll.

Tendrils of rage and embarrassment snuck up my neck and colored my cheeks. My jaw hung slack in awe. I was unable to verbalize my indignation. Instead, my mind was spinning, focusing only on Aleks' confident hold of my waist.

I tried to count to ten, but kept losing track as waves of competing emotions crashed through me. The only thing grounding me was the chill of the bowl in my hand and the new bite of the countertop into the soft part at the back of my knees. Everywhere else was fire. My shins, braced against Aleks' thighs. My waist, trapped in his hands. My eyes, locked on his. Our faces only inches apart.

The waves continued to crash through me, and I wondered whose emotions they were. All mine? Or was Aleks feeling what I was feeling? What happened to the murky black cloud that normally surrounded him? I grabbed desperately at these questions, hoping logical thinking might break the spell my body was under. I couldn't move.

We stayed suspended like that for what seemed an eternity.

"What is happening?" I finally managed to whisper aloud to the room. Of all the rotations of that question in my mind, finally my tongue loosed it into the supercharged air between us.

Aleks slowly removed his hands from my waist, placing them on either side of me atop the counter. His eyes never backed down from mine, but his previously stoic face now sparkled mischievously with a slight smirk of his lips.

Lips. No. We are not going to think about his lips.

Too late. Aleks must have noticed my eyes dart down to his lips because he smiled more broadly.

"You seemed uncomfortable," Aleks said. His voice was soft, matching the intimacy of the three inches between our faces. "Is this better?"

I pressed my lips together, finally bringing my jaw back up

from the floor. I inhaled deeply through my nose, attempting to slow my racing heartbeat before I passed out.

The amount of sensory input was overwhelming. I was having trouble separating the physical from the emotions and thoughts bombarding my consciousness. The more I tried to name and catalog what was going on in my mind, the more I felt the darkness of unconsciousness creeping into the edges of my mind.

I was on the verge of complete shutdown.

Normally, I would just throw up barriers haphazardly to push away the unwanted and overwhelming feelings. The sorting and boxing trick Dean Moriarty had offhandedly taught me didn't seem to be working either, as there were too many things to sort in a short period of time.

What would Noah do?

Instantly, I thought of her. Noah would not tolerate such emotional turmoil to color her thoughts. She took charge of her mind. If she came up against an unknown, she would attack it head on. She would strategize, and she would execute. I needed offense, not defense.

I held my breath.

Amidst the cloud of emotion, I cleared a small path, letting the waves of emotion swell around me at the disturbance, but not limit them to a certain space as I had tried with the boxing method. They flared out but remained predictable. Good.

My eyes remained caught in Aleks' stare, and I used that connection to gain access into his mind. Much like my attempt with Eli, I had to work my way around some unintentional barriers to finally break into his mind. A slight tinge of guilt hit me in my gut, but I let it melt into the other waves of emotion around me.

Once I was inside, I found Aleks' motor center, leaving his memories and thoughts well alone.

Step back, I directed, offering an image of Aleks stepping backward the two feet to the opposite counter.

Immediately, Aleks stepped back as I had imagined, except the look on his face was pure shock. I couldn't imagine him looking any more surprised than if I had kicked him between the legs.

As soon as he was a foot away from me, the cloud of emotions dissipated with a pop in my internal ears. The murky cloud reappeared around Aleks' feet, and a wave of sadness raged up within me. The wall was back up between us, and I should have been relieved. Instead, the bile rocked in my stomach as I watched shock, anger, and fear flash across Aleks' face. My own emotions began to beat me down further. What little relief I had gotten was eclipsed by my own disgust and fear for what I had just done. And it hadn't been that hard.

My ice cream bowl crashed loudly to the ground, shattering the blue etched ceramic design I had been admiring only minutes before. I stared through my violently trembling hands at the mess of half-melted ice cream and shards of dishware and let the sadness take me.

Sound rushed back to my ears, and I realized I was sobbing uncontrollably.

My hands snapped to my mouth, trying to smother the noise echoing back to me in the sterile kitchen, reflecting my guilt a hundredfold in the form of audio torture. I curled into myself, hiding my face behind my curtain of hair, my forehead pressing itself firmly into my kneecaps. I couldn't bear to look at Aleks. His expression was permanently seared into my memory, and my mind was looping it on repeat.

"Evangeline," Aleks said softly. "I'm so sorry."

I sprung out of my curled position, another punch of guilt causing my stomach to convulse. "I—"

"It's okay," Aleks said, shaking his head softly side to side. "Take your time. Just breathe." He was crouched about where I had instructed him to retreat, staying on the far side of the mess on the floor. His posture reminded me of someone trying to coax a distressed animal into trusting them.

Another wave of guilt rolled through me.

"It's my fault," Aleks' warm voice said, winding through the murky cloud of emotion swirling around me. "I pushed your boundaries too far. I am very, very sorry."

"I should never," I stressed aloud, "never do that to anyone."

My body continued to tremble, but the tears slowed as I tried to put into words what I was feeling.

"You have every right to protect yourself," Aleks said. "Whether it's me or a stranger, whatever their intentions are, you have the right to do what you need to do to feel safe. Do you hear me?"

I shook my head back and forth.

"If I could just build better barriers, I wouldn't have to put myself in those situations," I said, more to myself than to Aleks. "I need to do better than that. I can't be taken by surprise by anyone. I'm not safe."

"Hey," Aleks said, "that is not true."

"Aleks, I could have made you do anything," I whispered in horror and disgust. "If that's not a monster, than I don't know what is."

Aleks reached toward me but stopped himself. The pool of black mist darkened around his ankles. Even without the full strength of my abilities, I could tell he was really angry. I would be, too, if someone had just taken control of my mind like that. Maybe I should be locked up if this is what I was capable of doing to people. It had seemed so unfair before, but it was looking more and more practical the more I realized I couldn't control myself as well as I had thought I could.

I felt a light pressure on my ankle, and my eyes refocused to see Aleks standing in front of me. As I had spiraled down into my own thoughts, he must have approached me. I looked at him, slightly confused. Why would he want to be anywhere near me after what I had done to him?

Aleks tentatively took one of my hands in his, testing the boundaries of what was safe and what was not. A knife of anguish sliced through my gut.

Even Aleks was afraid of me now.

I was so spent, I didn't even think about my barriers until it was too late. Our connection flared to life and the dark cloud dissipated once we shared the same common space. Aleks squeezed my hand lightly, drawing my attention to it.

Nothing bad happened.

The sky didn't fall.

Aleks didn't keel over dead.

I was so tired, I could barely manage to be relieved. As I stared at our hands, I felt a light brush on my cheek.

Aleks tucked my hair behind my ear. His thumb brushed the remaining moisture from my many guilty tears and held my face. His eyes searched for mine, waiting until we were locked back in once again.

"Evie," he whispered, sending an excited chill down my spine. "I will do whatever necessary to protect you. From others. From yourself. From me."

His hand squeezed mine again. Through our connection, I felt a surge of warmth. This was not the fire from last time but rather a more muted glow. I sighed out loud, allowing myself to sit in the warmth for as long as possible. Another tear escaped down my cheek, and I closed my eyes to try to concentrate. I needed to be vigilant so I wouldn't slip up again.

Then, I felt a light kiss on my cheek where the trail of the tear had started. The warmth flared a little more strongly, but remained a neutral shine. It didn't seem nearly as dangerous as before.

Aleks pulled me into a comforting embrace, and I buried my face in his chest. I clung to him as I let all the anguish and fear and guilt leak out in my tears. After a while, though, my tears dried up, and I was left holding onto Aleks, never wanting to let go.

THIRTY-ONE

"I don't know what to do," Aleks said, his voice muffled through the mostly closed door to my bathroom.

I had fallen asleep briefly after expending all my energy on crying and being beaten to death in an emotional hurricane. Aleks had carried me back to my room, even going so far as to pull the curtains down around the bed to give me further privacy.

The light from the bathroom glowed a vibrant orange against the deep red carpet, and I stared blankly at the strip of light as his words floated through my hollow mind.

"No, no, she's fine now. Sleeping," Aleks said to the person on the other end of the phone. His voice had woken me from my exhausted stupor. Little spikes of worry darted out from his dark aura, and all I could wish was for the darkness to just cooperate and keep everything on the other side of it. Aleks was usually one of the few people I didn't have to manage so directly, but the closer we became, the more his cloudy aura seemed to open to me. As if I didn't have enough other puzzle pieces to maneuver.

"What did I do?" Aleks repeated, a guilty pause speaking volumes for him. "What do you mean?"

You know what they mean.

"She fell apart as soon as she used her commander mode on me. I don't know how else to explain it," Aleks continued. "I don't get it. If it was anyone else, they would use that power to their advantage widely and loosely. She reacted like...like her body was rejecting it."

Aleks fell silent, but I could hear him fidgeting in the bathroom. The clank of various objects being picked up and sloppily set back down tinkled back through the cracked doorway as the voice continued.

"I guess that could make sense," Aleks said. He sighed. "I just don't know what to do to help her. She almost completely cracked. I don't know how much longer she can handle both Elevations."

The sliver of orange carpet grew larger, and I heard Aleks' bare feet pad softly on the plush carpet toward me. I snapped my eyes shut, hoping he hadn't seen the whites of my eyes in the darkness.

"We're going to need to make a decision soon," Aleks said to the other end of the line. "I'd really hate for us to lose the Queen. We can play without a few of the others, but not her. Without her, we've got virtually no chance."

Aleks sighed.

"Yeah, agreed. I'll keep my eye on her," Aleks replied in finality. "We'll talk again tomorrow."

I felt the corner of the bed sink as Aleks sat at the foot of my bed.

My muscles tensed, trying not to show the movement had registered to my supposedly sleeping frame. I was sprawled facing slightly away from him, but somehow, he could tell I wasn't fully asleep.

"Evangeline? Are you awake?" Aleks whispered across the bed. He was close enough that he reached out to lightly touch my ankle. I could feel his concern through the sheets and comforter. Or maybe I had just imagined it.

I stirred, feigning just waking up. I shifted my frame slightly toward him while pulling my ankle out of his reach. My hand draped over my eyes slightly, as if I were trying to clear my field of vision. It was quite the Oscar-worthy performance, if I could say so myself.

"Aleks?" I said, my voice naturally scratchy after a long crying session.

Icing on the cake.

I tried to analyze him through my hooded eyelids in the dim light. Beams of light from the bathroom fell far enough into the room for me to read his face quite clearly.

The phone call made me extremely uncomfortable and on edge. I wasn't sure who I was talking to anymore. The Aleks who made lame references and kissed me like the world was ending or the Aleks who was the heir to a prominent Elevated family trying to stay one step ahead in the race for power among the supernaturally gifted.

I was not amused by being compared to a chess piece.

But Aleks' face looked concerned. His eyebrows creased, forming a cute series of V's on his forehead. His clear eyes darted over me, surveying me for any signs of distress. Maybe both Aleks' could exist in the same place.

I wished I could believe him. A bitter taste lingered in my mouth. As much as I wanted to rely on him, to trust in his words and intentions, I couldn't quite reconcile in my mind who I thought I had come to know and the person who had been talking strategy on the phone mere feet away from the person stuck in the middle.

Even in the half-light of the room, I could make out the swirling mass of energy surrounding Aleks. As much as I wanted to rely on it for my barrier between our thoughts, the more I realized how complacent I had become. Before, I could rely on my own senses and intuition to know a person's true intention. Sure, I had difficulty turning it off and separating myself from it when I needed to protect myself, but I was always one hundred percent sure of what I was dealing with. Beneath convincing facial expressions and body language, I could read the truth.

Not with Aleks. The clouded aura of loose Elevated energy blocked that flow of information. I had thought my other instincts were strong enough to determine his motives, but I was seriously beginning to doubt myself. I couldn't trust anything that had happened between us.

It was tainted now.

I was just a chess piece after all.

"Did I wake you?" Aleks asked, small blips of worry leaking through both his barrier and mine.

"What's going on?" I asked. I waited for the answer, knowing he wouldn't interpret my question the same way I was asking it.

"You passed out in the kitchen, so I brought you up to your room. Are you feeling any better?" Aleks said.

"Do you feel it?" I asked. I waved my hand toward the swirling mass I was fairly certain only I could see. Offense didn't quite suit me, but I was willing to try again.

"What?" Aleks said, looking around him like he had spilled something on his shirt.

"The energy," I said. "Or whatever you want to call it."

"The black stuff you mentioned before?" Aleks said. "No. Why?"

"It changes sometimes, you know," I said, half to myself. The changes had been bothering me, but I'd been thinking about so many other things that I hadn't thought through the possibilities of what Aleks' aura changes could mean. At this moment, it seemed like the most important answer I needed to find. Maybe it would unlock everything else or at the very least give me an answer to the ball of questions that had become Aleks.

"It does?" Aleks replied, his tone overly cautious. "Like how?"

"The texture sometimes," I said. "It used to be sticky and thick, like oil or tar. It's more smoke-like now. Wispy. But the color darkens sometimes. I wonder if it's your mood…"

My voice trailed off. The answer couldn't be so simple as a mood ring.

"It used to be wilder," I mumbled, finding the effort of explaining my infantile theory extremely draining. The words weren't right. "Now, it behaves more when I'm around. Like a stray puppy that bites at first, but warms up to you later." I started to chuckle, the laugh lasting only a few seconds until a wave of exhaustion derailed my amusement.

Suddenly, it was nearly impossible for me to keep my eyes open even to slits. In moments, Aleks disappeared in front of me. The blackness of sleep pulled me under, and I never did get an answer to my question.

THIRTY-TWO

Eli burst into my room and marched straight to my bed. Her anger had woken me from down the hall, so I was both mentally and physically prepared for the covers being ripped off from on top of me. Still hated it though.

"Your boyfriend is coming," Eli seethed. "So much for the appointment rule. Real great boundary setting, by the way. Your tantrum was so worth it."

"Technically," I began, lounging back on my elbows, "the appointment rule was for Aleks' uncle, not his lackeys."

"This is your ten-minute warning," Eli spat. "You're lucky I even care to give you that much of a heads up."

"Your disdain is showing," I said, my words pointed and fierce. Eli's body was shaking with agitation, but she remained sentry at the side of my bed. To make matters worse, Aleks and Niko appeared in the doorway.

"Any idea why your friend would be coming?" Aleks asked. His fingers were busy unrolling his shirtsleeves and buttoning the cuffs closed. "A bit unexpected."

"I'm an empath, not a psychic," I said, shrugging to no one in particular.

Niko coughed in the doorway, his hand covering his face quickly to mask his smirk. Eli growled at me from the edge of my bed, and I bristled at the vibration. It didn't help that her normally well-tamed emotions were rocking against my barriers insistently.

I turned to Eli, gathering my legs underneath me.

"You need to keep your animosity to yourself," I said, holding her gaze coolly.

She bristled again, but I was already walking across the mattress, leaping down from the foot of the bed. I snatched a few articles of clothing from my wardrobe and marched into the bathroom.

I poked my head back out to my audience.

"If anyone wants to figure out why Brendan's here, maybe you should be there to greet him at the door and ask him yourself," I said. "In the meantime, I'm going to get dressed."

"Yes, ma'am," Niko said, his eyes sliding to Aleks, whose fingers had frozen trying to button his non-dominant cuff hand.

Niko disappeared down the hall, and Eli dodged past Aleks in a whirl of anger and embarrassment. The energy of the room quieted substantially once she had left. I let out a breath and began to close the door to the bathroom.

Then the door bounced back. I looked down to see Aleks' foot stuck in the way.

"Everything okay?" he asked, his eyes searching mine intently. The concerned V lines were back. I wasn't going to fall for that again.

"Fine," I said, waving my pile of clothes at him. "Mind if I clothe myself before entertaining visitors?"

"Okay," Aleks said, his frown deepening. "Meet you downstairs."

I nodded, shutting the door again. My fingers twisted the lock home with satisfaction.

That was not very nice, a voice floated in the back of my head.

Tiny prickles of guilt itched the base of my skull, and I shook my head to dislodge them. Even though I couldn't quite figure out who was friend or foe these days, the little voice in my head knew better than to let me treat people like that. I had to be more careful with the words and attitudes I let loose. What I did carried much heavier weight than the average snide comment.

I sighed heavily into the bathroom and caught my reflection mid guilt trip.

"You need to get your shit together," I lectured the mirror image. "Not everyone's motives are pure. You just have to tread lightly until you figure out what's going on. No need to throw tantrums."

My slender finger poked out, emphasizing the reprimand. Upon seeing the puffy dark circles staring back at me, I could only sigh again. Ten minutes wouldn't be enough time to do a decent enough cover-up job. Whatever Brendan was here for, he would have to deal with me in my natural state.

I had one leg in my pants when a soft knock came at the door.

"Tsaritsa," Niko said through the door. "I'm ready whenever you are."

"Just a moment, please," I called back through the door, all my bite already expended from earlier. I wiggled into my pants, doing a couple stretching poses to make sure the painted on jeggings settled correctly over my hips. "Do I have time for eyeliner?"

"Doesn't matter to me," Niko replied. "You might need some war paint today."

"Oh?" I said, pulling at my eyelids to swipe a quick smudge of black at the lash line. "What makes you say that?"

"Brendan is under the impression he is taking you with him today," Niko said. "The pretense is your grandmother's wake, but Aleksander is hesitant to believe that is his only motive."

"Hmmmmm," I replied, wiping some color back into my face. "I see."

"Ready?"

I opened the door to find Niko leaning comfortably against the doorframe.

"Ah, that would be a yes," Niko said. A brief smile flashed across his face, but was soon replaced by his typical brooding expression.

"Can I ask you a question?" I blurted out suddenly.

Niko didn't strike me as someone who did anything he didn't want to do. I had never heard the story of how he came to work with Aleks, but if it were anything like the brief glimpse I got from Eli, maybe I could believe in Aleks' seemingly good intentions. Chess piece or no chess piece.

Niko nodded.

"How did you come to work for Aleks?" I asked. "Or with. Sorry."

"And why do I stay?" Niko replied, pushing the question further into the territory I had been aiming for.

"Yeah, something like that," I said, slight embarrassment coloring my cheeks to a deeper pink.

"Originally, I worked for one of Aleks' cousins, rest his soul," Niko said, making the sign of the cross across his broad chest. The movement surprised me, more for its sincerity than anything. "It was natural for me to serve under the next master after his passing."

"Did you have a choice? Or was it one of those choices that isn't really a choice?" I asked, daring to dig to the heart of the question. The word "master" had irked me.

"Aleksander released me from my contract. Under that condition, I was offered employment. All previous debts had been forgiven, so yes, I was free to choose," Niko said. He bent over me a little from his perch against the frame. "And I can leave whenever I would like."

"But you stick around," I said, pulling my hair over one shoulder.

"I like having a purpose," Niko said. "I like that the purpose is a positive one."

"So you trust Aleks?"

"Yes," Niko said. "With my life."

I bit my lip, not wanting to press further. I had gotten my answer. Whether I chose to believe it would be completely up to me. Pushing past Niko, I grabbed a fur-trimmed hooded jacket from the wardrobe.

"My phone," I muttered to myself, patting my pockets forgetfully. "Huh."

"Here," Niko said, offering me a phone. "I believe yours was left quite some time ago in a snow bank in Indiana."

The sleek black phone looked new, much newer than my old phone.

"Oh, yeah," I said. "I can't believe I've been without it all this time."

"It had a tracker in it. No good." Niko shrugged. "This one has no GPS tracking."

"Kind of silly with you and Eli, huh?" I said with a smile.

"Exactly," Niko said. "I've programmed our numbers in there. In case today—"

"Isn't just the wake?" I said, dread coloring my voice.

Niko stood to his full height and waited.

"Thanks," I said, tucking the phone into my pocket.

"Shall we?" Niko asked, offering his arm. "We are late."

"The diva needed to put on her eyeliner," I said saucily. "What could you have done?"

Niko chuckled, offering his arm to me.

"Yes, I was completely helpless," Niko replied.

"Whatever," I snorted at him. "I can read you like a picture book. You're all warm and squishy on the inside."

"Don't tell anyone," Niko said, his face darkening. "Teddy bears make poor bodyguards."

"I promise."

I held my pinky finger out to him, and he hooked his massive hairy knuckled finger around mine before we popped into the downstairs hall to my unexpected sendoff party.

THIRTY-THREE

"They are holding off the wake for her." Brendan's raised voice bounced off the wood paneling and trim. "She has to go."

"Get her uncle on the phone, and I'll consider it," Aleks shot back coolly. "How do I even know you're going to take her there? You're probably just going to send her right back to that institution and collect a nice reward for your troubles."

"How dare you question my motives and my word!" Brendan said. I could feel his whole aura vibrating in agitation, even through the wall separating Niko and me from the argument. "I have known Evangeline since we were kids. I've known that family even longer. I have every right to escort her to the wake. Who are you to say whether she stays or goes?"

"I have her best interests at heart," Aleks said. "I'm not sure you do."

"Oh, so she's a prisoner here just like she was in the institution. The dressing's a little nicer, but it looks the same to me," shouted Brendan.

Niko raised his eyebrows at me, but I held my hand up. I wanted to hear this without getting in the middle of it.

"I'm not the one making her life dangerous," Aleks growled back. "My interests and Evangeline's safety fall neatly on the same side. I don't know if you can say the same."

"I want what is best for her," Brendan said. "That will always be my side. And what are we, competing little league teams? What sides are you even talking about?"

"I can't tell if you're playing dumb on purpose or you really have no idea what is going on in our world," Aleks said, the disbelief leaking through in stronger beams from his normally silent clouded aura.

"Our world? Last time I checked, you weren't Elevated," Brendan shot back ruthlessly.

"My family's business is my business," Aleks said. "And Evangeline falls into that category. I don't trust you farther than I can throw you."

"Luckily, whether you trust me or not is irrelevant. Evangeline is coming with me. The end," Brendan launched back.

The boys continued shouting at each other. I turned to Niko, pulling on his collar lightly to bring him down to my level. He obliged without hesitation.

"I have to go, but you'll be able to find me, right?" I asked, a tinge of worry coloring my feigned confidence. I had been so sure in my bedroom I was making the right decision to go. My stomach was flipping over and over again. Maybe I wasn't thinking this through.

"Of course," Niko said. "We are on speed dial. Any of them. Eli and I are on standby for you."

I nodded, letting my hand drop from Niko's lapel before he could tell it was shaking. Suddenly, I was terrified to leave the safety of the Navratil manor. Surely I could just stay here, tinker with my research, slowly make plans to track down potential Elevated people, make sure they were safe or at the very least aware of what was afoot. I shoved the cold fear down from my stomach into my toes. I didn't have time for that nonsense.

I popped up on my tiptoes and placed a thankful peck on Niko's cheek before he could straighten fully.

"Thank you," I said. Niko inclined his head.

"Ready?"

I exhaled deeply, waiting for a break in the shouting match before I turned the corner.

Queen. You are the queen chess piece. Act like it.

"Are you both done?" I said, walking into the cloud of heated emotions.

Brendan's energy field was pulsing menacingly, and his aura was crowding out the thick black smoke attached to Aleks. In my Elevated mind's eye, I could barely even see the boys beneath their emotions. I swiped the air.

"What are you doing?" Eli piped up from the staircase. Her curiosity flared out briefly from her lounging posture up the stairs.

Both Aleks and Brendan stopped arguing long enough to see me swiping through the air like a maniac. From an outside perspective, I bet it looked ridiculous.

"Brendan, calm down before you suffocate me," I ordered, my tone sharp. "You know better than to act like this around me."

Brendan's aura field immediately shrunk, the color changing to a muted guilt tinge, a stark contrast to the rage and indignation from moments before.

"Sorry, Evangeline," Brendan said. "I got carried away."

Eli snorted on behalf of everyone.

"Aleks, can you come with me for a second?" I asked, kicking at the dark cloud around his feet. "Brendan, wait here. Don't embarrass me." I looked pointedly at Eli and Niko watching him from the two entrances further into the manor.

Brendan nodded quickly, the desperation for approval leaking out from his quickly built shields.

I walked into the dining room and waited for Aleks to follow me. He was on my heels and shut the door softly behind us. I spun around to see his hands stuffed awkwardly into his pockets. The rest of his body language read as impassive, but I knew he was trying really hard to hide behind that mask.

"You're going, aren't you?" Aleks stated, his tone deflated.

"You know I am," I said, my hands reaching farther into my

own jacket pockets in avoidance. Strong shoulders. Confidence. Deep breaths.

"And you're not worried at all," Aleks pressed.

"I'm going to take Brendan at his word," I said. "I have no reason to doubt him."

"You're not serious," Aleks said, his hands flying out of his pockets to emphasize the other side of the wall. "He was supposed to take you back to the Association after the wake. And now suddenly, he's not going to do that a week later?"

"I guess we'll have to see," I replied. My fists clenched tightly in my pockets, but I hoped the rest of my expression was as blank as I intended. "Not going doesn't seem to be a viable option."

"I can't let you go," Aleks said, shaking his head. "Absolutely not. We don't know what will happen. We can't risk it."

"We?" I asked. "Risk what, exactly?"

Aleks stiffened. His mouth moved as if to explain, but the silence stretched on. The heaviness in the air dug into my heart.

"What am I to you, Aleks?" I held in a sigh, but emotionally I felt myself sink a little into the disappointment and grief of the answer I could feel coming.

"You're—"

"The Queen?" I said, my words slicing through his explanation.

His jaw snapped shut at my words.

"You were awake."

"You talked about sides earlier," I said, rushing my words before I could change my mind. I had to let this out before it ate me alive. "But I don't really know what sides you're talking about. And I really don't appreciate being referred to as a game piece, whether it's the Queen or what everyone is in the end—a pawn. I will not be moved around the board at your command."

My voice wavered with anger. Tears prickled the edges of my eyes, and I struggled to clear my throat. I hated that I cried when I was angry. I needed to say what I needed to say without tears ruining the power of my words.

Aleks stepped forward, his hands out ready to comfort, but I put up my hand and stepped back a pace.

"I wanted to tell you," Aleks said, the dark matter at his ankles licking at the distance I had tried to keep between us. "I was trying to find the right time. You're not some pawn in the game, Evangeline. You're the most important one. I'm not the player moving you around at my will. I didn't know if you were ready."

Aleks growled, his fingers flexing in the air in frustration.

"I'm not explaining this right," he said desperately. "Evangeline, I'm on your side. You're the chess master, not me. I'm just the placeholder until you're ready. You're going to be the great unifier. That's the 'we.' That's why you can't go."

"I have to," I said simply, the thickness in my throat making the statement sound weaker than I wanted it to.

"I can't promise I can get you back," Aleks said, shouting out his frustration. "I don't want to lose you."

"What, then you're back at square one? Trying to find some great unifier according to some prophecy no one has a copy of or any proof that actually exists?" I shouted back. My own frustration colored my voice.

Aleks stepped back, his face flinching at my words. I could feel the air heat around me with my anger. Somehow, it was in the air, causing my face to glisten with sweat.

That wasn't good.

"We'll find the answers together," Aleks argued, his own temper matching mine. The clouds at his feet turned black, and a warning bell went off in my head. "There's no other option. It's just you. That's why it's imperative you stay safe."

The warning bells ratcheted up a notch. That really wasn't a good sign.

"I'm so tired of being shuffled between houses. Between families. Between prison cells," I spat back at him. My tongue lashed out, and I realized however true the words were, I wasn't sure where they were coming from. The nagging voice in my head was sending out panic signals, but my mouth continued to move of its own volition.

"I am my own person. I have my own problems. I have a right to decide how I deal with them," I screamed.

My vision blurred in front of me, and I felt my tenuous grip on reality stretching too thin. I was just so angry.

Muted banging added to the din, and I realized someone was trying to get into the dining room.

While I was momentarily distracted, a blurry figure filled my vision.

Aleks' dark eyes glimmered in front of me, and I could tell he was focusing intently.

On what? I thought to myself in a detached voice.

His hand was on my cheek, and he closed the distance between us, pulling me close to him.

All I could see were his eyes, so all my anger channeled directly into our forceful visual connection.

I know, I heard in my head.

The voice snapped me out of my fury trance. That was Aleks's voice. Why was Aleks' voice in my head?

I understand your pain, Aleks said in my mind. *I didn't mean to hurt you. Please believe me.*

I tried to pull myself out of his embrace, but he held on firmly.

Just let it all go, Aleks said. My eyes focused on his lips, still in shock that he had somehow managed to penetrate my mind, especially as a human. His lips weren't moving at all. He was definitely in my head, behind my protective barriers. My mind started and stalled over and over again to register this new phenomenon.

Suddenly, Aleks leaned even closer, and my eyes watched as his head dipped near mine, my eyes slowly going out of focus again as Aleks' lips met mine. What began as a firm lip lock changed into a hungry exchange of anger and relief and understanding.

Just as my anger began to dissipate, a loud bang erupted in the room. And everything went black.

THIRTY-FOUR

It's not too often you get woken up by a literal pain in your butt, but the first thing I noticed when I came to was the shooting pain radiating down my legs. I sat up, trying to rub the pain away. Aleks lay on the floor of the dining room a few feet from me, and I yelled out an obscenity in surprise.

I crawled over to him, checking him for breathing and a pulse. Both were weak, but there. More pounding came at the door until I heard a little pop. In moments, Niko was on the other side of Aleks, also checking for vitals.

"I think he's fine. I don't know if he hit his head though," I said under my breath. "Damn it. Why does he always have to poke his nose in other people's business?"

Niko clicked his tongue at me.

"You should be thankful to have such a...friend," Niko said, avoiding my eye deftly, focusing instead on checking Aleks for injuries.

My hands dropped from Aleks' wrist as Niko took over first aid. I sat back on my heels to observe him and immediately toppled backward with an unceremonious screech.

"What?" Niko said, his hands moving more swiftly over Aleks' prone body, trying to find the source of my distress.

My hands were clasped over my mouth as I tried to make sense of what I was seeing.

The murky cloud that had grown from the tar-like black

energy around Aleks had transitioned yet again to a solid black aura around his entire body. The energy moved and hummed like everyone else's, minus the color. I had never seen such darkness mask a person before. While most humans had a series of halos around them, the Elevated tended to have a purple wave surrounding a pure white core.

Such a little detail hadn't seemed so important. At least, not until Aleks' core had become black.

Black did not seem like a good color to have as a core energy color.

"Please tell me I didn't kill him," I said through my hands.

Niko glanced briefly at me.

"What makes you say that?"

"His energy is...concerning," I said, my voice hitching with anxiety.

"Hasn't he always been unusual to you?" Niko asked, straightening Aleks' limbs one by one after checking for breaks.

"Yes?"

"He's not dead," Niko assured me. He waited patiently for me to explain further.

"Yet," I said darkly. "There is no way he can survive like that. It doesn't feel...right." My eyes watered from not blinking enough. I couldn't help but follow the ebb and flow of his energy, dark as it was. It was almost like Aleks was wrapped in shadows. My stomach felt like it had turned itself inside out. Just looking at it made me extremely uneasy. I couldn't place what seemed so... wrong about the aura.

Banging erupted once again on the other side of the door. Niko ignored the noise. My shoulders jerked as if someone had punched me in the stomach.

"Aleksander is very durable," Niko said, straightening from his medical survey. "But if he comes to and you are still not gone, you will never leave."

"You want me to leave him like this?" I squeaked. A variety of half-realized thoughts spun in my mind. What-if scenarios collided with worst-case scenarios, and I was left with a thick cloud of unease. My gut was silent.

"Will you staring at him give you answers?" Niko retorted.

I scowled at him, his crisp words snapping me from my reverie.

"Evangeline! Are you all right?" Brendan yelled through the door. "Answer me!"

The directive drove through the ruckus in my mind, poking at the core of my being. A flash of red colored my vision as an uncontrolled wave of anger licked out at the impact.

Don't tell me what to do, I shot back in my mind.

The knocking stopped.

And I realized my words had ridden the wave of rage out into the minds of those around me. I counted the auras in the house. Eleven. Eleven people had just heard me in their minds unannounced.

My eyes grew wide, and Niko shook in a silent chuckle.

"Did I...?"

"I think we all heard that," Niko said, tapping his head. "You should compose yourself before you visit your family. I'll be right back."

Niko gathered Aleks into his arms and popped out of the room.

I sat cross-legged on the floor and began a breathing exercise. Niko had a point. Flying off the handle immediately upon meeting my family after a long time was not going to help me keep my freedom. Abuela's wake was also not the time or place to go off like a loose Elevated cannon. I would apologize to Aleks for leaving after knocking him unconscious when I got back. After all, I would only be gone a few days. Hopefully, by that point, he would have regained consciousness and maybe even some appreciation for the fact that I came back as promised.

Hopefully.

I could feel agitation radiating from the other side of the door.

Between Eli and Brendan, the foyer was becoming quite heated. I didn't have time to stroke their egos and make them feel better.

Beginning with the localized emotions, I brought up a hallway of doors in my mind. The boxes the dean had suggested did not work for the amount of complexity I was working with. The energies needed unlimited boundaries with a firm access point, and a series of cosmic closets was the only thing that came to mind. They had worked a whopping one time before. I sent a silent prayer out that they would work again.

Slowly, I unpacked all of the external emotions and escorted them into the appropriate doorways. Once the outer ring around me was solid, I thought through what I had been feeling lately. A lot had happened the past few days, and I had not done any emotional check-ins with myself. I had been too busy trying to solve the puzzle of the Elevated hierarchies and the implications of a poorly played chess game.

Had I even stopped to decide I would help?

I wished I had Noah around to bounce ideas off of.

Even our brief time together at Windermere had been a godsend. Noah's logic weighed options against each other with facts and practicalities. Some might say she was cold, not taking emotions into account, but the distance she helped me build let me make better decisions. Before my Elevation had manifested, I could pride myself on solid common sense decisions. I could manage myself quite well in the world from an early age. Once the emotions came crashing into me at all sides, that part of me had been lost. Common sense didn't seem so common with so many new variables introduced.

Only a few months without Noah and I was back under the waterline.

I pinched my thigh, bringing my mind back from another needless thought tangent. I needed to focus.

What really needed to happen was a secluded place, like Switzerland or the Library of Congress. I needed to exist in a vacuum where no one was trying to acquire me and no one was threatening in-patient treatment. The Navratil mansion had been as close to that as I could get, but the problems I had abandoned along with my phone and the car in the snowy ditch had come back. They too needed to be sorted neatly and put in their places behind doors. Some of them more heavily barricaded than others. I would come back to those later.

So what were we going to do?

Aleks was right. The wake was likely a trap. It was an excellent trap considering I had no way to avoid it unless I was sedated or in shackles. The need to say my goodbyes to Abuela and grieve with my family far exceeded any concerns I had for my personal safety. Aleks had been right to point that out, but it didn't change my decision.

I was going. I let out a long, intense breath.

Aleks. Brendan. That was a whole other mess.

On both sides, I could feel they were doing what they felt was best for me. Between Aleks' inky barrier and my promise to not snoop in Brendan's mind, I didn't know as much as I wanted to. Was this a serious enough concern for me to break my promise? If I breached Brendan's mind, the trust we had built from childhood would be destroyed. The weight of that decision caused me to sigh again.

"Is that helping, or are you just messing around?" Eli's voice said from my right.

I jumped an inch off the floor. My eyes locked on hers. She sat looming in a chair pulled out from the dining table. With her elbows resting on her knees, she looked almost casual. Her aura screamed in tightly wound agitation, so at least I knew her façade was just an extended poker face.

Eli was ready to launch at any moment.

"When did you get here?" I didn't bother to ask how.

"About ten minutes ago. Your boyfriend was driving me up the wall, and he just couldn't believe me that you were just sitting inside the room, completely unharmed. Niko deposited me to keep an eye on you. But I could have broken in if I wanted to." Eli leaned back in her chair. "Are you almost done, or am I going to listen to you sigh all day?"

"I was processing," I replied.

"It must be nice to have that luxury," Eli said.

The words swiped at me like a cat's paw. Even with my carefully barricaded thoughts, I could feel Eli's envy attacking me with force.

"Do you want to do this right now?" I asked in a flat tone. I didn't even have enough energy to add snark. "You were much lower down on my priority list than whether or not I was walking into an ambush, but no, it's fine. We can do this right now."

I turned my body to face her directly.

"Have at it," I said, letting my arms rest comfortably on my crossed legs. My chest was open and confident, so even though I was seated, the power posturing could not be misunderstood. I was ready for whatever Eli needed to launch at me to get over her little fit. I was over trying to dodge her barbs and her unreliable aid. Apathy was a great temporary shield.

"Seriously?" Eli replied, her laugh ringing through the dining room. "You think you matter enough to me for me to have a problem with you."

"You're wasting your hot air on an empath," I said. "Do you want me to catalog your current feelings for you? I can even give you specifics on percentages of energy you are putting into them. You've got quite an array of colors going on. I'm sure I could find some really dirty details to air if you need supporting evidence."

"Well, aren't you the princess?" Eli shot back. "One peek behind the curtain and you think you know me."

"So it is about Aleks," I said, recalling the memory I had brought up with her first encounter with the Navratil boss.

Eli's aura flared red before returning to a vibrant green.

"You may have him fooled, but you don't fool me. You don't have any idea what's going on, yet you insist on meddling around with plans that we have built up for months," Eli said. "You're going to ruin everything."

THIRTY-FIVE

"You're nuts if you think I asked for any of this," I said, holding Eli's intense glare. My throat was warming, but I held back the venom. I already knocked one person unconscious this morning. Body counts this high before breakfast were inadvisable.

"Well, here you are," Eli replied. Her mouth twisted from her sour words.

The amount of negative energy floating around her perplexed me. How could so much anger and pain exist in one person and still have that person be able to function? As unstable as I felt I was, at least I was aware. Eli seemed oblivious to the danger.

"Then tell me exactly what I'm ruining," I said, "because honestly, I have no idea what I could possible impact by just existing."

"I can't even trust you enough to explain what's going on," Eli said. "It doesn't matter. You're going to the other side in minutes. I'll probably never see you again, so all I have to do is wait for you to burn them down from the inside."

"How kind of you," I muttered. I pinched the bridge of my nose. Within one intake of breath, I had reinforced the barriers between me and Eli's poisonous aura. My eyes were closed, but I heard Niko's distinctive pop.

"What did I miss?"

"Apparently, I'm the new and improved pyrotechnic Trojan

horse," I mumbled through my hand. "Eli was just wishing me well on my latest mission."

"Oh," Niko said.

I could see a slight blue overlay of curiosity in his aura, and I wondered if he was able to play around with his aura colors. Niko was the only person in recent months who did my barricading for me. He kept all his emotions close enough to his chest that his aura was barely a shimmer of colors. Somehow, that flicker of blue reminded me of his silent shoulder-hunching chuckle.

"Are you laughing at me?" I asked, turning to look at him.

His eyes opened a little wider. Such a minimal difference read as shock for the stoic teleporter.

"Nevermind," I said, my hand in the air between us. "I was attempting to sort through this huge clusterfuck of a situation when Eli unloaded her nonsense onto me. I don't need another what if from you."

Eli's eyes darted between us, slightly off put that her rage was being so easily dismissed.

"Actually, no, now this is going to bug me," I backtracked. I leaned back on an arm, catching Niko's gaze. "Can you manipulate your aura on your own? Or is it unintentional?"

"What's she talking about?" Eli asked Niko. "She keeps babbling about colors."

"You should really pay more attention when Birdie tells stories," Niko said to Eli, an edge of reprimand to his tone. "How else are you supposed to learn about all the other Elevated manifestations? And most of them are funny."

Eli grumbled to herself.

"So you do know what you're doing," I said, my eyes squinting into slits. "I don't know if I like that."

"I have had some training in mental barriers. It is helpful when encountering Elevated on the sentient plane," Niko said, offering another shrug.

"That's why you're so quiet," I said. "Not that you're loud normally or anything."

Niko grinned.

"Don't compliment him," Eli barked. "He won't shut up about practicing if you do that."

"See? It is useful," Niko said, his eyes weighing heavily on Eli.

"How many others do you think can do what you do?" I asked. Now my curiosity was hooked. While it should have occurred to me long ago, I never thought about people manipulating the information I was reading from their aura. Quentin had learned to project, but in terms of his emotions, he was still as bright as twinkling Christmas lights in the dark. Adair had taken me by surprise by completely cloaking himself.

He didn't count though. His Elevation was on the sentient plane.

"Not sure," Niko said. "If an Elevated person learns, I'm sure they can shield themselves better than most. Plain humans? I don't know that they could do it consciously."

"I do not need another snag in the fabric of my being right now," I growled, burying my face in my hands.

"You're doing better than any empath I've ever heard of," Eli said suddenly.

I jerked my face upright so fast that a zing of pain shot down my neck.

"What did you say?"

Eli's face colored.

"From the stories." Eli cleared her throat awkwardly. She looked at Niko. "You didn't tell her?"

I looked intently at Niko.

In all my spare time, I heard in my head.

My eyes bulged.

"Niko!"

His eyes slid to mine.

"Did you do that on purpose? Don't change the subject!" I said, hitting the carpet in agitation.

"What?" Eli asked.

"I think Evangeline heard me," Niko said.

Eli's face crumpled into a series of confused frowns. Then Niko tapped his temple. His head was cocked slightly to the side.

"Can you not send her back over the edge? Do you know how much sighing I had to sit through before you got here?" Eli replied. "If she talks about another color, I'm going to think she's really cracked wide open."

A warm pool of anger boiled beneath the surface of my mind.

I was so far beyond information overload.

"It is impolite to do that without asking permission," I said pointedly at Niko, my voice loud and pinched. "It's like walking in before knocking."

"She's got rules," Eli said, trying to hold in a giggle. Finally, some of the darker aura layers were broken up with joy. "Maybe I will practice some more."

Glad I could be of help, I growled inside my head.

"That is the extent, that I know of," Niko said, bowing his head in apology. "I didn't mean any offense."

I glared at him, my anger still licking at the corners of my mind. He held my gaze, and I could feel his sincerity, which only made me angrier.

And I could also feel his mind pressing against mine. Without realizing it, I had begun to probe around his mind, trying to figure out what else he wasn't telling me.

"Knocking works both ways," was all he said.

"Sorry," I let out with a sigh. I rubbed my face in agitation. "Can you just be honest with me? I can't handle any more unknowns right now."

"Let's just say that my family is as large and gifted as yours," Niko said. "When this has all been resolved, remind me to tell you more about it. You'll need firsthand sources for your research anyway."

"Ha! Research," I said. My fingers traced the patterned carpet idly. "I just wish I could hide in the library and never come out again."

"Nah," Eli said. "That's not true. You need to go say your goodbyes. You'll hate yourself if you don't."

My fingers stilled. I glanced up, finding a dusty coating of regret around Eli. It was there only briefly, probably as she recalled a memory. It broke apart within seconds, and her multi-faceted colors flared back up again.

I abandoned the hope I would be fully pulled together before heading off to Abuela's wake. Whatever work I had completed would have to suffice. Every new realization was a distraction, and it was silly to drag my feet and go down rabbit holes chasing currently irrelevant information. I was coming back anyway. When I did, you bet I would be grilling everyone until every last secret was squeezed out of them.

"You'll come find me, right?"

I was starting to doubt the speed with which I would return.

"Yeah, I guess," Eli sighed. Niko shot her a look, and she rolled her eyes. "Promise."

I took a deep inhale, and released as much disjointed energy as I could in the exhale.

"Screw it. Let's go."

THIRTY-SIX

Whoever was the travel agent for the Association had learned I was not to be trusted in cars without heavy supervision.

As I filled empty minutes next to Brendan on the way to the airport, I amused myself with the statuesque features of our two "chauffeurs," who filled up the entirety of the front bench of the luxury old model black sedan, and their deep inner lives. Their shoulders almost brushed in the small space, and I wondered what exactly they thought those overdeveloped chest pectorals and biceps would do to protect themselves against the likes of Elevated teenagers. Maybe they had not been fully read into the situation.

"Friends of yours?" I said to Brendan, inclining my head toward the two in the front. At least Blue Eyes had some personality buried behind all that bulk. Nothing interesting came back from my lazy foray into either jughead mind, and nothing good to manipulate either.

Brendan glanced up from his phone, taking a break from typing. I had assumed it was texts based on the short bursts, but the screen held a wall of text in a different format. The question of who he could be so intently emailing at a time like this made my stomach drop. My idea to go along with the plan, trusting that Brendan wouldn't steer me wrong, was beginning to feel like a bigger and bigger mistake the more distance we put between ourselves and the Navratil mansion. I swallowed hard, trying to dampen the bitterness rising from my stomach.

"Mr. Navratil offered to arrange your itinerary once he heard you hadn't been able to pay your respects yet. It's his token of appreciation to your family," Brendan said. The words marched out of his mouth like a computer reading a teleprompter. Most of his energies were still concentrated on the email.

In that moment, I realized I didn't know Brendan as well anymore. The thought slammed me hard in the chest.

I had no idea what he was doing with the Navratils or so closely tied up in the Association. Beyond his visits to me and his talk of "getting well," we had no time to talk about his world and what he was up to. And with our previous arrangement, I still felt uneasy poking around his mind, even for something so mundane as his college major. Or his internship.

A shiver streaked down my spine. I pulled my jacket tightly around me against the cold, even though I knew from the heat blasting in the front of the car that the sensory snap wasn't caused by a poor heating system in the well-maintained car.

Why do you always have to do things your way? I asked myself. *Your intuition warned you this was going to be a bad idea. Yet here we are. Are you trying to prove you can still survive doing things on the highest difficulty setting?*

"Do you think everyone will be there, or have they all left by now?" I asked out loud as I stared at the variety of greys on the bleak Midwestern highway. I had been curious by what Brendan had said earlier. Had they really put everything on hold? For me?

"People have been coming by the house all week, but the family is still there," Brendan said, his fingers stilled over the smudged screen.

I bit the inside of my cheek hard.

Don't overanalyze body posture, I scolded myself. *Brendan is your oldest friend. You asked him a question, and he stopped what he was doing to answer you. Plain and simple. Tons of people can't talk and type at the same time.*

I could feel the stiffness of Brendan's posture. He was in a suit, which seemed out of place with the easygoing personality with which I was accustomed. This was not us hanging out on the weekends or a school break. This was his internship, so it was only natural for him to wear a suit. This was not the time for track pants and henleys.

My fingers found their way to my favorite pressure point at the corner of my eye and the beginning of the bridge of my nose. I let my hair fall over my face to hide how desperately I was jabbing my thumb into the bone. As the anxiety rose in me from the back and forth about exactly how poor of a choice I had just made by trusting a childhood friend and the seesaw of guilt from doubting a close trusted ally, the blur of a migraine crept into the corners of my mind.

I hadn't had a migraine since I'd left the Association's medical facility. With the rollercoaster of medications I'd been on, my body was in a constant state of getting over a migraine or beginning a new one. The mental clarity of the past week hit me, pulling into focus exactly how much and yet how little I had accomplished.

My decisiveness and sporadic actions seemed manic at the Navratil mansion. If I listed it out, I actually had done a lot in such a short time. I imagined it had looked like a wild animal coming to from a harsh sedative. Sure, my processing ability was severely dampened by information overload, and I felt like I was drowning in Elevated riddles, but I was thinking.

A lot.

Looking back on the past few months in the Association's medical prison, other than my infrequent outbursts, the days blurred together. Nothing monumental could distinguish one day from another and another. I had been on pause for months. The transition to double time speed in just catching up to the present of what was going on had been rough.

But I could not go back. Would not.

In an answering call, the rumble strips of the airport parkway assaulted our silent car. The vibrations jarred my elbow from its perch against the door, and I poked myself in the eyeballs.

"Damnit," I muttered, exasperated with myself.

Suddenly, I felt three pairs of eyes on me. I quickly brushed my hand through my cascading hair, schooling my face before revealing it to the car. My mask of innocent nonchalance fooled two of the three. The chauffeurs navigated us to the curb, focused on their immediate task. I could feel Brendan observing me intently.

"What, am I going to get the appropriate language lecture now?" I asked, turning my head enough to glare slightly out of the corners of my eyes to match his stare.

Brendan had chosen to wear his glasses today, which made his ensemble look much more GQ than intern lackey. I could still see his emotions flickering across his hazel eyes, although I blocked my reading enough to remain in the dark about what exactly they were. I knew all the curves of his face from all the hours of staring I had done in middle school. Although Brendan had banned me from his mind, I knew him better than any obsessed fangirl.

Did I not know him well enough to tell if he was about to betray me? My stomach gurgled.

Our gazes locked for an uncomfortably long time. I refused to blink or turn away. In my peripheral senses, I could tell the driver had gotten out of the car to retrieve the luggage from the trunk. He had made it all the way to the curb, back to close the trunk, and waited patiently outside Brendan's door. I continued breathing steadily, waiting.

Brendan didn't look away.

"You know I'm the youngest. I can do this all day," I said, breaking the tense silence after the first blip of agitation rolled off the front seat sentry. Both the statues had been emotionless the whole time. Only now did they have enough of any emotion for it to materialize, which meant the agitation level must be quite high if Rock Number Two had let it slip.

But I didn't break my gaze.

Brendan's eyes pinged back and forth between mine.

"I'm worried about you," Brendan said suddenly.

My eyebrows popped up a half inch before I could stop them. That was not the tactic I had been expecting.

"You always worry about me," I said. Brendan let the next silence press in.

By this point, the outer chauffeur was arguing with an airport attendant about moving the car. Had we been sitting there that long? In a direct conflict, the chauffeur let his feelings be known. His emotions flared out as the two argued outside the car. Behind Brendan, I could see an aurora borealis of anger, and the halo effect distracted me enough to break my intent stare as my eye deadened to assess the argument outside.

Brendan pressed his hand lightly over mine against the leather seat. The warmth, usually a comfort, made my palm sweat instantly. I felt pinned to the seat, and I itched to move my hand.

Guilt lanced through my gut.

My mind raced ahead to all the possible reactions Brendan might have to me removing my hand, and all of them made me sick. No, I would deal with it. He seemed to think it was comforting me, and I would let him have that comfort himself.

I locked back in to Brendan's gaze, trying desperately to ignore the escalated issue on the other side of the heavily tinted window. My skin crawled in agitation.

I didn't want to be stuck inside the car much longer, but I knew once we exited the car, I was one step closer to certain doom. Sure, I didn't know when exactly I'd be whisked away back to the institution, but at this point, I felt it was an inevitability.

Would I even make it on the plane to Chicago?

As stubborn as I was in my ways of doing things, that's the level of determination Brendan had for following through on his convictions. If he gave his word, he would die to keep it. Or at least he would die to keep a promise he thought he had made at some point in the past. Aleks might have underestimated his uncle's latest intern, but I knew what I was dealing with.

Which is why I couldn't blink. The decision had been made for me before I got into the car. I knew it, but it was only now I felt in my bones that there really was no other way. I took a deep breath in through my nose.

"Ready?" I asked.

Brendan's eyes squinted imperceptibly. The question was more for myself, but I felt it only fair to fire a warning shot. I loved Brendan, but if he went against me for my supposed best interests one more time, I was ready to snap.

I couldn't placate him anymore.

I couldn't choose him over my safety. Not when it was clear he thought he was saving someone who only existed in his mind. This Evangeline could no longer be the family martyr.

I said a silent apology to the Brendan I thought I knew. He was still in there somewhere, after all. Just too deep to speak to in such a short amount of time. We had reached an impasse, and I could no longer choose him over me. I let him have one final comfort, one final win.

And then all hell broke loose.

THIRTY-SEVEN

The lightshow of emotion that had haloed Brendan's head moments before was now a full-blown situation. I had been too focused on Brendan to pay attention to the particulars, other than the most obvious one, which was that I should have intervened much sooner.

A flurry of bright hazard work vests fluttered against the lone suit, and the front seat attendant finally abandoned his post babysitting us to go help his friend. Waving arms turned to swinging fists that blurred the reds and blacks of a tumultuous fight.

Brendan was still staring at me, oblivious to the danger outside. I'm sure he hadn't intended to start such an altercation, but the underlying truth was that if we did not exit the car, it was only going to get worse.

I sighed heavily, annoyed I had to lose the staring contest to protect my protector.

Before I could count to three, I was out my door and around the other side of the car. Three airport attendants and one security guard were up against two walls of muscle. The odds were not in their favor, but their righteousness fueled their anger.

The front seat guard noticed me first, and he moved to block me from the inky octopus of anger and imminent assault charges. I caught his eyes behind his sunglasses and entered his mind immediately.

He stepped to the side, allowing me to grab the handle of my waiting rolling bag.

With each footstep toward the fray, I was able to break through into the minds of the angry men, forcing them to lower their arms and step back from one another. I dialed down the anger to mere agitation, not wanting to take away the emotion completely. I would have been even subtler if I'd had the time, but I couldn't risk someone flaring up again and setting the others off. I let the excess emotion eek out into the chill air instead of absorbing it. Definitely did not have time for that drama.

The other suited chauffeur was the last to fall to me, being the only other one with any semblance of mental guarding it turned out. In my mind's eye, I had to pin him down forcefully.

Stand down, I told him, my tone thick with authority.

His shock snapped him out of his rage, and he stepped back enough for me to squeeze through with my bag. I found the supervisor in the group of airport attendants and addressed my audible words to him. Behind the scenes, I was dampening the others' anger and turning up their understanding and forgiveness.

"Thank you for your understanding," I said to the supervisor, his mustache twitching in slight agitation. Good, I didn't want to take it all away. "We didn't mean to cause a disruption. I apologize for any disrespect."

Two of the three attendants' auras flared gold in appreciation. Loyalty to their comrades was the only thing bringing them into this fight, and in the end, they just wanted to be recognized. We had admitted fault, and that was the deepest point of contention they held with us. Even without any extra oomph to my words, just acknowledging others' humanity seemed to go a long way.

It wasn't even that difficult.

Brendan had exited the car sometime during my exchange, his hand gripping the door tightly enough to outline his knuckles through his thin gloves. I glanced back at him. His coloring was not good.

I turned my attention back to the group of workers.

"We'll get out of the way now. Again, I apologize for the disruption."

My hand signaled Brendan to come get his luggage. I smiled brightly at all the workers, sending them another small wave of righteousness to allow them to remain amenable. In their reminiscence of this scene, I wanted them to retain a little indignation to make it seem as normal as possible. It didn't take much. Even in my brief encounter with them, I could tell they were good people. I wanted to leave as little impact of my gift as possible.

A sour taste filled my mouth, and I tried to swallow the rising bile without drawing any attention. I hated myself for manipulating people to this extent, but it was the only course of action that had the safest outcome. A little mental tinkering had been better than a brawl and several hospital beds, right?

I nodded toward the chauffeurs, unsure if they were planning to escort us further or not.

I gripped the handle of my rolling bag tightly, letting all my anxiety focus on that point as I slowly unwound myself from the minds of the men around me. Once I was free of them, I strode confidently toward the automatic doors, not checking for Brendan behind me. As long as he kept his mouth shut, the spell of positive vibes would carry us all through to the security line, at the very least.

Even though I had detached myself from their minds, I could still feel the presences and emotions of the airport attendants and chauffeurs acutely as they dispersed. The aftereffect made me cringe even more.

The reminder was clear: once you intervene, you are responsible for all those you touch.

A slight pressure brushed against my coat at the small of my back, and I turned to find Brendan directing me subtly to the security checkpoint. His face was set, and I wondered if the wrinkle on his brow was from anger or concentration. Mentally, I reached out, only to pull back again as soon as I realized what I was doing.

I tucked my hair behind my ear, letting my fingers trail through the sleek strand all the way to the end.

"Your hair's gotten really long," Brendan said, his eyes purposefully avoiding mine. I felt a wave of déjà vu pour over me. Had it only been a week ago? Two? We had already had this conversation.

"I guess," I said. "I like it long."

"I think we'll have time to get your hair cut before the wake," Brendan said. "I'll look up some places in Chicago for you."

"It's fine," I said, turning to Brendan for my travel documents. As our fingers brushed, I felt a strong wave of fear overtake me. I lost my balance, and Brendan steadied me instinctively. The wave of fear left as quickly as it had come, but my body was no longer responding to my directives to stand tall and confident.

"Are you all right, miss?" the TSA agent asked, his hand stilled over the ID I had handed him at some point in the past few seconds. I didn't remember getting to the front of the line, so I shook my head, trying to clear my thoughts.

"She hasn't eaten much today," Brendan's voice said. "Come on, babe. We'll get you a frappe on the way to the gate."

My eyes kept shifting back and forth, the image of the TSA agent's frown of worry flickering in and out like I was battling shoddy reception. I smiled weakly at him. I needed to keep it together.

"Sorry," I said, my voice making it out at a whisper. "I'm fine."

The agent continued to frown, initialing my ticket hesitantly. I flashed another brief close-lipped smile at him. His eyes glanced behind me at the growing line, duty forcing him to dismiss me on my word.

"Take care of yourself," he said. "Safe travels."

"Thanks," I heard Brendan respond. His firm hand rematerialized at the small of my back, propelling me forward.

In a blink, we were past security. I tucked another piece of hair behind my ear.

How did we get here?

It was like someone had fast-forwarded me through the security line. The lack of memory set off alarm bells in my mind.

I was not okay with this.

This did not feel right.

I was left in the middle of the bustling terminal hallway. My ticket was nowhere to be found, meaning Brendan had likely taken it back once the TSA agent had signed it. I didn't know which flight or which gate, so I just stood in the middle of the hallway, allowing the sea of people to flow around me.

My eyes caught Brendan as he walked out of a newsstand shop with a small bag of items. Everything I was seeing seemed slightly blurred around the edges, more so than usual. Even with people's auras, I could still see where their physical bodies ended. At the moment, the halo effect was too strong, and the sharp lines of reality were lost in the flow of colorful energy.

I could really use a pair of magical Elevated sunglasses right now. Dampen the lights and the auras. A dark chuckle echoed in my mind. Good one.

Brendan was in front of me, and I felt the cold of a chilled water bottle in my hand.

"You must have a wicked migraine right now," he said. "I got some ibuprofen for you. Here."

Diligently, I held out my hand, letting the small blue orbs rest there patiently as Brendan cracked open the bottle of water for me. I took the pills, knowing they wouldn't do much to stave off the already massive migraine crowding out my thoughts. Based on what they had given me at the Association's facility, I would need elephant tranquilizers to get through my level of brain trauma.

I didn't have the luxury of sleeping for two days to recover. And there was the small matter of getting on the plane. The thoughts snapped smartly against my mind like a taut rubber band.

This was really not good.

Brendan led me to a seat, and I crumpled against the awkward dimensions of the faux leather modular form. Colors and lights were assaulting me from every angle. Any armor I had installed for myself at the Navratil mansion had been eaten away by the silent car ride and the curbside altercation. Between limiting my powers too strictly and overreaching, whatever balance I had been able to strike was disrupted. I was stumbling through this blindly. I couldn't even tell what should work to bring me back into equilibrium, but I was willing to pay a heavy price to find that answer.

Isn't that why I had agreed to come?

"Evangeline," a voice whispered. I tried to backpedal from the dark interior path I was spiraling down.

I hated feeling this weak. The days with Aleks had been an alluring dream. They had been too safe. The moment I was in any stress, I flared out like a supernova. Two hours outside that safe zone and I was practically catatonic.

Anger surged within me. I had to handle this. I had no other choice.

Hey, I scolded myself. *You are stronger than this. You don't know all the answers…yet. Breathe. Build back the walls. Protect yourself at all costs.*

"Evangeline?"

Slowly, I opened the hall of mental doors in my mind, shoving emotions and visuals and sounds willy-nilly behind each door before it filled up. I worked steadily to close as many doors as I could to redistribute all the everything that was pressing against me from all sides. As I focused internally, my muscles relaxed, and I slumped deeper into the chair.

My fingers slipped against the seat of the chair. Slowly, I traced the double diamond-shaped symbol of the Elevated that Birdie had drawn for me only a few days before. What had we talked about?

Balance.

Balance.

Balance.

My eyes flew open in clarity.

Brendan's face hung within inches of mine. I could see the little flecks of amber in his hazel eyes, even with the slight glare from his glasses from the over-bright florescent lights of the concourse.

My field of vision had stabilized. Along with the normal outline of people, I could see their auras rippling as they moved through physical and emotional space, but they were clear and contained. There was distinct separation between people and energies and most importantly, myself. I leaned back, suddenly overwhelmed with exactly how close my face was to Brendan's.

His hand reached out and cradled my face. I froze.

I was just far enough away from Brendan to see his aura. Under normal circumstances, I took extra care to block him. A mental blanket was always covering his aura and dampening his emotional flares.

But I had not had the presence of mind to do it this time.

Brendan's face creased in desperation as he came to the same realization as I had.

I could see Brendan's aura.

And it had a white core…when it hadn't been white before.

"Evangeline, I can explain," Brendan said, his hand still lightly touching my face.

Rage erupted from me, intermingled with fear and pain. I tried to push away from Brendan, needing as much physical space as I could to fully unpack what I had only just realized. My body had been nagging at me all along. Even Aleks had said his uncle took on an Elevated intern. Brendan appeared, and I hadn't made the connection, assuming just like Aleks that his family connection might have been enough.

My childhood crush, my brother's best friend, the person I had trusted more than my own family was tainted. He was part of the monstrous organization killing innocent people---children---and lining up to reap the rewards. My chest felt hollowed out. Tears leaked from the corners of my eyes.

As I braced my hands on his chest to get a good push off and get as far away from him as possible, Brendan's fingers tightened around the base of my neck, halting my forward progress.

I felt a slight pinch at my neck.

Everything went black.

THIRTY-EIGHT

The jerk of wheels on uneven ground threw my mind back into consciousness. I had felt like I was falling in a dream, but found my limbs braced against the cold steel of a wheelchair armrest. The wheelchair navigator mumbled an apology, but I could tell it was in response to a reprimanding glare and not directed at me at all. I stilled my fingertips, careful not to grip the chair or draw any attention to the fact that I was awake.

After several months in the institution, I was excellent at playing possum.

"We just landed," Brendan's voice said. His tone sounded strangled to my ears. He was clearly not in control, but was feigning that everything was well in hand. Whoever was on the other end of the line hadn't called him on his bluff. Yet.

The whirring of wheels against carpet bounced softly in the backs of my ears. Another jerk, and the soft purr of the wheels turned sticky as the rubber battled against the heavily waxed laminate of the main concourse hall. The overall din of the crowded concourse faded into the background as I focused more intently on Brendan's phone conversation.

A flare of white assaulted my mind's eye as I remembered what I had found out right before going under.

Somehow, Brendan had developed an Elevation.

I bit the inside of my cheek hard. Focus. I had to remain under control. The rage tickling the corners of my mind was tamped down. Now was not the time to fly off the handle. But, boy, was I ready to tap into that deep well at any moment.

Thinking back, I had no idea when Brendan had changed. I'd been so focused on not seeing him that I had no gauge to figure out when exactly he had been gifted with abilities. Certainly not when Tomas was alive. Not that that narrowed the window by very much.

Tomas had only been gone two years.

"Of course," Brendan said into the phone.

I quietly seethed about what I was going to do next. I needed to confront Brendan. Not only that, but I needed to do it before anyone else joined the next leg of our travel party. I was certain the person on the other end of the phone had arranged an escort similar to what we'd had in Minneapolis. Or worse—this time they could be Elevated.

Like Brendan.

I just wanted to scream. Of all the people to keep something from me. Of all the lies to keep hidden. I didn't know if I could ever forgive Brendan. The betrayal ran too deep.

I argued with myself. What I wanted to do was eavesdrop mentally on the phone conversation. What better way to hear the other side than to invade the mind of the person hearing it? But the method grated at my sense of loyalty and ethics. Just because Brendan had hurt me didn't give me the right to invade his privacy. My word was still worth something. The righteousness felt hollow though.

"That wasn't the arrangement," Brendan said crisply over the line.

That's it, I thought to myself. Personal safety clause enacted. I had to know what was going on.

Brendan's agitation left cracks in his mental barriers. I had never tried to get around them before, but I felt like I had actually done Brendan a great disservice. His barriers sucked. He was so easy to crack, anyone else with half a spoonful of charisma could have swayed him. If I were a kinder, more understanding friend, I would help him seal up the cracks.

But at that moment I was not very understanding.

I wove into the background of Brendan's consciousness. No thoughts hiccupped. No gut feelings set him on alert. I was just a fly on the wall of his mind. A very, very curious fly.

"Wait for assistance at the house," the voice said over the line. "Another escalation is being resolved, so you're on standby until further notice."

"How long?" Brendan asked, his throat closing against the high levels of anxiety his body was battling. I could hear his mind telling his body to calm down, but the directive was too weak, and his body had other ideas.

"Could be hours. Could be a few days," the voice said. "Is there a problem?"

"She's a lot stronger than she was two weeks ago," Brendan said. His eyes glanced at my limp frame in the wheelchair. A lance of profound sadness stabbed Brendan at his core. His mind spent a few too many seconds lingering on the pain of it. "I'm not sure keeping her sedated will work for long."

"I thought you said you could handle her?"

"I can," Brendan said, clearing his throat. "I'm just saying I'll need to know if it'll be longer than a day or two."

"You'll be kept up to date," the voice said. It paused. "Did something happen?"

"Nothing newsworthy." Brendan hesitated. "There was an altercation in Minneapolis, but she diffused it before anyone took notice. She had a break shortly after. Energy drain, I figure."

"Keep her calm and slightly sleepy," the voice directed. "I'll let the director know we need to bump up the priority level. If she's smart enough to intervene and leave no trace of her influence, the director's going to want to hear a full report on it."

"Already typed up and submitted," Brendan said, a sigh escaping him. "I'll text in updates in real time."

"Noted," the voice said. "And Brendan."

"What?"

"Keep your barriers up at all times. I don't have to tell you what a dangerous combination that girl is. Double Elevated is no joke, especially on the Sentient plane."

"She won't hurt me," Brendan said. Doubt pinged back to me internally, and I could tell Brendan was still worrying about what had been revealed earlier. "You know she doesn't read me."

"Until she does," the voice said, its tone argumentative. "Stop looking deeply into her doe eyes before she kills you."

"Is that all?" Brendan said, a wave of anger and defensiveness building in his mind. "We've got to meet the driver."

"Check in is every two hours. Don't be late." The line disconnected, and I could feel relief flood Brendan's mind.

Being on the inside was much more intense than I had predicted. My inner monologue had been silenced, although I had plenty to say about this exchange. I slowly extracted myself from the tangle of emotions knotting themselves in Brendan's mind. I had to get out before he realized I had let myself in.

My guilt was waiting for me in the peace of my own mind. Brendan had so much faith that I would stand by my word and never overanalyze him. Even though he felt worried I might not react well to his being Elevated, the undercurrent was firm. As much as he was warned about me, he thought he knew me better.

I was torn.

Part of me really chafed at his certainty of knowing me. Sure, we had grown up together, and to some extent, he did know parts of me more than others. But did he know me well enough to anticipate my mindset? My moods? Clearly not if he thought I would never break my word no matter what. I was still human. The Evangeline in his mind was a little too pure, a little too angelic. I couldn't resolve his picture of me against my true self. The comparison made me extremely uncomfortable.

Then again, I could feel how devoted he was to me. I knew he looked out for me, but I had assumed it was some misplaced sense of duty. As if he felt he had to take Tomas's place. But the level of despair that had assaulted Brendan from seeing my limp frame...

My stomach dropped.

After pining for Brendan since the age of seven, I could not believe my intuition. Around the time of Tomas's mysterious death, I had put aside my love for Brendan and tried desperately to move on. Nothing was worse for an Empath than enduring a loved one's funeral. I could tell everyone saw me through the lens of the little sister left behind. At the time, I couldn't imagine Brendan ever coming to love me just for myself. Even the dubious future possibility had been clouded by his best friend's death.

Two years later, here we were.

Somehow being on this side of the unrequited love made me even more uncomfortable. I wondered if I could scrub my own memories. I'd heard horror stories of Commanders making people forget huge chunks of time. Were the stories myths? Or was there some element of truth to it?

Clearly Eli was not the only one who could have benefited from more Birdie story time.

"Did you need assistance to your car?" the wheelchair attendant asked.

Both Brendan and I were snapped from our respective internal reverie.

"No, thank you," Brendan said. "I'll be able to get her into the car myself. Thank you for your help."

I heard the crinkle of cash exchanging hands and then felt a warm presence behind me. Fingers slid through my hair, and I tried not to tense up my shoulders. Now did not feel like a good time to pop awake. I had to bear everything until the right time.

Slowly, Brendan gathered my hair together, twisting it into a loose bun before tucking it into an oversized beanie. He carefully adjusted the band of the hat around my face, hiding my ears from view. Next, he wrapped a long knitted scarf loosely around my neck, discretely hiding the bottom half of my face. My skin tingled as he prepared me for the biting winter air. I felt like a doll being used for dress up. Even though I knew he was doing it for my benefit, the agitation remained.

Finally, Brendan pushed the wheelchair through the automatic doors to the curb.

"Bags are right inside," he directed to the driver.

Then I was in his arms. His gloved hand secured my face against the lapel of his jacket, making sure it leaned there instead of rolling out and straining my neck. Or would have, if I hadn't had the wherewithal to brace it imperceptibly.

The smell of Brendan's aftershave overwhelmed me. This time, instead of comforting me as it had in the past, especially on his occasional visits to the institution, all I could think about was Aleks. About how I wished he were here instead of Brendan.

Immediately, I felt guilty. Brendan placed me gently in the back of another unmarked luxury sedan. He adjusted my legs discretely, making sure my posture was as natural and comfortable as possible. A wave of love rolled off him, and I lost it.

A tear rolled down my cheek just as a gust of wind rocked the underground covered lanes.

Brendan wiped it away, sighing into the wind. He shut the door softly, walking to the other side to get in.

I didn't know where we were heading next, but I didn't care. I needed some time to process Brendan's feelings—and my own. The drive would never be long enough.

THIRTY-NINE

I must have fallen asleep on the ride. The warmth of the over-heated car and the slow stop and start of rush hour traffic had caught me off guard, and I surrendered to my possum play a little too easily. My body stiffened as soon as I felt a light touch. I peeked through the millimeter slits between my eyelids. I had to regain my bearings. Fast.

Brendan cradled me in his arms again, closing the short distance between curb and aging three-flat in several confident strides. I could see the surrounding brick buildings standing sentry with their cracking concrete stoops. What little grass that could be seen through the chunks of leftover snow and ice was mottled with dead leaves and bare patches. Having only been to Chicago in the summers, the street felt subdued in contrast to the loud vibrant memories of block parties and family reunions.

A murmur of voices leaked through the solid wooden front door. A gust of warm spiced air wrapped me in a wave of memory and homesickness before Brendan could even step across the threshold.

"Leave her in the downstairs bedroom. We'll keep an eye on her until she wakes up," a smooth voice said. The low male timbre tickled my memory, but I was still fighting the pull of sleep. The name sat stubbornly on the tip of my tongue. Blurs of color flickered through my eyelids as my barriers sagged along with my energy. The most prominent color told me my host was also of the Elevated variety, and my stomach rolled in apprehension. I really hoped this person was on my side after all.

Abuela's face popped into my head. Even seeing her in memory form calmed my anxiety.

A tear slipped from the corner of my eye. This might have been Abuela's house before, but it didn't hold much of her warmth. For once, I wished I could feel inanimate objects like Ms. Xavier. A soul's mark on an object seemed more stable than the fleeting energies of consciousness. I laughed at myself and my Elevated envy. Of course I would want almost the complete opposite of my power.

"It's colder than I remembered," Brendan said, his tone colored with mild embarrassment. I felt his gloved hand wipe at the tear stains on my cheeks. "This wind, huh?"

The other man chuckled.

"The space heaters may seem old and noisy, but they work wonders. Once you settle Evangeline in, come into the kitchen. We'll get some coffee for you while we wait for her to wake up."

My eyes were able to track him from his aura color blur, which went all the way down to his white core, the grey disrupting the normal ebb and flows like a layer of dirty snow.

Grief.

The answer smacked me upside the head.

Some of the kids at school had had a similar grey cloud. The thicker the cloud, the more I was convinced they had been suffering from depression. The whole campus had caught the grey sludge after the tragic accident that had almost killed Colm. It had seemed insensitive to pry too deeply at the time, although I realized I'd missed a great opportunity. If no one was going to teach me, I had to do better about learning on the fly.

Like today.

Brendan's fingers lingered on my hair after he settled me on the bed. I could feel him taking off my boots and repositioning my legs back onto the bed. A thick blanket that smelled of Abuela was laid over me, and I began to feel overwhelmed. The weight of the cable knit afghan against my several layers of sweater made it hard for me to breathe. Between the persistent ebb of the sedative pulling at my consciousness, the smell of home, and the too many layers of restrictive comfort, my mind was pushing a mental break.

"Brendan!" a voice called brightly from across the apartment. Brendan's hands stilled before pulling away. I heard the soft click of the door shut behind him, and I let out a ragged sob.

The soft tears that had begun at the first smell of the old house were now a steady stream of anxiety and frustration. My mind was spinning further and further askew, and I didn't know how I was going to right myself. My throat was constricting painfully. I couldn't swallow the tears that were escaping from every possible pore, and as I started having trouble breathing, I panicked more.

The soft swish of the wooden door against the carpet alerted me to someone entering the room. I tried to pull myself back inside, back into my shell, hidden.

Another painful sob escaped, and my heart sank at the noise. No use in hiding now. I was clearly some form of awake.

I awaited the pinch of another needle. Brendan had been instructed to keep me sedated, and I knew I was in no state to fight him off. I moaned, torn at the agony of being awake enough to feel everything, but not awake enough to put it away in the farthest corners of my mind.

The air next to the bed filled with a presence, but the tears blurred my already limited sight. The colors bent together, and I wasn't sure what I was supposed to be reading. I desperately hoped they were a friendly instead of a potential adversary.

"Evangeline," the low voice said. A warm hand rested on top of mine, and I instantly felt lighter. The emotional tension in the room popped, like my ears on the airplane. The fog from my partial sedation broke enough for my mind to zip through the past few hours, collecting all the important information and linking it together neatly in an outline for me.

"Tio," I choked out, my throat still swollen with tears.

With my free hand, I wrestled my upper body free from the constrictive blanket. My fingers made quick work of brushing away the trail of tears that had left a spider web on my cheeks. I glanced over and found the white of Tio's aura flaring against the damp grey of grief.

"Welcome home," Tio Manuel said. The crow's feet at his eyes danced as his cheeks rose in a toothless smile. If eyes could hug, I would be wrapped up in the strongest embrace right now.

I let out a huge sigh. The weight from only a moment earlier was almost completely gone. If anything, I felt a little too light. My mind whirred in a million directions. Fight or flight had kicked in, and I wasn't sure which one I was leaning toward.

"What's happening?" I asked aloud. The warmth surged around my left hand where Tio's hand still covered mine. My eyes bounced back and forth between my hand, completely encased in a bright white aura, and Tio's chest, where I could read the source of his emotional health.

"Almost done. Just hold still," Tio Manuel said softly. The grey around him thickened a bit, and I could see his overall health take a slight hit. It was like he had gone from completely healthy to fluish in a matter of minutes. Again, the juxtaposition caught me off guard. When I had seen Abuela from my sensory tank exercise, she had a similar chronic static around her energy. Anyone battling long-term health issues had weird energy breaks, but other than Abuela, this was the first time I had experienced it in person, or at least in real time.

"Tio," I pressed.

He squeezed my hand, and I saw the white flare up before being absorbed back into our respective Elevated auras. Flares of color licked at the outer edges of each of our forms again. I looked up, and Tio's smile was even fainter than before. He looked like he needed a nap.

"Please tell me what's going on in this family. I really can't handle any more surprises."

"Yes, it is past time you heard everything," Tio Manuel said, a sigh escaping him, his hand idly patting mine. "But right now, it's not important."

"Not important?" I shrieked, a zip of anger flaring out around me and causing Tio to flinch. I slapped my hand over my mouth, aware I was still supposed to be asleep. My eyes darted toward the door, feeling past it to the other energies in the house. Brendan was with someone in the kitchen, likely Tia or one of my many cousins. They were talking loudly enough they had not heard my outburst. I bit hard on my lower lip.

How could I be so sloppy?

Tio raised an eyebrow, but didn't say anything. I let out a deep breath. My mind was scrambled again, and I took several cleansing breaths.

"Okay," I said, dropping my voice. "Then can you tell me what is important right now?"

"Getting you out of here before anyone notices you even came," Tio said, his small smile twisting slightly in sadness. "Ah, but you're so grown. I wish I didn't have to send you away so soon."

"Why can't I stay? What about Abuela's wake?"

Tio shook his head.

"The services have been done for a week. The only people about to gather at this house is the team of bodyguards here to escort you back to an Association controlled facility. Only me and your tia even knew you weren't at school. My sister made it clear that our intervention wasn't necessary," Tio said. At the slight mention of my mother, I felt my stomach convulse. I couldn't breathe.

"Mama told me you visited," Tio continued. "I was so proud of you. She wasn't all there in the end, but that day, she was like her old self. You gave her peace in the end. And I gave her my promise that I would take care of you."

"I don't understand," I said. I felt numb. Besides the prickling of my skin, all my other senses had shut down. My mind scrambled to make sense of what I was hearing. "My mom said you weren't Elevated. She said it was just my dad. She said you wouldn't understand."

"One of our many regrets over the years." Tio sighed. "The distance between you and your brother and the rest of the family…"

Tio cleared his throat.

"I wonder how much of this is our fault. For not standing up for you kids," he said. His eyes wandered off toward the wall, and I wondered what he could be remembering.

Part of me thought it would be easy to find out. His energy was shaken from whatever he had done to wake me up. The cracks were enough that I could weave myself in before he even thought twice.

I shook my head hard. Absolutely not. *Not okay*, I told myself. These are not okay thoughts to have. Just because it's easy doesn't make it right. He's your uncle. He's allowed his privacy and his memories.

I squeezed his hand. He squeezed right back, his eyes sliding back into focus.

"Ah, I'm wasting time," Tio said. "Forgive me."

"So what's going to happen now? Am I going back to the lab in New York?" I asked, fear bleeding into my tone. "Or Montana?"

At least we would be closer to Noah, a voice said in my mind.

The cold shiver that shot down my spine rallied against that fleeting silver lining.

"Do you want to go back?" Tio asked. Curiosity colored his weak aura, and I couldn't help but smile.

"Do you think I'm that crazy?" I asked. "I'm a bit tired of learning the hard way."

"I wasn't sure if you had a plan," Tio said. "Or some need to prove yourself. You wouldn't be the first de los Santos to fight their way out of enemy territory just for fun."

"You owe me so many stories," I said, wagging my finger in Tio's face. "I'm not going to take no for an answer."

Tio chuckled.

"Of course," he said. "So now we agree that your place is not in New York. Or Montana." He paused. "Oh, I'm too old for all this nonsense," he muttered to himself. He shook his head, leaning down from his chair to reach under the bed.

In his hands sat a brown paper wrapped box. The stamps looked recent, and domestic, but the style seemed out of place. Tio's large hands wrapped around the box effortlessly, but it took both of mine to take it from him.

The handwriting was jagged cursive. Beautiful, slightly illegible, and very memorable.

"Is this from…"

"Jasleen." Tio sighed. "Fascinating woman. I play it safe and do what she says without many questions, so I can't help you much. Didn't dare ask."

My fingers hovered over the crisp paper. The date on the package was from six months ago.

"That's not scary intimidating at all," I said out loud.

Another rumbling chuckle emanated from Tio's chest.

"Whenever you find the Seer in your generation, be sure to play nice," Tio warned.

Mags' angry face popped into my mind.

"Whoopsies," I said. "Already messed that one up." Tio harrumphed to himself, but I could see the laughter dancing in his eyes. He was just too tired to let it escape again.

"Jasleen mentioned you would need this. I'm sorry I'm the one to have to give this to you instead of your abuela. She was looking forward to your visit ever since we got it last fall."

My fingers traced the outer dimensions of the package.

"Jasleen didn't say anything about this when she met me," I muttered darkly. Even amongst allies there seemed to be many, many secrets. "Heads up would have been nice."

"The only instruction she gave us with this is that you would need this if you went into hiding. That you would be able to hide in plain sight." Tio shrugged. "She seems to know the players on all sides, and that you might know what that means. I know you're frustrated that you don't know as much as you feel you should about the Elevated, but I think it's been a blessing for you up until now. Between your parents' divorce and the accident and losing your brother, you didn't need to be worrying about this, too."

I looked up from my obsessive stroking of the mystery package to see the sincerity in Tio's words. His aura flickered with caring, protection, and another wave of grief and loss.

"Maybe let me decide from now on," I said. A tendril of anger licked at the corner of my mind, but I stomped it out immediately. Throwing a tantrum right then was just plain dumb. Nothing could change what had led up to all this, or at least nothing someone with my Elevation could do. I was just cranky and in dire need of an Elevated-free vacation.

"Fair enough."

A zing of fear flared out from the kitchen. My attention snapped to the wall between me and the wave of anxiety.

"Evangeline?"

"Where's my phone, Tio? I need it."

"I don't know…"

My neck snapped over to lock eyes with Tio.

"Do you want to do this with or without the cavalry? Because I'm pretty sure I'd prefer the cavalry," I said, throwing my mental net wide to catch all the consciousnesses in the nearest three city blocks.

I hissed. This was not good.

"Tio!"

"I heard you," the old man grumbled, lumbering up from his perch on the uncomfortable sewing chair. His large hands pawed through the bags by the door just as the air from the front door opening rattled the old door in its frame.

Tio paused.

"Tio!" I growled through my gritted teeth. He waved a hand at me, continuing to search the outer pockets of the carry-on bags with his other hand.

Then, he turned, tossing the phone toward me on the bed.

"Stay here. Lock the door," Tio said, his hand on the doorknob. "Don't come out for any reason, do you hear me?"

"Why are you saying it like that?" I said, my voice a tight stage whisper.

"Because you are a de los Santos, and that means you do stupid things for the ones you love," Tio Manuel said. "But you need to get out of here. Count of three. Remember we love you, mija."

Tio signaled the countdown, opening the door and strolling out as if he had just put a child to bed, shutting the door softly behind him.

Apparently, a flare for the dramatic also lived strong in the de los Santos line. My cheek pulled at an almost smile. Before it could bloom fully, I was across the room, my hand twisting the lock home just as a scream ripped through the building.

My stomach dropped.

I pressed my phone hard against my cheek, and I counted the infernal rings as the phone dialed out.

The phone clicked.

"About damned time."

FORTY

"Missed you, too," I hissed into the phone. "Now is not exactly the time, Eli."

"I was about to lose the bet. You called right before the end of my time window," she replied, a little petulantly. "I almost had to wash Niko's delicates for a month. Do you know what that would do to me?"

"Eli!" I hissed into the phone.

"Yeah, yeah, SOS," Eli replied. "What level of extraction are we talking?"

"Depends on if you want me to bring the party to you," I said, counting the consciousnesses again within the neighborhood. "There was nobody until there was everybody."

"Fun times," Eli said. "So coming in guns a-blazing then?"

Another scream launched through the walls from the kitchen.

"What the hell was that?" Eli said, all snark gone from her tone.

"Did you think I just called for a girl chat?" I growled. My teeth were clenched so tightly I was beginning to give myself a headache.

"What happened to Sir Lancelot? Is he the one screaming?"

"I don't know because I was told to stay out of the way and not get involved," I said, my forehead braced against the cool frame of the old carved door. "And I can tell you right now, I am about to go rogue."

"Stop that," Eli said, the phone line rustling. "Describe to me in detail what's going on."

"I hate you," I said, the thought making bile tickle my throat. I was keeping a big wall between me and the kitchen goings on, and I knew the second I dropped that barrier I would absolutely lose any resolve I had to stay out of it.

"Okay, and?" Eli said. "Peel back layer by layer. Not the hatred. I don't need a blow by blow of that. I get the gist."

I let out a massive sigh.

"Who and how many?" Eli said. The phone muffled again, and I could hear her shouting orders. Only the tone made it through the phone, and I wondered what was happening on that end of the line. "Hello? Earth to the Empath!"

"Yeah, yeah," I shot back. "Give me a second."

In my mind's eye, the loose map of people in the neighborhood flared brightly. Starting from the outside, I discarded people on the periphery who were clearly not involved. The couple arguing and the lone man doing laundry two blocks over were weeded out, which allowed me to focus on the closer consciousnesses in greater detail.

"Tio, Tia, Brendan."

"Friendlies?"

"Mmmmmmmm," I said. "Yes, yes, maybe…not."

"What an asshat," Eli said.

"Not now, Eli."

"But am I wrong?"

I sighed. Tia was in a lot of distress. She had been the one screaming. Her aura was pulsing with fear and sadness and anxiety, but I didn't see her body react in physical pain. Tio stood in the doorway, and it looked like he was being restrained by two normal guards. No Elevated. Plenty of anger, which was warranted. From my perspective, I couldn't quite tell what was happening.

"A dozen trained suits on the first floor," I counted aloud to

Eli. "Two per floor doing sweeps, probably for me. The rest are in the kitchen with—"

"The hostages," Eli finished for me.

I swallowed hard against the lump in my throat.

"Breathe," Eli said, her voice full of calm and strength. "What else do you see?"

"Brendan…"

"Sir Assclown."

"…is also in the kitchen," I said, my tone going up in a question. "He seems afraid, too, even though no one is bothering him."

"Maybe Sir Assclown has a conscience and is not okay witnessing the torture of loved ones," Eli spat at me.

"I'm not calling him Sir Assclown," I muttered, losing myself in my web of consciousnesses again. "And I don't know if Tia is being tortured or not."

"Fine, we can pretend she likes to scream in agony for fun," Eli shot back at me. She sounded out of breath. "Where are they coming from? Do you see any more than the twenty or so you already tagged?"

"They keep flickering in," I muttered into the phone. Every time I went to count them, another one or two seemed to pop in from the periphery.

"That is not…good," Eli said, her voice tense. "How well can you read objects?"

"Objects?"

"Yeah, like can you tell if a person is traveling by bike versus motorcycle versus car, for example?" Eli said.

"Depends on if they're thinking about it. Or sometimes their body position…"

My mind went off on that thought, trying to remember exactly how I distinguished them, if I did at all.

"Can you tell me if there are people outside waiting in cars?"

"Let me—"

"Damn it, Niko! I'm going to put a tracker on you that rips you through time and space. Did you crawl here?" Eli bellowed into the phone.

I flinched, pulling the sweaty screen from my cheek.

"It's like I sent smoke signals," Eli muttered to herself in exasperation.

"Um, I can't tell if there are cars…where did they come from?" I squeaked, suddenly accosted by two people on the other side of the door.

I bounded toward the bed and launched myself onto the pile of afghans and decorative throw pillows. The corner of Jasleen's box stabbed me in my ribcage, and I buried my face into the knitted blankets to stifle my pained groan.

My phone squawked from underneath me. I palmed it clumsily back to my ear.

"Evangeline!" Eli was yelling at half-second intervals.

"Shhhhh," I hissed into the phone. "I now have a team of guards outside my room. They don't know I'm awake."

"Niko is coming. Can you distract them to cover the pop?"

"What?" I hissed. "Don't you think that's—"

Another scream rattled through the wall. All the color drained from my face right as Niko appeared in front of me.

"That's so messed up," I said into the air.

"Nice to see you, too," Niko said, his grim determination clouding the potential and familiar snark of his comment.

"We can't leave them here," I said, my eyes already pleading with him. "Niko, I can't leave without them."

"I'll come back for them," Niko said simply. "I have to save you first."

"Just shut up and listen," Eli said from over the phone. "I know you're not a fan, but you're very important. Without you, there is absolutely no hope for the rest of us, your aunt and uncle included."

My eyes darted to the door handle that was clattering violently against the lock.

"I think they know I'm awake now," I said to Eli. "And I've got six visitors about to make it a party in my room."

"You get out of there right now," Eli said. "Don't you dare get Niko killed. I won't ever forgive you."

I locked eyes with Niko.

"I'll have to live with that," I said simply, my thumb savagely tapping the screen to end the call.

Niko's eyebrow rose.

"If I promise to cooperate in fifteen minutes, would you trust me?"

"This does not sound good," Niko replied. "I'll give you five."

FORTY-ONE

The problem with going up against professionally trained extraction experts is that they got the blueprints ahead of time.

I was not so lucky.

It had been years since I could recall toddling through the hallways of the divided building. Luckily, the building had been filled with family for decades, so the doors remained unlocked between apartments, and coming and going was not seen as an intrusion of privacy. Each floor was the same as the one before it, so the only real variable now was furniture. And people. People who may not be involved and therefore should be avoided at all costs.

As I rested my hand against the smooth wooden doorframe and braced myself for a surprise attack, I took a moment to scan the building.

Tia, Tio, and Brendan were being "chaperoned" in the kitchen, painted into the breakfast nook and frozen with fear against a wall of clone-like security detail. While Tia remained seated, Brendan seemed to be standing near Tio, who looked to be pinned up against a wall. The second floor was nearly empty, save for a cat lounging in the front window. A pain jabbed at my stomach as I remembered Ig at Windemere. He would most certainly have inserted himself by now. Or flagged the cavalry. Clearly, we weren't getting any additional help today.

I watched as a few invaders peeled off, jogged up the stairs, and cleared the remaining apartments. They were already marked un-friendly though, so I ignored them and continued on. Third floor was empty, and I took a deep breath. During my childhood, Abuela had insisted on staying on the top floor. The stairs kept her moving, she had said. In the end, I doubt she had enough energy to do that, and Tio had likely moved her downstairs. Another lancet of pain streaked through my gut, and I took in a sharp breath.

"What?" Niko murmured behind me. "Too many?"

I took a measured breath in, and a silent exhale out through my mouth.

"It's fine. Just us," I said with a nod. "Round everyone up and get them back in this room. They'll think we're trapped, but you can safely transport us out."

Niko nodded, then froze. I looked back at him.

"Do you have a human capacity for ride alongs?" I asked, picking up the slight ping of worry he had let escape through his barricaded mind.

Niko shrugged.

"Oh, good. Good to know," I muttered darkly to myself. "Not like my entire plan hinges on that assumption. It's fine."

"Only one way to find out," Niko said. "Also, you underestimate my speed. I can flicker back and take multiple trips if it's too much."

"Pinky promise," I said, the doubt weighing down the question mark in my tone.

"I will make sure everyone is safe," Niko replied with a solemn nod. I blew out another deep breath through my mouth, and tapped the doorframe impatiently, my other hand on the doorknob.

"Final note," I said, fear beginning to creep in up my spine. "We are entering a no judgment zone for Elevations, okay? Anything that needs to be done will not be held against us later, kapeesh?"

"You'll do fine," Niko said, reaching out and squeezing my shoulder. "Trust your gut."

"That is a binding yes," I said, the tension leaking slightly from the squeeze of solidarity.

The door banged against the frame as my honor guard tried to break through the deadbolt. They must have heard our voices, as much as we had tried to keep them low. I set the wrapped box from Jasleen on top of the dresser against the wall. It looked inconspicuous near the door, so if my plan went to hell, I could grab it quickly on my way back. I patted it twice, trying to reassure it I would be back for it.

I counted to five on my fingers as I held Niko's gaze.

I better live to tell my grandchildren about this, Niko warned in my mind.

I nodded once.

You need more hobbies.

The door banged again, and this time, I was ready. I flipped the old lock open, pulling the door open slightly after the latest push. The crew outside my door were unprepared and already destabilized from their last battering ram attempt. As I stepped out, I grabbed the weighted ram from the black clad assailant, and entered their mind when it opened up with a ping of surprise. I asked them politely to step aside in my mind, and they bustled against their comrades on their way towards the front entry hall. We were in the front bedroom, so the small space of wall between me and the front door held a bench for shoes and hooks for coats. I directed the battering ram operator to sit nicely on the bench, and they complied.

While this was happening, I registered surprise on the other three comrade's auras. In part from me, and in part from Niko entering the doorframe. They were clearly not expecting him. As quickly as I moved on the first assailant, I pulled the other three into line quickly, moving them to the side and having them take a seat. The ram thunked heavily on the ground as I briefly forgot about it, letting one side pitch down out of my grasp. The noise did not register on the placid faces of the team I had subdued.

Niko tapped my shoulder, grabbing my line of site and

pointing upwards. I gave him a nod, and he crept silently through the front door and around to the staircase to eliminate the other mobile threats. I turned my attention back to the seated team, feeling a flicker of fear as they realized they couldn't move against me. Their brains were being overridden by me.

"Everyone take a deep breath," I said softly, not wanting to alert the remaining infiltrators down the hall that I was outside of my room yet. The team complied. I sent a small wave of assurance to them, keeping them calm. "Thank you for cooperating. Please stay seated for the time being. If at any point I feel you may be in danger, I will release you so you can protect yourselves, understood? I just need you to stay out of the way for now."

The fear from earlier had turned to unease and confusion, but I could live with that. I needed to move fast. As much as I scolded Niko for not knowing his limits, I too was unsure how long I could hold a variety of people in different states while still keeping myself conscious.

As Niko had said, only one way to find out.

Leaving my peaceful charges on the front bench, I tip-toed down the hall, hoping against hope I hadn't forgotten where the creaky boards were in the hardwood flooring. I passed the open living area. Barren as it was, it still held a lot of life. Brightly colored blankets covered well-worn sofas and chairs. A mural was painted over the fireplace, and pictures and old art prints speckled the walls. There were more books than I could count lining the low shelving along all the walls. I so wanted to come back here when all this was over. I could picture myself sitting on the floor with books scattered around me, Tio in the big corner chair excitedly talking me through one of his many adventures in far-flung forests cataloging plants and animals for his job. Tia would be on the floor with me, her arm pumping rhythmically at her mortar and pestle as she ground fresh pigment for her pottery studio. The picture faded from my mind as a thud echoed from above.

"It's probably just the cat," I could hear Tio's voice call out.

"He likes to knock books off the shelf upstairs." His voice sounded strained, and I imagined he was probably still pressed up against the wall. Not because he was a real threat, but because people in power liked to let you know they were in power sometimes.

I froze, vulnerable in the middle of the hall. Tracking Niko, I found him next to a sleeping person, likely his doing, with the cat winding around his feet. As I found the other bodies in the stairwells, all asleep or otherwise unconscious, I realized Niko had been catching them and letting them down softly. The cat must have gotten underfoot, and he had not wanted to potentially harm the cat. I let out a soft snort through my nose, the puff of air barely registering even to my own ears. Big softie, indeed.

Through the door to the kitchen, I could still sense an overwhelming crowd of people. I wouldn't be able to take them on all by myself, especially not with my mind already holding four people.

I sent a soft ping to Niko, requesting an opening. He complied easily.

Can you take the back stairs and come in from the back porch through the kitchen? I can't take on everybody alone, I volleyed over mentally.

Sure you can. But I'll make my way over. Top levels are clear.

A radio chirp echoed through the flat, and my eyes focused back to the closed kitchen door.

"Team B, status. Team A, stand by," a voice said, quickly drowned out by crackling silence. The channel chirped again, and they repeated their message. After another silence, they moved on. "Team A, status. I repeat, Team A, report status."

Tio let out a howl of pain, and I imagined his arm being twisted further behind his back. A bolt of anger slipped out from me, and I watched as the kitchen reacted to my slip up. Two guards peeled off toward the door. I stepped slightly to the side, the backs of my legs up against the couch so that I was out of the line of sight for the hallway. My hand brushed back, knocking against the high table along the back of the couch, normally filled with pretty knickknacks and plants.

Next to the pile of remotes was a small cylinder, and I recognized it as a laser pointer. My fingers wrapped around it, and I darted against the wall right at the opening between the hallway and the living room. I slid in line with the wall, facing the front of the apartment.

The door creaked open, and I heard two pairs of boots take slow measured steps out of the kitchen. Their minds were focused, scanning and cataloging what they saw with very assured, clear minds. They were far enough away they didn't quite notice the group sitting quietly at the front, so I beamed the laser pointer onto the wall, moving it every few seconds. For their training, they likely assumed it to be a long distance weapon instead of a harmless laser pointer. Question marks of surprise rose in each brain, as they did not expect a third party with weapons on this mission. In that moment, I was able to sneak into each of their minds, pausing their footsteps.

I stepped out in front of them, waving the laser pointer at them. I shook my head and tutted my tongue against my teeth. Putting my finger to my lips, I directed in my mind for them to walk over to the couch and take a seat. Fear rose up hard in one, and I sent a wave of calm to him. I sat them nicely on the couch, forcing them to holster their handguns and place their hands nicely on their laps.

This time, it was too risky to assure them out loud.

Hello, I said awkwardly into their minds. Two pairs of eyes bulged back at me. *Sorry about this. You must be very surprised. The good news is this is the extent of the mind play for today. Please sit nicely until I leave. If any shenanigans happen, I promise you will be released in time to protect yourselves. I don't want to hurt you. Okay?*

The eyes blinked back at me, and I nodded.

Yes, I agree, you are clearly not getting paid enough for this. Hang tight.

I left my two newest charges on the couch and tip-toed back to the edge of the hall. I listened through the door, and didn't hear any further expressions of pain. Taking a deep breath, I reached out to Tio. His mind was wide open, as if he had been waiting.

Tio, I'm coming, I said.

Mija, we already talked about this.

And we already agreed I wouldn't be listening. So. I took a deep breath. *Don't be scared, but I have everything under control. Or everyone, I should say.*

I could feel Tio sigh through our connection.

I'm just letting you know Niko will be coming from the back. I'm on the other side of the kitchen door. The plan is to rendezvous in the front bedroom, and Niko will pop us out. Are you okay?

I'm sorry we weren't there to teach you, to protect you, mija. Tio said. *I trust you. Your abuela would be so proud. Your dad, too.*

Sadness lanced through me, and I couldn't distinguish if it was coming from my own reaction to his words, or if Tio was sending through those feelings as well. I swallowed hard, trying to clear the lump in my throat. I had to remain focused.

I don't know how much longer I can hold everyone, I warned. *We have to be quick.*

At your ready, Tio said.

Ready, I heard Niko send over from behind the kitchen door.

Everyone knows the plan, I sent to Tio's connection and Niko's. *Brendan is not a friendly. Subdue, but don't hurt.* Much, I added to myself. A ping of surprise came from Tio, but no rebuttal came through. It seemed he would trust me on this count, too. I would have to explain later. We would all have to explain a lot to one another later.

I took one final steadying breath. I closed my eyes, thought of Abuela, and Noah, and Birdie, even Eli and Aleks and all the people counting on me to get this right. The pinch of a migraine started between my eyes, but I pushed it away. Exhaling, I opened my eyes and walked straight through the door to the kitchen and unleashing my next volley.

"Tia, is there any cafecito? I have a wicked headache."

FORTY-TWO

"Is that a no then?"

Seven pairs of eyes swung to me, and I sighed internally as their minds cracked open from such a small surprise. It worried me more that I was getting better at this, but I shoved that thought deep down and made quick work of driving the three closest guards toward the back door and Niko's waiting choke-holds. The back door swung open to reveal his broad frame, but they didn't need much push from me to go towards the biggest, most obvious threat. I tried not to be offended.

The only tactical guard left was pinning Tio against the wall. He was a bit harder to crack, but also the closest.

So I walked a few more steps and kicked him as hard as I could in the shin.

He howled, immediately loosening his grip on Tio, who twisted easily away. The guard staggered down onto one knee, and through the open door of pain, I instructed him to just sit down cross-legged, which he complied quite readily. I looked up, immediately catching Brendan's eyes. His jaw was agape, and the shock was evident in every crease of his expression. In my peripheral vision, I saw Tio grab Tia's arm, pulling her towards and then past me, out of the kitchen and into the hall. The scuffle continued at the back door as Niko worked steadily through his share of assailants.

Brendan's eyes dropped to the grown man sitting cross-legged on the floor.

"He's fine," I said aloud. "You should probably worry about you."

"How are you doing that?" Brendan said, forgetting to mask the absolute horror in his tone.

"Easily," I fibbed, feeling an icepick wedging its way into my skull. I was deteriorating, fast. My control would not last much longer. "Are you going to cooperate, or do you also need to criss-cross-applesauce on the floor?"

"I don't understand."

"I'm not staying," I said simply. "And if you are going to get in the way of me leaving, then I'll have to break our promise. Not like you haven't already broken your side."

"What?"

Brendan's face contorted in betrayal, but at his core, I could tell I had landed on the truth. The feeling didn't make it past his outermost layer.

"Also, you need to work on your acting," I said, taking a moment to loose my true feelings. If I never had a moment alone with Brendan again, I wanted to make sure he knew where we stood. "I can tell you don't mean it. And I'm not even trying."

"What happened, Evie?" Brendan searched my eyes, a deep sense of loss blooming from his core. I felt some satisfaction that he understood on some level what was going on, that maybe now he could see me a little better as I actually was. "This isn't like you."

"No," I said. "It's not. I don't have that luxury anymore. I can't sit quietly with my books in the library and mind my business. People, and that now includes you, won't let me be. But what happened to you, Brendan?" I couldn't hide the disgust on my face or in my tone. My sneer pointed right at the glowing white core of Brendan's soul, right at his new Elevation. One that did not belong to him.

"Give me a chance to explain," Brendan said, his eyes darting to Niko, who had the final enemy in a chokehold, counting down until he passed out.

Time was running out.

"I think I already know," I said. "And even if I'm wrong, I don't want to hear it right now. I'm going, and you're staying right here."

A chirp echoed from a radio, this time a different, very recognizable voice came over the channel.

"Evangeline, aren't you tired?" the Dean's voice warbled over the line, fighting through a body lying over it to be heard. It was clear enough in the room, Niko, Brendan, and myself froze. The icepick in my head dug deeper, causing me to wince. My eyelids felt heavy.

Immediately, I slammed up all my barriers, fortifying them with as much desperation and fear as I could. My eyes caught Niko's, and a wave of understanding rolled off him.

"I think this is more than enough," the Dean's voice called out, honey laden and annoyingly self assured. "Go ahead and let go. It's time for you to come home."

My mind drifted to Tio and Tia in the front bedroom. I was calculating, watching the guard on the floor fidget a bit from his seated position. If the Dean was sneaking in the back door of everyone's minds and loosening them up, we had a lot more to get through in order to make it to the back bedroom. Instead of fighting her for their consciousnesses, I was ready to let go.

I just had to time it correctly.

I sent a mental image to Niko of the front porch of Ms. Xavier's residence at Windemere, complete with Ig on the porch. I zoomed out, and sent over a general map view of Windemere as well, as best as I could remember. Niko stilled, receiving the information, and gave me an affirmative nod. In two full strides, he wound around the fallen bodies, behind me, and through the door, leaving me, Brendan, and the walkie talkie in the kitchen.

"You've taken my home away from me," I said aloud to the

walkie talkie, my eyes locked back on Brendan's. "I'm not going anywhere with you."

"Evie," Brendan said, standing up from his seat at the kitchen table. Finally. "Please come back with me. Dean Moriarty and her team can help. They have everything you need."

In answer, I held my hand out as a final warning.

"One more step, Brendan, and I am no longer responsible for whatever action I have to take to protect myself. Please stay out of my way."

I sent a wave of emotion out, hoping that either way, he would be able to understand.

But the emotions bounced off him. I could see he was being shielded, although not by himself. I took in a deep breath quickly through my nose. I was really, really out of time.

Brendan took another step, and my boundaries snapped.

I launched the seated guard toward him, putting a literal body between Brendan and myself as I rocketed through the swinging door. Loud crashes and groans echoed behind me, and I released that guard from my control. Even on his own, it would take some time for them to become untangled. Those few seconds were all I needed.

My toes launched me down the hall as I leaned into my sprint. As I passed the living room, I released the two guards on the couch. They sat still, however, not realizing they had control over their own bodies once again. Not knowing what was coming, or how quickly, I didn't want to leave them to be forcibly released by the Dean. I wasn't sure how kind she would be given their mission failure.

I was at the door to the front bedroom in no time. My breathing was ragged as my lungs caught up with my efforts. I felt light headed, and even after releasing half of my mental burden, the pounding in my ears intensified. My migraine was getting worse.

The kitchen door cracked loudly against the plastered wall after Brendan pushed it open with all his might. I watched him stride toward me, a manic sheen in his eyes. I wasn't sure if the desperation was to save me or to stop me. I'm not sure that those things were mutually exclusive.

"Sorry," I muttered to the two nearest guards on the front bench. "I'm going to need to borrow you for a moment. Again, so sorry."

I requested they stand, marching forward to blockade me from Brendan's advance as I darted into the bedroom for Jasleen's package, and Niko, I hoped.

Hold him off, please, I sent to their minds, and I could feel them work with me instead of against me. Even though they had the excuse of my mind control, clearly Brendan had not made friends with these guards. I loosened my hold on them, ready to break the tie cleanly as soon as I was ready to jump.

I rapped quickly on the door, opening it to find Niko standing sentry between the door and my aunt and uncle, who peered at me around Niko's broad shoulders.

"Set?" Niko said. "Harder to track if we only jump once."

"Two seconds," I said, grabbing the box from the top of the dresser and leaning back out to release the two remaining seated guards. As I pivoted to release the two lightly held guards blockading Brendan, his face loomed before me. I clutched the box to my chest, fearing I would drop it.

"Evangeline. Wait," Brendan said, his arms reaching out for me.

Instead of landing on me, his hands landed on the package. White light flared from his core, and I could see his eyes deaden as he looked at something inwardly. Like Tio, I could see his Elevation in action. It felt like a bucket of ice water had been poured over me. This was not something I wanted to be able to see.

Brendan gasped as he let go of the package.

"What did you see?"

"Where did you get that?"

Our words overlapped, but I caught Brendan's intention to

reach back out and grab me. I moved the box to one arm, and stepped back. I could hear my name being called from inside the bedroom, but I froze. I was torn. Would rummaging through Brendan's brain to find out what he saw be worth the risk?

Brendan lunged at me, his brain registering my moment of hesitation.

I said a silent apology, more for my future sense of guilt than for Brendan. Just as his body broke the outer ring of my personal space, I loosed a solid right hook that landed perfectly on his very attractive, very surprised jawline.

As Brendan's body crumpled against the hallway wall, I dropped what remained of my connection with the two blockage guards and stepped backwards into Niko's arms, clutching the box tightly to my chest.

My stomach lurched as Niko pulled us away to safety.

FORTY-THREE

A pair of green lantern eyes greeted us as Niko popped us in front of the humble teacher's cabin at Windemere Prep. My feet sunk deeply into several inches of snow, and I could hear retching noises behind me in the dead grassland landscape. Bile churned in my stomach as well, but with practice, I had been able to keep it down. Tio and Tia were not as lucky.

"Ig!" I called out, jogging through the snowdrifts to the porch. Ig's black tail switched back and forth in as much of a tail wag as he was willing to allow. I bounded up the porch steps and scooped him into my free arm, cradling both the box and the cat equally. I buried my face into his fur, demanding full cuddles. "I missed you!"

A slightly indignant yowl got lost in my hair, but Ig remained in my arms, permitting my cuddle even though he wasn't the biggest fan. All the tension in my body melted after holding him for a few moments.

"Did you tell Xavier we were coming? Huh? Could you tell?" I cooed at him. I turned around, finding Niko with his head cocked slightly to the side, and Tio and Tia brushing themselves off before taking in the surrounding area. I looked between Niko and Ig and back again. "What?"

"Is that only a cat, or..." Niko raised an eyebrow.

"Hard to say," I said, burying my face back into Ig's soft fur. "Not part of my specialty, I'm afraid."

I looked at Ig, and he squinted his eyes at me.

"You're right. Not important," I replied, turning back toward everyone. "Come on inside. We can put the fire on if it isn't already. You can camp out here until things settle down."

"Did I just port us behind enemy lines?" Niko asked, trotting up the stairs. "This doesn't feel...like a welcome place." Tio and Tia followed close behind.

"Also hard to say," I agreed. "I don't want to ruin the surprise for you though. Gotta test those spidey-senses of yours."

I opened the door to the cabin, scooting my dirty feet on the mat earnestly before heading further into the house. I set the box on the counter in the kitchen and let Ig out of my arms to do whatever he felt like doing as I moved around to make tea and coffee for everyone. The house felt warm and lively, and I smiled as the kettle and the water faucet hummed at me.

"Missed you, too," I said to the objects I touched. Niko froze in the hall, causing Tio and Tia to run into his back.

"Are you...why am I even bothering to ask," Niko muttered. "I will await further instructions. Although we may want to call Eli."

"Do you want to get yelled at twice or just once?" I asked the mugs. I gave them a knowing look as I pulled out the tea leaves and coffee press. Niko harrumphed behind me. "Who wants tea and who wants coffee?"

"Anything is fine," Tia whispered. I turned and caught her slight smile. She looked shaken, and I could tell she was having a hard time keeping it together. I left the various beverage paraphernalia and walked to where she was seated at the big kitchen table. I crouched down next to her and took her hands.

"Tia, would it be okay if I helped? Just a little," I said. My eyes darted to Tio, whose expression looked a little pained. "I know Tio can't help with this kind of pain, but I can give you a few moments of peace, if you'd like. Otherwise, I'll leave it alone."

"Don't waste your energy, mija," Tia whispered, patting the

top of my hand. "You have many more important things to be worrying about."

"I'm not going to be able to stay with you long," I warned. My eyes slid to Niko's. "I'm going to have to move on as soon as Ms. Xavier gets here. But she'll make sure you're safe. Are you sure I can't help? I feel partly responsible anyway."

Niko checked his watch, and gave a slight nod.

"Please?" I asked again. After a moment, Tia relented, giving a slight nod.

I opened up my mind again, checking that we were still in the clear. Ms. Xavier's energy was en route, and I knew she would walk through the door any moment. Otherwise, it seemed like the normal bustle of campus. Not too many of the other far flung teacher's cabins were occupied. I felt an energy outside on the perimeter, but it was still. Since it didn't feel threatening, I let it pass.

Taking in a deep breath, I poked slightly around Tia's energy, seeing where was causing the most pain. The grey cloaking her core was deep, and I knew I wouldn't be able to move that energy. Her grief for Abuela was her own, and I had no business messing with it. There were some murky clusters latching on outside of it, so I focused on those. Slowly, I focused my attention on them, and they broke up into smaller pieces, scattering and being absorbed elsewhere in her energy.

I opened my eyes, and watched as Tia let out a huge sigh.

"Better?" I asked. "I didn't take anything away, so it's still there. But now should be more manageable." Tia smiled, her eyes watery as she nodded in understanding.

"I'm used to it, mija," she whispered. "I'll be okay."

I looked to Tio, and he reached out, placing a hand on his wife's shoulder. After a moment, he seemed to determine something and looked directly at me.

"It's a shame you didn't inherit my gift, but I am so thankful you have yours," Tio said. "The emotional wounds are not things I can heal with my energies."

"I don't know if we can call what I did healing, but I am always happy to help," I said.

The floorboards beneath my knees hummed.

"Xavier's home!" I said, a smile escaping me. I sent a happy blip toward the front door, where Ig was already waiting.

"I know I said I had an open door policy," Ms. Xavier called out from the front hall as she relieved herself of hat, gloves, and scarf, "but you could maybe let me know you're in the neighborhood first."

"Surprise?" I called out. "Sort of."

"Ah, and guests," Ms. Xavier said, feigning surprise. "You're lucky it's exam break. Normally, I would be in lecture right now."

Tio and Tia looked to get up from their seats, but I swatted them back down. Popping up from my crouched position, a wave of vertigo hit me. I gripped the back of Tia's chair briefly, waiting for the feeling to subside. When my eyes caught back up, I found several pairs of eyes watching me intently. I ignored the concern and wandered off back toward the whistling kettle.

"I'm just stopping by, but they'll need to lay low for a while. Couldn't think of a better spot," I said, busying myself in the kitchen. Ms. Xavier walked in, surveying the motley crew of refugees.

"Welcome!" she said, pinging back and forth between the guests. "For however long you need."

"Niko, Tio, Tia," I recited, pouring hot water into the teapot and French press. "This is Ms. Xavier."

"Yes," Ms. Xavier said, stopping at the edge of the counter and absentmindedly resting her hand on the package Jasleen had left for me. Her brow furrowed, and she pressed her lips together. "Please excuse me, but whose is this?"

"Mine," I said, turning to face her. "I haven't opened it yet."

She hummed at me in response.

"Should this be a need to know thing?" I asked. "I don't want to tell you more than you want to know."

"It's alright," Ms. Xavier said, her eyes pulling away from the package to meet mine. "I recognize this. I'll leave it to you. Everything else though, may be best to leave me in the dark."

I nodded and looked at Niko.

"Shall we?" I asked. Niko looked slightly taken aback.

"Now?"

"You can come back after dropping me off to transport Tia and Tio. They'll be safe here for a while. No one would ever expect they'd be here," I said. "I don't want to involve Ms. Xavier more than we already have. I'm a bit of a hot commodity, and I don't want folks storming in here and ruining her lovely home."

The objects around me hummed in agreement.

Niko paled.

"I'll loop you in when you come back for your second trip," Ms. Xavier said, offering a knowing smile. "But it's probably what you're imagining."

Tia twisted in her chair to face me.

"Come give me a hug before you go," Tia said. "I never did get a proper hello."

Blood rushed to my cheeks, and I bit the inside of my cheek. Pressure rose up behind my eyes, and I felt my ears pop. Something was telling me we were cutting it very close again.

I walked over to the table and melted into Tia's embrace. Tio's arm joined, and I felt cocooned in love and safety. I didn't want to leave it.

When I pulled away after several minutes, my cheeks were wet. I sniffled and offered Tia a reflection of her own watery smile.

"We will meet again soon. Until then, take care," Tia said.

"And give them hell," Tio said with a firm nod.

I looked up, and Ms. Xavier was holding out Jasleen's gift to me. In her arms, Ig purred.

"Good luck," Ms. Xavier said. "And don't worry. I'll take good care of everyone."

"Any spoilers?" I asked, shaking the box slightly at my favorite mentor.

"You have your ethics, and I have mine," Ms. Xavier said with a chuckle. "Just because I know what's inside doesn't mean you get to skip the fun part."

Another wave of nausea hit, and my field of vision blacked out briefly.

I could feel Niko behind me, and he rested his hands on my shoulders.

"I think we've found the limit. Come on. Time to go," Niko's voice rumbled.

I took a deep breath, unable to clear the swirling mass around me. Worried I might freak out everyone, I turned around, leaning into Niko's chest and pressed my forehead against his sternum. His arms wrapped around me, and I felt confident I had masked my impending fainting spell.

"Surprise me," I said. "Just not, like, the beach, okay? I really hate sand."

"It's going to be sand or Eli yelling," Niko warned.

I muttered against his chest and let out a sigh.

As soon as I felt the pull of Niko's jump, pain crashed through my head, ricocheting down my limbs. We swayed, and I knew we had landed somewhere. I smelled saltwater, and I sighed, surrendering to the overwhelming pain that had blanketed me. My body slumped, but I wasn't awake to know if someone caught me before I hit the ground.

EPILOGUE

If my vision had also included temperature information, I would have worn thicker layers.

I found myself shivering under Ms. Xavier's kitchen window, knee deep in snow and dead shrubberies, just because my stupid vision told me I'd be here. And that I wouldn't want to miss it.

I blew into my mittened hands, rubbing them together violently before sticking them back underneath my parka-coated arms. New England winters were stupid. The second I graduated, I promised myself, I would escape to warmer climates, preferably some place I could be as far away from the Association and all their shenanigans as much as possible. Maybe I could make a living reading tarot cards and predicting the future for tourists on cruise ships or retirement communities in the deserts of Arizona. Sounded like as good of a plan as any.

Ever since Noah and Evie were sent away, I had not had a moment's peace.

I had fallen out of favor with Dean Moriarty, Adair had gone off somewhere to "study abroad," and senior year was filled with studying and tests and other meaningless things. My visions had grown stronger, not that anyone cared. I only cared because now I had ulcers and acid reflux and couldn't eat anything. Sleeping was difficult, too.

So here I was, trying to squeeze blood out of a rock. I had lost access to reliable intel, and without it, I couldn't make sense of my visions. What was true, or maybe true. Or more likely to be true than not. What was still able to be changed versus what was bound and determined to happen. I had chosen the side that promised me safety and prestige and a place to prove my skills. But that side had tossed me aside, but not far enough away that they didn't have complete control over my life.

I needed to know which side to pick now.

Should I double down, get scrappy, and win my way back into the dean's good graces no matter the cost? Or should I run as far away as I could, likely for the rest of my life?

"How much does she know?"

The voices had been quiet for some time after the big burly man, Nick or something, had teleported Evie to the next safe house. I hadn't gotten much from their earlier conversation other than to gather Evie had gotten ridiculously powerful, and even more surprisingly, even more in control of that power. No wonder Dean Moriarty was up her ass so much.

"More and more each day, but not enough," Evie's uncle said. "I'm worried we haven't left enough clues."

"Evangeline is a very smart girl," Ms. Xavier said. "It will be enough. Jasleen's gift will push the odds in her favor."

"I don't want to know," Evie's aunt said. "All I can do to protect her is to not know and not get in the way."

"I'll keep an eye on her," Ms. Xavier said. "She's with the right folks. It's all up to her now. She has time."

"We'll do our best to buy her as much time as she needs," Evie's uncle said. "You know how to find us?"

"Of course," Ms. Xavier said. The man chuckled.

"Silly thing to ask you, of all people."

"I like that some people forget. My life would be much easier if more people forgot."

"All our lives would be easier if people forgot and just left well enough alone."

A clear pop punctuated the wishful thought.

"Ready?" the teleporter's voice said. "Your house is still a mess. Do you have another place you can go?"

"Yes, just drop us off at the cathedral down the street. We'll take our time coming home from mass. If they're still there, we'll deal with it then."

There was a dramatic pause, and I squirmed, punching blood back into my thighs. I couldn't feel my toes in my shoes anymore. Boots, while more practical, hadn't seemed as stealthy. Lesson learned.

"I'll be here whenever you're curious," Ms. Xavier said. "Open door policy extends to you now as well."

After a round of thank you's and farewells, another pop resounded in the brisk early evening air. I waggled my jaw back and forth, worried the vibration had somehow messed with the pressure in my own ears.

A whoosh erupted above me as Ms. Xavier raised the window pane above her sink.

I tumbled over in surprise, landed on top of a mound of dead leaves and snow.

"Are you going to come in and regain feeling in your extremities, or should I ignore your eavesdropping?" the professor called out into the frigid air.

"Depends on if I'm in trouble or not," I said, feigning bravado. My chattering teeth undercut the mood though, and my fingers and toes ached for relief.

"Oh, we'll see," Ms. Xavier said. "At the very least, you owe me a favor."